THE LAST ROAD TRIP

The Journal
of Brett Tempest

Bardolf & Company

The Last Road Trip: The Journal of Brett Tempest

ISBN 978-1-938842-28-3

Published by Bardolf & Company
    5430 Colewood Pl.
    Sarasota, FL 34232
    941-232-0113
    www.bardolfandcompany.com

Cover design by shawcreativegroup.com

**To my Creator
and
Guiding Light**

Other books by Michael Judge

CAPTURED HORIZONS
An Artist's Journey

THE LAST ROAD TRIP

The Journal
of Brett Tempest

Michael Judge

Bardolf & Company
Sarasota, Florida
2016

Prologue

The light of dawn was peeking out from under its nighttime blanket, promising a new dance of color and time in the cobalt blue Carolina sky. I loved preparing my motorcycle at this early time of day because it afforded me plenty of time to work the wax into the steel hide of my metal steed. I used a golden cloth and buffed the black and yellow surface of the *Valkyrie* with smooth, curved strokes. Before long I started to become hypnotized by the large, purple wax circle and I changed hands thinking that would break the spell. But I continued to feel a hypnotic pull. I was both enchanted and captivated by the violet halo that seemed to lift off the paint and float towards me.

Feeling a strong sense of déjà-vu, as if I had already performed this grooming of my *Valkyrie* in another reality, I eventually managed to ignore the purplish ring and focus on the road trip I was about to embark on to still my burning wanderlust.

Day 1

The bright, clear, mid-October morning was just right for the start of my journey to discovery. North Carolina in the early fall is a sight to behold and on this day it did not disappoint. The sky was the pale blue of a robin's egg, bringing out the yellows, golds and reds of the maples, oaks and Bitternut Hickory trees that lined the street from my home in Durham.

Thirty-one previous trips across the continent had given me a commanding knowledge of America's blue roads, where I looked for suitable subjects for my photographs. By now I had settled into a planning routine of letting my fingers trace the various red and blue lines on the coffee stained, dog-eared maps ahead of time. I always had a notebook in which I wrote down the route I would be taking in my quest to rediscover my homeland and record on film some of the storied treasures of the past. The mapping process usually took a week or two and, inevitably, I would make minor changes to the plan once I was out on the road. Sometimes my choices did not yield the character I was looking for but, most often, I found that my research paid off, and I always managed to capture a variety of visual treasures from bygone times.

Sitting at my wooden Shaker breakfast table and looking over my road worn atlas while sipping a cup of coffee was akin to watching three decades of personal history come to life. The names of small towns that would mean nothing to most people awoke fond memories in me of a flirtatious waitress, a corny joke told by a pig farmer, or a particularly evocative photographic subject. In any case, I always garnered attention because I was doing what most people only dream about—flying across the American landscape free as a bird. I often encountered envious stares of locals, reflected in the side mirrors of my motorcycle, as I pulled away from a stop sign or left a parking lot and disappeared from their reality to become one with the horizon.

This trip would be my last, however, because by now I had a cornucopia of photographs. I only needed to get one last set of images to complete my book of travels through 9all 50 states, which I had given the working title, *100 Reclamations of the Past.*

My ritual for packing the motorcycle always started the night before the trip: two pair of jeans, one black, one blue; five tee shirts; four woolen socks; five pair of underwear; an extra set of long johns and driving gloves that could handle both rain and snow; and last but not least, a rain-suit. I also toted along enough camera gear to handle almost any situation I might encounter.

This morning I wore a thick leather motorcycle jacket and pants over thermals and a sweatshirt. The fall weather can create quite a chill and there is nothing worse than riding cold! I wore a nylon skullcap under the yellow and black helmet to keep my curly hair from becoming a tangled mess during the hours of riding.

The motorcycle, my customized, mega-powerful Honda *Valkyrie,* was equipped with two good-sized leather saddlebags, one of which contained the full complement of cameras, lenses and film that I would use on the road. But the main storage container was a thick canvas duffel bag with a pocket sewn onto its back so it slipped over the rear seat backrest to sit securely on the passenger seat. The bag could expand by another third to accommodate any new acquisitions I might find on the road. Bungeed onto the back of the "sissy bar" was my emergency sleeping bag wrapped in a canvas tarp, which kept it dry in inclement weather and made for a decent shelter when needed. Strapped on top of the saddlebag with my cameras was a small but sturdy tripod. The final piece of luggage was a stiff canvas tank bag which held a Swiss Army knife, matches, flashlight, cell phone, my wallet, change for tolls, a pair of all-weather gloves, plenty of protein bars, a couple of bottles of water, and a few small packs of Kleenex. The last item was the journal I always kept during the trip. I had logged thousands of miles on six different motorcycles with more or less the same equipment.

I always felt a special thrill straddling the Honda *Valkyrie*, my metal maiden, and settling into her seat, ready for take-off. I tapped my right upper thigh to make sure my gold pocket watch was secure. It had belonged to my grandfather on the old Chesapeake and Ohio railroad where he worked as a conductor. I gave a quick peek to see if the map was folded and in place under the clear, rainproof covering on the tank bag. I had topped off the gas the day before to allow me to go 175 or so miles before my next fill-up. All the lights were in working order, the fresh oil was at optimal level, and a brand-new set of Dunlop tires promised a smooth ride.

I always did one final check-over before snapping down the tinted helmet visor and getting going. All seemed ready as I pushed the starter button and the big six-cylinder engine sprang to life with a deep roar. After letting the oil warm for a moment, I was finally ready to hit the road. The colorful trees along both sides of the driveway stood like an honor guard as I started my journey. I wove through downtown Durham to get to a southbound highway until I reached U.S. 15 South. This smaller highway coincided with one of my long-standing resolves: to avoid, if possible, the congested Interstates and keep to the older, red and blue line roads. This allowed me to unearth a more authentic culture that was, in a sense, isolated from the concrete and fast food joints along major highways and Interstates.

Twenty minutes later Durham was no more than a memory as the cool October air brought a new scent of farms and fallen leaves. This fresh aroma replaced the smell of tobacco emanating from the giant processing plants that dominated Durham's downtown area. I always found the odor of freshly shredded tobacco intoxicating, but now the pungent smell of agricultural fields and farm animals greeted me with the promise of new and unknown adventures.

In Pittsboro, I joined U.S. 64 West, which would be my paved road for the next 600 or so miles. I loved this highway which snaked through the picturesque Nantahala National Forest and the Great Smokey Mountains, and then meandered through a string of small towns on the way to Memphis, Tennessee and points west. The scenery was breathtakingly beautiful as the Blue Ridge Mountains were in full autumn bloom. Because the road had little traffic, I could take it easy and enjoy the intoxicating surroundings.

Around two o'clock my stomach started to growl in tandem with the rumbling of the engine. I knew that just ahead was the town of Chimney Rock, a major summer vacation spot. I figured it would be relatively quiet at this time of year but that all the eateries would still be open, and I looked forward to a good meal with a tasty piece of homemade fruit pie. Imagine my annoyance at the hordes of sightseers that greeted me as I cruised into the little village. All the restaurants were packed with gawking tourists. Irritated, I tried to coax my grumbling stomach into settling down for a bit longer and headed towards the tiny dot on my map that indicated the next town, Bat Cave, North Carolina.

By the time I finally got there and found the *Bat Cave Diner*, a small eatery in a worn-out, gray, three-story building, I was famished. I pulled into the adjacent parking lot and dismounted. As I stretched and turned around, I found myself facing a crusty looking man standing by the side door to the kitchen. He could have been anywhere between 40 and 80. I figured he was the cook because the white apron he wore was decorated with bits of meat and brown sauce. He was having a smoke and stared at me with dark, wrinkled eyes. Then he slowly approached.

He spoke with a kind of whistling, chirping Southern accent that made him sound like Andy Griffith in an aviary. "What kind of motorcycle is that? Ain't ever seen one of those before?"

I gave him the 10-cent tour of everything I had done to the *Valkyrie* and said, with a touch of pride, "She's propelled by a six-cylinder engine."

That revelation left him scratching his balls through the greasy apron. He was using the same yellow stained fingers that held his burning cigarette. I'd seen that odd habit before—mountain men seem to pride themselves on the ability to do two things at once with the same hand.

I asked him, "What's your best dish?"

He replied with a wink, "Do you mean food or women?"

"Food, but I wouldn't mind hearing about the women as well."

He smiled, exposing a row of tobacco stained teeth the color of a canary's breast. I realized that the gaps from the missing ones were the cause of his whistling, bird-like speech.

After one last drag on his cigarette, he said, "Tell Ester that Joe already has your order." Then he flicked away his stub and headed inside.

I went around to the front where an old screen door had a rusted "Wonder Bread" sign attached on one side. The frame had seen better days. It squeaked as I entered the *Bat Cave Diner*. Ester, the only person in the place, had dark, shoulder length hair and matching brown eyes. She appeared to be in her late 40s and had more wear on her than a poor man's shoes, but she still displayed some sex appeal. Her lean body accentuated pillow-like breasts which were exposed just enough to generate interest. The rest of her was mostly hidden under an off-white, nylon waitress uniform that had long ago lost its sheen. A well-worn black apron, cinched at her waist, completed the outfit.

Ester tried to seat me at a table designed for one, which faced directly into the partially open door to the men's room. But with my size and temperament—I am 6'1" and weigh 200 pounds and can be easily irritated—I was not about to settle for a small table with an unpleasant view. Since I was the only patron in the place, I asked for one of the three booths that lined the far right wall. Reluctantly, and with an air of exasperation, Ester seated me and handed me a plastic-coated menu, which looked like it had been dropped into the chili and then wiped off with a greasy rag.

I said, "Joe is preparing something special for me."

She nodded and smiled at me with her own set of tobacco stained teeth. They were three to four shades lighter than old Joe's and seemed to be, for the most part, intact. I realized she had forgiven me for demanding one of the "group" tables when she leaned against me while placing a frosted, red plastic cup of water in front of me. I could feel the warmth of her body on my shoulder as she lingered for a brief moment. Then she grabbed the menu and sauntered off in the direction of the kitchen. I admired the way in which the nylon of her dress clung to her shapely, swaying behind. This old gal still knew how to work her stuff.

Tossing my jacket and helmet on the opposite bench seat, I made my way to the men's room to freshen up. Five hours of riding with only one stop for gas had left me looking a bit disheveled. My dark brown hair, normally combed straight back and settling into a mass of waves and curls on my neck, had flattened. I looked like some washed-up European royal with way too much pomade in his hair. But the fresh mountain air had imparted a reddish complexion to my face, which made my eyes seem much bluer than usual and took 10 years off my appearance. I looked like someone in his early 40s. I cleaned myself up as much as possible and left the bathroom in much better condition than when I entered it. In fact, Ester gave me the once over as I made my way towards the table.

Waiting for my food to arrive, I wondered why so many of these small eateries always served beverages in dark red plastic beverage holders. In the *Bat Cave Diner*, at least the ruddy color balanced with the mottled gray walls and tattered brown leatherette seating. The aroma of chili beans and baking meatloaf wafting from the kitchen mingled with the scent of pine trees coming through the diner's open windows.

Ester reappeared carrying a rather large plate of grub. At first glance, I could not tell what it was, but it smelled of beef. It turned out to be Joe's special corn beef hash with diced tomatoes, cut corn and mashed potatoes, buried under a thick, brown sauce. It looked awful but tasted great, and there was enough to feed an elephant.

About three spoonfuls in, Joe appeared without his apron and plopped down opposite me and asked what I thought of his special hash. When I ventured that it was quite a tasty dish, he seemed pleased.

Then he asked. "Would you mind if I try on your motorcycle jacket?"

I said, "Have at it."

He stood up and draped the heavy jacket on his frail, slender body. It was at least three sizes too large for him and gave him the appearance of a baby wrapped in a large black leather blanket. Nonetheless, he called to Ester, who was in the back booth counting her tips, to admire his imitation of Marlon Brando in *The Wild One*.

She started to laugh and said, "You look like a wet rat in that jacket."

He ignored her remark and said, "I have always wanted to ride a motorcycle but had no idea the jacket would be so heavy."

When I asked Ester if she had any homemade fruit pie, she said, "We don't do any baking on the premises." Then she added with a twinkle, "But if you stick around, I might be talked into making one for you."

Despite such a sweet offer, I felt the call of the road and reluctantly asked Joe for my jacket and Ester for my check. Joe said that it was on the house and I thanked them both for a great meal. Ester gave my jacket a little curiosity feel and wanted to know where I was heading. When I said that I was on a cross-country journey to capture a part of

America that was disappearing in photographs, she and Joe both got a far away look in their eyes.

I dropped a fiver on the table and turned to leave when my curiosity got the better of me and I asked Ester, "How long have you been working as a waitress?"

She replied, "The better part of thirty years. I started when I was sixteen. The only other jobs around here are in Rutherfordton in the mills, and I ain't about to do factory work." Then she wrote her name and phone number on the back of one of her "Guest Checks," and handed it to me with a wink. "If you ever get lonely out there on that road—give me a call."

I folded it neatly and tucked it into my jacket pocket. As I looked into Ester's dark, misty eyes, I was saddened by what I discovered there. She had given up on life and was just "marking time."

Nodding to Joe, I said, "You'll have to fill me up with your other dish when I return."

I left with a phone number, a full stomach, and a surprising feeling of well-being. I snapped down my visor just as Joe was coming out for a smoke, so with a parting wave I left the parking lot and headed out.

It was now mid-afternoon and I figured I had two to three hours of safe riding left. One of my rules when cruising in the mountains was to avoid driving into dusk or dawn. At those times all kinds of animals come out to eat, turning the roads into an obstacle course. On the other hand, the early morning and late afternoons were prime time for taking photographs as the light performed its special magic then, rendering even mundane subjects in a flattering radiance.

I encountered my first interesting subject just past the town of Cashiers, North Carolina. It was a defunct restaurant where a neon chicken sign that used to beckon people into the old coop had partially fallen down. It had come to a rest above a discarded cigarette advertisement, making it look like the chicken was smoking. It was a cute image but it didn't convey the right message for my book on America.

Another 30 miles down the road, I pulled into a motel with the catchy name, *Dew Drop Inn*. I could not resist the invitation and made my stop there just as the sun was disappearing behind the mountains. That night, lying alone on a lumpy mattress, I coaxed myself to sleep thinking about a waitress named Ester.

Day 2

Slivers of dawn's light slipped through the partially separated drapes and gently nudged me awake. It took a moment to realize that I was in a strange room somewhere outside of Murphy, North Carolina. Once I got my bearings, the anticipation of a new day's adventure replaced my morning drowsiness. I wanted to get an early start, hoping to dodge the Chattanooga congestion and navigating through the unavoidable section of the Interstate quickly. I gave my motorcycle a little wipe down and marveled at how the early morning light played over the yellow and black *Valkyrie*. The chrome refracted the sun's rays like a prism, giving it the appearance of a radiant crystal. I was packed and on the road by 6:45. The early morning chill mixing with the fragrance of the surrounding pines tickled my nostrils. It was a scent you wouldn't find in any perfume boutique, no matter how pricey, and reminded me what a pleasure it was to ride a motorcycle.

Late morning I was a good 50 miles past Chattanooga and back on U.S. 64. I had breakfast at the *Country Boy's Restaurant* in downtown Winchester, Tennessee, the birthplace of Dinah Shore. They'd named a boulevard after her. While I enjoyed a very good cup of joe, I looked over my map and the route I had chosen. I had passed plenty of postcard type, photographic opportunities already, especially in the mountains, but none of them had offered me what I was looking for. This didn't come as a surprise. On a previous trip I had traversed the entire United States without finding a single image for my book. Still, I had a feeling that this trip would not remain an empty-handed escapade for long. Since the restaurant didn't have any homemade fruit pie, I topped the meal off with a slice of Butterfinger cheesecake. Although it tasted crunchy and sweet, it didn't satisfy my craving.

When I finished I gassed up the bike and made my way back to the old highway. The overcast day eliminated any glare from the noonday sun and let me relish the spectacular views. I loved the hum of the *Valkyrie* as the wind gently pushed me back into my canvas duffel backrest and allowed me the luxury of becoming one with the road in comfort. The trick to riding a motorcycle is to not force anything and let your eyes control the bike. If you don't trust yourself and try to drive, you will only wear yourself out and miss the fun of being liberated from the mundane. That's what motorcycle Zen is all about. I was in the zone, and soon the road became a direct route into my spirit center and I found myself looking at my life from the perspective of my soul. I had known from an early age that my time on this Earth was only a vacation from eternity and that, before long, I would be returning to the Light for yet another adventure.

I was torn from these reflections by a giant sign which announced the next 25 miles as "Antique Heaven." If you like to browse flea markets, then U.S. 64 is the road for you. I must have passed at least 20 such "emporiums." Some of them covered acres of land, while others merely occupied somebody's front lawn. I did stop at what promised to be a nifty antique mall, called *The Peddlers Pride*. It must have been at least 5000 square feet in size but, hard as I looked, I could not find one true antique. My special interest is in old paintings, prints and sculptures. There were several studies of cowboys, but they were Remington knock offs, hung alongside a still life that looked like someone's attempt to paint by the numbers. I also found loads of old offset prints, copied from Audubon etchings. These pseudo reproductions crop up all over rural America. It seems that our forebears sure loved their birds.

As I was about to leave, I came upon a booth that displayed some older cameras, and I spotted a 1950s vintage Rolleiflex Twin Lens camera sitting near the back of the counter. I asked the shopkeeper to take it out for me. The twin lenses looked to be in good condition, as did the ground glass focusing screen, and the shutter seemed to work fine. Film was readily available. In fact, I used the same film in my Hasselblad camera. The Rollei had a price tag indicating $45. I felt I could not go wrong with it.

I asked the woman at the counter, "Would you take thirty dollars for it?"

She said, "The best I can do is twenty percent off."

While we were haggling, I started to frame her in the camera. She had a pretty face, but her makeup and the old-fashioned, green and yellow flower print dress she wore gave her a matronly look. My best guess was that she was in her late 30s or early 40s. The camera's 80-mm lens cropped most of her unfashionable outfit, leaving a nicely framed head shot. She was surprisingly photogenic and her image on the ground glass had the bygone look of a 1930s Hollywood movie star, giving me an uncanny sense of déjà vu. She reminded me of Marlene Dietrich; she had the same kind of hair and lips.

When I told her that, and how good she looked in the camera, she blushed and said, "I used to do some modeling back in my high school days."

I introduced myself, "My name is Brett Tempest."

"Kathryn Bailey."

I told her about the trip I was taking and let on that I would like to photograph her. As we spoke she seemed to change and get younger looking by the minute. She agreed to let me "snap a few photos" of her after she closed the shop, in just 40 minutes. I suggested that we could shoot right in the store and she agreed.

I went around gathering what I thought might be enticing clothes for her to model and ended up with a bundle of silky scarves. I went out to my motorcycle and got my Leica, two lenses, a 35 mm for full body-work and a 90 mm for portrait shots. Since I didn't have lights with me, I had to rely on the illumination in the store. It was times like this that made me wish I had switched to a digital camera, but I was old-fashioned in my own way and not ready to give up on my beloved film yet.

The last customer was out the door shortly after closing time, and half an hour later we were ready to shoot. I don't know what Kathryn did to herself in the ladies room—she was in there no more than a few minutes—but she emerged a different person. Her hair, which had been kind of straight, now had a slightly wavy quality. It brought out the highlights in the golden strands that were laced through her dark, sand colored tresses. Her green eyes were now highlighted by dark-gold mascara and her lips were the color of a red sunset. She looked terrific—from all business to all pleasure—and had me instantly in her spell.

I took her to a booth with a four-poster bed completely draped in white. It was a great set that would allow Kathryn to melt into a white nothingness. I positioned her on the bed and had her trade the frumpy dress and stiff bra for about 20 or so scarves that flowed around her in a profusion of silky color against her pale white skin. The store's track lighting provided just the right amount of shadow to create a film noir feel.

I took about five photos before Kathryn started to react to the setting. She was a good model and by the twentieth frame, she was removing scarves like Salome discarding her seven veils. The nipples of her breasts were so erect that they created valleys in the gossamer fabric. By the end of the roll we were down to three veils and her skin was gleaming with a fine mist of sexually percolating perspiration.

While I was changing film, I asked, "Would you like me to shoot some nudes?"

She replied quickly, "I don't want to be photographed completely naked." Then she looked into my eyes and asked huskily, "Would you like to make love to me?"

Without speaking I removed my leather pants, sweatshirt and briefs and entered her at once. In my entire life I had not experienced anything like it before. Kathryn was so hot that she crescendoed to climax the moment I started to push into her. Time seemed to disappear as we gorged ourselves on one another. When we were finished and lying on the old bed exhausted, Kathryn started to revert back to her old self. The bloom was off the rose, so to speak.

I got dressed and met her up front.

She said, "Can we hurry and leave now? I have to get home."

I thought that we would at least spend the night together, but when I pressed her, she said, "That's not possible. I am married."

Feeling disappointed and a bit dejected, I gathered up the camera gear along with my latest acquisition. Realizing that I had not yet paid for the Rolleiflex, I offered Kathryn the money, but she refused.

"You have given me something I have fantasized about for a number of years."

I looked deeply into her green eyes. "Me too."

As Kathryn was getting into her car, a late model silver Audi A-6, I asked her where I might spend the night.

She said softly, "About thirty miles west there's a motel and a good restaurant."

We said our farewells and I drove away savoring the sweet memories of unbridled fervor.

After checking into the motel and unloading the motorcycle, I took a long hot shower. The nozzle had a pulsating attachment that acted like a mini water massage. I had been in countless motels that featured a similar mechanism, but there was something about this evening's experience that was totally satisfying. I decided to shave, something I almost never do when I'm on the road. I thought about going to the restaurant for dinner but did not feel hungry. The afternoon's lovemaking seemed to have given me everything I needed for a good night's sleep. The only thing missing was a warm body next to me.

Wearing clean briefs and a tee shirt, I climbed into bed and started to channel surf on the television, trying to find the weather channel and get an update on tomorrow's forecast. I almost didn't hear the soft knocking on the door. It had an unusual rhythm, like an uncertain woodpecker trying to decide if it had the right tree. Peeking through the scratched and cloudy eye hole, I saw a rather tall woman vaguely resembling my afternoon lover. I opened the door and it was Kathryn in full radiance. She was wearing jeans and a white blouse. I invited her in and as she entered the room, her lips brushed my cheek and her scent filled my nostrils with the faint bouquet of gardenias, a fragrance I did not recall from our earlier rendezvous.

To say I was surprised would be an understatement. "What's up?" is all I managed to get out.

She said, blushing, "I've come to get the roll of film. I don't want the photos to end up on the Internet or in some cheap girlie magazine."

I could not believe what I was hearing but, rather than act offended, I said, "Of course you can have the film. I would never publish the pictures unless you wanted me to." Then I looked into her eyes and asked, "Is that the real reason you've come?"

She started to mist up and, after a sharp intake of breath, said, "I had to see you again. I haven't been able to stop thinking about this afternoon."

She came into my arms and we shared our first kiss.

Feeling suddenly hungry, I grabbed her hand and said, "It's time for dinner."

I slipped on a clean pair of jeans and grey sweatshirt. Kathryn smiled and we headed outside.

A gay hunter must have decorated the restaurant adjacent to the motel, because it was a cross between a hunting lodge and an English tearoom. All the tables in *The Foxes Crumpet*, were draped in deep red fabric and had candles burning in red lanterns with Edwardian ladies painted on the glass sides. The collection of animal heads decorating the walls were in total contrast to the British chintz. But it was a quiet place and we found an out-of-the-way table tucked in a back corner. The wine menu included a nice vintage bottle of Jordan Cabernet which would have cost $90 more in a city restaurant. According to the waitress it was "the last of the Mohicans"—it had been lying in the back for over two years and they'd began to think they would never sell it.

"People around here don't cotton to paying sixty dollars for a jug of red," she said.

Sharing wine with a beautiful woman is one of the great pleasures in life and Kathryn was glowing. The first three buttons of her white blouse were open, allowing me to enjoy the line of her neck as it flowed into the gentle swell of her breasts. The candlelight played in a flickering arabesque across the multi-jeweled barrette she was wearing on the right side of her shoulder length hair, perfectly placed to bring attention to her lovely face. It reminded me of the Vermeer painting, "Girl with a Pearl Earring" and it would not have had the same effect if she'd worn the barrette on the other side of her head.

My curiosity aroused I asked Kathryn, "How did you manage to get out tonight?" Her green eyes danced with a devilish look and she admitted, "I have told you a little lie. Yes, I am married, but I've been separated for over eleven months and will soon be divorced."

I felt a little chill run through me.

As the evening passed we shared events of our lives and discovered one another in newfound passion. At some point looking into Kathryn's eyes I saw her life in another place, another dimension.

Kathryn reached across the table and covered my right hand with hers and asked softly, "Brett honey, you look like you just saw a ghost—what's wrong?"

"Oh, it's nothing, I found myself having a frazzled thought. Your beauty takes me to places I haven't been before and I don't quite know how to handle it."

She squeezed my hand and gave me a mischievous wink, "Let's eat. You must be starving after your afternoon workout."

Over a fine roast beef dinner we sipped the last vestiges of our musky Cabernet, savoring every drop as if it were a special gift. Unfortunately, when it came to dessert, *The Foxes Crumpet* lived up to its British reputation and did not have any homemade fruit pie. We finished our date with two snifters of Grand Marnier.

We left the restaurant in the glow of infatuation, holding hands as we made our way back towards my room. Kathryn insisted we stop at her car to "pick up a few things." The few things turned out to be an overnight bag that contained everything from a change of clothes down to her items of toilette. It even had few bottles of water tucked into it.

When we got back to my room, Kathryn seemed very interested in my map, which lay open on the table, she asked, "I'm curious. Where are you going, and was it fun being on the road all alone?"

I told her it was exciting and talked about the trip so far and some of my past travels. I finished by saying, "You are by far the most thrilling part of the journey!"

She rewarded me with a glorious smile and said, "Why, Brett honey, you sure know how to make me feel good."

I found her soft southern drawl enthralling, including the way she said my name and an endearment in one breath.

At some point, we made our way to the bed and gently caressed each other until our passion drove us into becoming one. When we finally exhausted our mutual desire, we drifted into a lovers' slumber.

Day 3

In the morning light we rekindled our passion for one another with the ease of a butterfly mating with a flower. As I was about to culminate in my desire, Kathryn held me tight and, in a voice that was almost a whisper, asked, "Will you take me with you?"

The question hurled my mind into a vortex of confusion and I could not give her an answer. After a moment Kathryn slipped out of the room to fetch us some coffee and I went to take a shower. The pulsating stream of water had none of the magic from the night before. My mind was racing through different scenarios, none of them plausible or realistic. I knew I could not take Kathryn with me. Her presence, no matter how lovely, would change my journey of freedom into a very different kind of trip. At best, it would distort my focus; at worst, we could end up in flames. I had to find a way to let her down gently.

As I stepped out of the shower, Kathryn was waiting for me with a towel and started to rub me dry. For an instant I thought about changing my mind and finding a way to take her with me.

When I was about to speak, she put her finger to my lips and said, "Don't say what you are going to say. I was wrong to ask you to give up your dream just because I am lonely and you are charming. Yes, I would love to go on a road trip with you and shed my responsibilities at home, but it has to be your choice and not mine."

Having settled that issue, we spent the next 23 hours together, exploring one another, and our lovemaking propelled us to unimaginable heights.

Day 4

Kathryn and I shared our final kiss early the following morning. By 7:30 I was on the road again. I had planned on heading to Memphis for some lunchtime ribs but decided to put them on the back burner, so to speak, as I felt the call to join up with one of the oldest, most historic highways in America. The Natchez Trace Parkway was built all the way back in 1809 as a link between the southern Appalachian foothills of Tennessee and the bluffs of the mighty Mississippi. It would take me past Grinders Stand near the town of Hohenwald where Meriwether Lewis of Lewis & Clark fame met his mysterious end, perhaps by suicide brought on by severe depression. The road would offer plenty of beautiful scenery and loads of history, no stores or billboard advertising is allowed on the 444 miles of two-lane, black asphalt; nor are commercial vehicles permitted. I would take the parkway 165 miles down to Mathiston, where I planned to pick up U.S. 82 West and cross "The Big Muddy," as people around those parts refer to the storied Mississippi River.

It was warming up, with temperatures heading into the 70s. Crossing the Tennessee River at the old Colbert Ferry site near Lauderdale, Alabama, was breathtaking. The morning sun played with the rippling water, forming golden bands that mimicked the palette of the shoreline sand and rocks. Entering Mississippi was like driving into a tunnel of color. The fall leaves were singing the praises of life. Even the leaves that had dropped onto the black tarmac continued to display their fall radiance. And the *Valkyrie* was purring in harmony with this glorious day.

All too soon I reached my exit and had to attune myself to different surroundings. Leaving God's art gallery and turning onto U.S. 82 was a sobering experience. The vibrant colors of the forest were replaced by the cool blush of faded billboards and the garish glare of fast food signs that lined the highway entering Winona, Mississippi.

After passing through the town and crossing Interstate 55, I was back on the hunt for a more congenial road. I found it Greenwood, Mississippi. Riding through this part of the country was like going all the way back to the origins of the blues. That quintessentially American music started in these delta regions with the work songs and field hollers of black cotton pickers. The great blues artist Robert Johnson cut his reputed deal with the devil here. Legend has it that he met the devil at the crossroads of Route 49 and Route 61 just north of Greenwood and traded his soul in order to achieve musical virtuosity as a singer, composer and guitarist. He certainly became one of the great delta bluesmen but lived only a short life, dying in 1938 at the age of 27.

I turned off U.S. 82 and headed into Greenwood. Cruising through the downtown along Howard Street gave me a real thrill. I have always loved the blues, and it was a real treat to see the place responsible for enriching our musical heritage. Howard Street was the home of the first radio station in the south that played live black gospel music. One of the most popular groups were the Saint John's Quartet, which included a young guitarist named Riley King. He later worked his way up to Memphis, where he changed his name to B.B. King and became one of the greatest blues guitarists of all time.

I was about to leave this celebrated town when I caught an image out of the corner of my eye that caused me to stop and take a closer look. The building looked to be about 50 years old and had gone through many metamorphoses in the five decades of its existence. It had started out as an urban filling station, but most traces of its origin had disappeared. What remained was a whitewashed cinder block edifice which would not have been all that special if it hadn't been for what was painted on the outside wall. The latest entrepreneur to occupy it was apparently a street chef/artist, who specialized in hot tamales, burgers, fries and sodas. But his or her real claim to fame was "Shave Ice," which was hand painted in blazing red lettering across the top of the building. Underneath it were pictures of the other food items, depicted in a style that suggested the "Shave Ice" writer was responsible for them, too.

On closer inspection, I noticed that the previous tenant apparently had had a propensity for hand lettering, too. Under the freshly whitewashed façade, just visible to the eye, were enticements for Bubba's Peach and a word that shall forever remain a mystery because it was covered over with a giant painted hamburger. I figured the word must have been "Margarita," as I found a close cousin, spelled "Margarith," just below the Shave Ice advertisement. So here I had a new business that still kept its artistic ties with the previous establishment.

Stepping back to get a better perspective on the whole building revealed two rather tattered bathrooms on the same side as the depiction of food and shaved ice. The problem was that both of the doors had been removed, as had the toilet seats, leaving a rather nasty impression. I decided to shoot the place using a lens that would allow me to crop out the fresh air lavatories, leaving just the essence of the urban frescos. I opted for my Leica camera with a 50mm lens and a versatile, hand-held light meter. The sun was at its highest point, usually not an attractive angle for photography, but for this subject I wanted the harsh light. I chose Fujichrome RDP film for its ability to hold color on a white background and used an extremely small lens opening of F-16. Since everything I wanted to show was on one plane, I did not need any depth of field. I underexposed the scene by one full stop, firing the shutter at 1/125 of a second, and bingo! There it was—an image that lived both in the here and now and in the past.

I knew that I had the picture I wanted but decided to try out my Rolleiflex to see what she could do. I found a roll of 120 film in the bottom of the bag, loaded her up and placed her on the tripod. The camera came with a "fixed" 80 mm lens, so I found the right position, with all other options being the same as the previous shoot. Trusting my ear to judge that the shutter speeds on the camera were still accurate, I pushed the button, heard the distinctive click and captured "Shave Ice" for the world. It's hard to describe the feeling when you know that you have caught a piece of the past on film and transformed it into art, but I sure felt elated riding out of town.

My day had started with a kiss, followed by a ride through an autumn dreamland and an unexpected addition to my book—and it was only two in the afternoon. It looked like I would be crossing the most famous river in America with the sun acting like a beacon to the west. I thought about taking a little detour to B.B. King's birthplace in Indianola, Mississippi, but decided to look for a little café where I might grab a burger and a piece of fruit pie.

I changed my mind when a Chinese restaurant caught my eye on the east side of Greenville. The front of *The Golden Dragon* was typical oriental kitsch, right down to the painted dragon whose mouth opened wide enough to encompass the front door. But inside the décor was all fine representations of mid-50s southern hodgepodge with pictures of Dale Earnhardt where there normally would have been reproductions of the Great Wall. The tabletops were brown Formica sans any type of linen. My Chinese waiter sported a Metallica tee shirt with an inordinate amount of glitter and wore tight jeans that had the words "love" and "hate" embroidered on the rear pockets. I thought, *This is one confused Chinaman.*

The waiter plopped a menu down in front of me with the muffled comment, "Most people just have the buffet."

I followed his suggestion and moseyed over to the food table which, with its garish lighting, looked like something out of the TV show *The Twilight Zone.* There were no Chinese dishes whatsoever—no Lo Mein, no Kung Pao or General Tso chicken, no dishes with "delight" in the title, and most disturbing, no pork! They did have two kinds of rice to go with catfish, collard greens and mounds of fried chicken. I grabbed some, figuring it would go well with the black-eyed peas which were generously spiked with fatback. As I scooped the southern delicacies onto my plastic faux Chinese plate, I thought, *This may very well be the first Heavy Metal Chinese Chicken Palace in the world.*

Returning to my table, I noticed that my rhinestone speckled waiter had brought me some water in a red plastic container, identical to the cup in the B*at Cave Café*. The food turned out to be surprisingly tasty. Between bites I became occupied with the place mat which featured the Chinese Zodiac. I found out that I am a goat, which made me a little nervous, considering there was a sign over the cash register proclaiming Sunday as "Goat Roast Day."

I left the heavy metal *Dragon* with a full stomach and I headed west on the old highway. The air was fresh and the afternoon sky had that special glow that seems to be in hibernation during the summer months and only comes awake on special fall days. The sun's rays were dancing off my gold tinted visor, but not in a blinding way. No, this was a tantalizing sun that emitted soft beams that warmed both body and spirit.

After I crossed the Mississippi river at Greenville, the road shrank to a two-lane affair, but the view was magnificent as the river split around a series of small islands and wound its way toward "The Big Easy." Every time I rode across this historic waterway from east to west, I got a feeling of independence, and this time was no exception. For me, the western bank of the river represented "new Earth" the entrance to the openness of the great West and liberation from the congestion of the East.

I figured Lake Village, Arkansas would be a good stopping place and found a great cabin in Lake Chicot State Park about eight miles outside of town. As I checked in, an old coot named Buddy overwhelmed me with information on Lake Chicot. I took two things away from his 12-minute dissertation. The first was that the lake was the largest oxbow lake in North America. It seems that many years ago a renegade branch of the Mississippi river split off from the main stream and formed this 20-mile, U-shaped lake. The second item really peeked my interest. Legend had it that Hernando De Soto met his demise here and was buried in the lake to keep his body away from the natives. I wondered what the conquistador had done to piss off the Indians so much that they wanted to scalp or decapitate the old boy. Had he done a little "exploring" in the valley of the squaws? Old Buddy did not have an answer to that question.

Since my cabin had a full kitchen, I took the time to find a grocery store and stocked up for some home cooking. I enjoyed olive oil and garlic spaghetti with a liberal sprinkling of Parmesan cheese and a bottle of local red wine, which turned out to be a surprisingly good Merlot. Dessert would be a hot shower and a call to Kathryn.

Hearing her voice sent chills through my body, and when I told her so, she said the same thing was happening to her. We talked for hours about everything and nothing, telling each other about our dreams and aspirations. I wanted to finish this seemingly never ending photo project and start to earn a living by writing and painting. I was making a decent living selling art by the Masters, but that didn't provide the satisfaction of using my God-given talent to support myself.

Kathryn's wishes were a little more esoteric. She desperately wanted to find the spiritual answers to the mysteries of her life. When I pushed her for more information, she told me that she was childless and would remain so—she had lost her child-bearing ability when she had major complications giving birth to a stillborn baby boy. As Kathryn told me her heartbreaking story, I felt the deep sadness in her soul. I did my best to alleviate her despondency and felt that I made some headway.

But what she shared next aroused a level of anger in me that I had not experienced in years. Kathryn felt that God had taken her baby boy to save him from the abuse that he would have had to live with.

With a quivering voice, she told me that her husband had frequently beaten her. She believed that had she not been around, he would have taken his rage out on their child. She needed to know if her feelings were legitimate, or if life was just a crapshoot. I knew that the answers to such unfathomable questions were buried deep within each of us and could only be called out through intense meditation. On impulse, I promised that I would help her in her spiritual awakening and that one day she would have her answers.

As Kathryn lay softly whimpering on her bed hundreds of miles away, I made love to her with my voice until she fell asleep. I hoped she got a good night's rest. My own slumber was interrupted with dreams of abuse, destruction and resurrection.

Day 5

When I parted the drapes the next morning and saw my rain-soaked motorcycle, I realized that my streak of sunny weather had come to an end. I made myself an omelet and some coffee and flipped on the weather channel. The local forecaster informed me that temperatures would reach a high of 55 degrees and rain would accompany me all the way to eastern Texas. The one good thing was being able to dress in my rain gear here in a dry room without having to change on the road in a downpour. After my second cup of coffee, I headed out into my rainy day adventure.

Once I got on the open road, the raindrops hit my visor and ran off in a mad dash to join the rushing wind of my slipstream. Motorcycling in the rain almost always drove me inward, and today was no different as I started to reflect on the women in my life.

I had been married a couple of times but things hadn't worked out. In fact, my relationships with women always came down to trust issues. Ever since I was a teenager I had seen many moral women give up their values with a sexy glance for a good lay, regardless whether they were with someone already or not. I also knew I gravitated towards women I could master and had a knack for finding good prospects. I looked for the ones with a roving eye, who would shoot a backwards glance over their partner's shoulder as they left a party, club or church. I was always amazed that the House of the Lord proved one of the most fertile hunting grounds. I often told myself that I was looking for virtuous women but, in retrospect, I had to admit I tended to overlook those qualities in my rush to plant the seeds of my lust.

Immersed in these thoughts, I hardly noticed my surroundings as I sped through Crossett, El Dorado and Magnolia, Arkansas. Only when the traffic picked up as I approached the conurbation of Texarkana did I realize it was time to wake up, so to speak, and gear up for city driving. I figured I would be out of the congestion in about 40 minutes.

The rain continued to come down hard as I joined Interstate 30 just east of the city and cruised along at the speed traffic allowed. I was in the far right lane and started to pass a woman who was driving at a snail's pace to my left. I pulled alongside her and glanced over. To my surprise, she was incredibly beautiful and reminded me of a Greek Goddess from a faraway dream of mine. She was gripping the wheel hard and stared straight ahead, oblivious to anything but her fear of driving in the rain. Without looking right or left, she suddenly decided to pull into my lane. The problem was that I had another vehicle in front of me and there was nowhere for me to go. My only option was to accelerate rapidly and try to motor out of harm's way.

In situations like this you have no time to think, you must simply react. I dropped down a gear, pulled back on the *Valkyrie's* throttle and let it fly. I hit the right shoulder of the highway fast, quickly reaching 100 miles an hour. I felt the front tire start to "float" as I flew by the car in front of me. Then I saw up ahead a discarded, coffee-colored armchair sitting on the shoulder next to the road.

Suddenly, everything around me went into slow motion.

The bike started to drift on the wet pavement, forcing me to lean hard to the left. Somehow I managed to miss the overstuffed chair. I have no idea how. It couldn't have been by more than an inch. But the mile marker next to where the brown armchair was resting stuck in my mind. The number was 223 and I remember thinking it odd that I noticed it. The things that stick in your mind in moments of great peril!

Once I was past the car on my left, I managed to stabilize the bike and rejoin the right lane. I backed off the gas until I was cruising at 60 again. As things returned to normal motion, I felt like I had been in another world. I had experienced no fear until it was over and realized that, without the *Valkyrie's* horsepower or my motorcycle experience, I would have joined the graffiti that adorned the sidewall of the Interstate at mile marker 223.

I suddenly become aware that I needed to find a bathroom fast. I stopped at the Texas welcome center and had what an old friend of mine referred to as "a good clear out." Much relieved, I motored my way to New Boston, Texas where U.S. 82 finally left the freeway and became its own road again.

I found a cozy café to warm myself with a big mug of hot chocolate. The frothy liquid was doing a fine job of bringing me back to normal. While waiting for my body to thaw, I amused myself watching how far the waitress's already short skirt would rise as she bent over the ice cream trough to dig out the creamy treats. The skirt finally traveled all the way up her legs, exposing a tattoo of a snake, wrapped around her thigh. The serpent's head was not visible, exploring the world beneath her underwear. I mused that it was a sexy snake indeed, and would be a hell of a turn on for a panties sniffing herpetologist.

At some point I asked the waitress, "Do you have any homemade fruit pie?"

She shook her head and offered me some ice cream instead. I considered staying a while to watch the slithering serpent again, but as enticing as the thought was, I asked for the check instead.

The ride from New Boston to Paris, Texas was uneventful, but the weather started to clear up. The sky lifted its gray shroud and exposed a bit of light blue that held the promise of sunshine. I pulled into a parking lot to remove the yellow oilskins from my black leathers. The adjacent building had a 50-foot long mural depicting life in Paris, France. Standing in a puddle I felt like Gene Kelly in *An American in*

Paris, and I expected Leslie Caron to come dancing out of the mural at any moment.

I had been to Paris, Texas before, so when I cruised around town, it didn't take long before I ran into and old friend—one of the city's icons, a 65-foot tall replica of the Eiffel Tower. Now, granted the French original is 984 feet in height, but the Texas version sported a four-and-a-half-foot, red Stetson Hat sitting on top and casting quite a shadow with its 10-foot wide brim. For a few years the town billed itself as "The Second Largest Paris with the Second Largest Eiffel Tower." Unfortunately, the glory didn't last. Las Vegas built its own 540-foot version, eclipsing half of Paris' claim to worldwide fame.

I wasn't ready to stop for the night and drove on. After having an early dinner in a Mexican eatery in Bonham, I rode for another half hour until I reached Sherman, Texas where motels were plentiful.

I found a room in one of the look-alike slumber palaces and checked in for the night. One of the motel's amenities was an indoor pool and I figured that after my mostly damp drive, I could use a good soak. The pool was heated and had a Jacuzzi next to it. The only problem was the smell of chlorine vapors that were trapped inside the building, but I ignored them as best I could. Having the spa all to myself was both good and bad. I could swim in circles and flip around like a maniac without having to worry about running into someone. On the downside, "playing Flipper" got boring in a hurry.

On previous trips, I had found these concrete ponds to be a good place to pick up a partner for a little play in the hay, but on this night my mind kept flashing to Kathryn's sweet face. Although something about her troubled me, I found her mysteriously stimulating.

I was about to mount the pendulum of love and lust and swing toward a new romance, but my intuition kept warning me to back away and get a better focus on the situation. My passionate side kept pulling me towards the promise of Kathryn's sweet honey, but I worried that she might also have a vicious sting if I got too close to her hidden secrets. At the same time, she clearly needed someone to pull her out of her mire of sadness and was asking me for help. I wanted a little more time to see if her hunger came from a true desire to break free or just needy desperation. I also wanted to be certain that my craving for her was driven by Cupid's arrow, not just my desire to control another helpless female.

Despite my yearning to call her I decided that on this night I would not yield to my infatuation and went to sleep without hearing Kathryn's soothing voice.

Day 6

By the time I woke up, the weather gods had delivered a great day for motorcycling—not a cloud in the sky and hardly any wind, a rarity in the Lone Star State. Now all I needed was to locate a great photographic opportunity and maybe find a laundromat. I was wearing my last clean set of underwear. Traveling a little further west on Route 82 brought me to Gainesville. I decided to head towards New Mexico on an old country road, Texas 51 South.

I always loved the narrow, hilly corridor that ran from Dallas to Austin, with its picturesque rolling terrain. But I knew that while this old country road would give me a good dose of moist-scented, green pastures, it would not inoculate me against the rank smell of gas and oil in the barren, sage covered land beyond.

A little before 11 a.m., I found a laundromat on U.S. 380 in the town of Throckmorton whose only claim to fame is being the nexus of several highways. As luck would have it, the change machine dispensed five dollars' worth of quarters and the soap dispenser coughed up a box of Tide without a hitch. While waiting for my clothes to wash, I spent the time cleaning off the road dust and small specks of dirt which had collected on my camera lenses and filters.

I was on my third lens when I looked up and saw a young, blond-haired girl standing in the doorway. She was sucking on a straw sticking out of a super-sized cup with "Dr. Pepper" in large green letters on the side. I had no idea what kind of concoction she was drinking. She was dressed in cut off jeans and a black tee shirt with the head of Mickey Mouse covering most of the front and could not have been more than 15. I wondered what she was doing out of school. She surveyed the place as if looking for someone. When she saw that I was the only person there, she stepped cautiously inside and started to walk towards me. When she got close, she put her drink on top of a washing machine and pulled up her Mickey Mouse shirt exposing her small starter breasts for a few seconds.

Looking at me, she asked in a diminutive, uncertain voice, "Do you want to buy some pussy?"

I did a double take and replied in my sternest voice, "I came in here to clean my clothes, not my dick. And what are you doing turning tricks when you should be in school?"

Picking up her Dr. Pepper cup from the top of the washer, she said, "Don't be mad at me. My mom makes me do these things."

"Why would your mom make you into a whore?'

"So she can have money for drugs."

"How old are you?"

"Thirteen."

I could not believe what I was hearing. "Where is your mother now?"

"Getting high in the van."

I started to go and give that pimping bitch a piece of my mind, and maybe a piece of my boot as well, but the young girl stopped me by putting both of her hands on my chest and said, "My mother's boyfriend will beat the shit out of me if you say something to my mom or call the police and make trouble for her."

When I asked her where she took the johns to have sex—it was obvious that the laundromat would not do—she pointed to the van and said, "In the back."

I gave her 10 dollars and said, "Tell your pimping mother that you had no luck with the old biker dude in the laundromat and keep the money for yourself."

She looked at me with deep sorrow in her blue eyes, an emotion no 13-year-old should feel, and said, "Thanks Mister, I wish to God that you were my Dad."

And then she was gone.

I caught a glimpse of her mother, looking like a washed-out junky, as she drove the old, brown and tan Dodge van into the highway, no doubt looking for another score.

The episode so upset me that I sat dumbfounded in the laundromat thinking about it for a good hour after my clothes were washed and dried.

With a troubled heart I got on my bike and pushed on down the road, hoping that being on the move would lift my depression. Around four in the afternoon, I pulled into Rule, Texas, a tiny "blink of an eye" town, where Texas 6 crosses U.S. 380 on its long meander down to Galveston. The place is nothing more than a few old, dilapidated buildings surrounding a gas station. I had visited it a few years back and had the good fortune to capture a classic photograph of the Rule fire station.

Since then, somebody had had the good idea of turning the vacant stores that housed tumbleweeds and empty beer bottles into an outdoor art exhibit by having various artists paint wonderfully naïve depictions on the facades of what they thought life used to be. One of the paintings featured the front of a movie theatre, complete with a little boy reaching up to the woman behind the glass of the ticket booth. She looked like everyone's grandmother and was smiling at the young lad as she passed him his ticket. Unfortunately, somebody had added vomit coming out of her mouth. Across the street was a representation of a flower vendor next to a picture of a meat market. These two hadn't been vandalized.

But what caught my eye was a new mural on the wall of the volunteer fire department, a simple cinder block building. It depicted a hook and ladder truck and five volunteers in firefighter regalia hanging on in precarious fashion. The driver whose helmet was adorned with the word "Chief" had a severe expression, looking like a Kamikaze pilot about to crash into a destroyer. The interesting thing was that the background scene had turned into a mass of peeling paint from the intense Texas sun, casting deep shadows. I took out my cameras and captured just him to convey the feeling of what had happened to this ghost down.

I sat for a while on the shady side of the street, looking at the defaced ticket lady in the movie theatre mural on the other side and thinking about the pubescent prostitute I'd met earlier. I felt a strong urge to do something for this vulnerable child, to cast her a rope to get out of the well of shame into which her mother had cast her; but short of kidnapping her, I had no idea what I could do. Was it okay to interfere and commit a crime to save a life, or to sacrifice a life by not interfering? I wondered how I could find her again and what to do with her if I did. Then I began to wonder if I was crazy for even entertaining such a notion, which could lead to unthinkable consequences. Better to move on and forget her.

I left the cool shade of the curb, got back on my motorcycle and continued heading west. Maybe in a few days she would be out of my mind, and that would be that.

I drove all the way to the city of Brownfield, the "Star of the South Plains," and decided to hole up for the night. I found a room in the Best Western and opened a bottle of bourbon I'd bought. I turned on my cell phone and thought about making a call to Kathryn. There was no ice bucket in the room, so I poured a good splash of bourbon into a flimsy plastic cup that all hotels seem to supply to their guests and headed to the ice machine. Unfortunately, it was designed to fill an ice bucket to the top, no more, no less.

As I was standing there trying to figure out how to coax three or four ice cubes from the spigot, a woman came up with her empty bucket.

I explained my dilemma and asked, "Could I get a few cubes from you?"

She flashed a saucy smile, and said, "If I can get a few drops of what's in your cup."

Nodding in the affirmative, I said, "Why don't you come to my room for a real splash of Bourbon?"

She didn't hesitate. "I'll meet you there in a few minutes. I have to get my cigarettes."

The thought of someone smoking in my room did not please me. I'd had a hell of a time a few years back giving up that addiction. But I was curious what her story was and where our encounter would lead. I put her somewhere in her late 30s to early 40s. She was on the tall, voluptuous side and seemed to be in good shape. It occurred to me that she was quite hot for her age and had that "fuck me" look about her. I caught myself, a little shocked how fast my mind turned to sex. More than likely she only wanted a drink.

The cell phone chirped just as there was a knocking on my door. Looking quickly at the screen, I saw that it was Kathryn. Why did I always have to make choices when it came to my liaisons? I blindly toggled the phone to voice mail and answered the door.

A smiling, sexy woman greeted me, carrying a pack of Parliaments and a bucket of ice. She walked into the room, held out her hand and said, "My name is Karri."

I introduced myself, "Brett."

Then I grabbed the ice bucket, tossed a few cubes into another plastic cup, and splashed a good shot of the bourbon on top. When I handed Karri the drink and offered her a chair; she chose the foot of the bed instead. In no time we were talking about sex and what we liked and disliked. I told her a bit about photographing Kathryn and how sexy it had been.

She said, "I'm adverse to physical sex because it's dangerous as hell these days."

Pouring us another round of bourbon, I agreed with her, even though I still went with my vibes as to who was clean and who was not—a bit like Russian roulette, I realized.

Karri started to pull a cigarette out of the Parliament box and was about to put it in her mouth when I reached over and handed her the fresh drink. I pulled the unlit cigarette from her lips and said, "That's a no-no in my room."

For a moment she looked concerned, but my next question got her mind on to other addictions. "What do you do for pleasure if you do not have sex with warm-blooded people?"

"My big thing is phone sex. I have quite a few partners who share my view."

I was intrigued. "Who are these people and what do you talk about?"

"Every one of my phone partners has different fantasies and I love them all." She looked at me slyly and asked, "Have you and Kathryn tried it?"

"I have made love to Kathryn over the phone," I acknowledged.

Karri laughed and said, "We consider that missionary sex. Our group is way beyond straight stuff, and besides, I don't know if I could get off talking about a straight fuck."

As we continued talking, I realized that Karri was completely addicted to raw phone sex and I was getting turned-on by the thought of it all. After another shot of bourbon, Karri asked me, "Would you like to hear me in action? I am supposed to call one of my bitches."

I nodded.

"We'll have to go to my room—my 'equipment' is there," she said. "Besides, I'm dying for a smoke."

I grabbed my cell phone, the ice bucket and the booze and followed her like a new puppy down the hall. Her room was identical to mine, except for the heavy, permeating smell of smoke.

I watched in fascination as Karri pulled a giant dildo from her suitcase. "Here is my 'equipment,' my Steely Dan," she cooed.

She flipped a switch at the end of the make-believe monster cock and it started to twirl and dip in interesting patterns. The device was clearly designed to drive the recipient into the sexual stratosphere of pleasure. Still, I had a hard time believing that she could impale herself on the entire, 10-inch long, twirling log.

She mixed us a couple of fresh drinks and lit her cigarette. Then she said, "Just relax and enjoy yourself. I have to warn you, though. My friend Beth is a fast and furious comer who mainly loves to listen, but on occasion she lets fly with some randy talk. Don't be offended."

"There isn't much I haven't heard," I said gamely.

Karri slipped out of her clothes as if she were the only person in the room. She had a sinuous body with large breasts that splayed out to the sides as she leaned back comfortably on the big bed. Propping herself up on three pillows, she slowly lubricated the dildo, all the while looking at the front of my pants, which started to bulge with my enlarging penis. She put her cell phone on speaker mode and keyed in a number. After a few rings a soft voice answered with a sweet "Hello." Barely audible in the background I could hear the faint hum of a vibrator being turned on.

Not wasting any time on idle chatter, Karri started right in to drive "her bitch" wild, telling her what she is going to do to her. Most of what she promised I had used myself, but there were some unusual techniques to bring someone to a thunderous climax I had never heard of before.

After a while Karri started to insert the fake penis into her vagina and copulate with herself while coaxing Beth to her first orgasm. I could not believe how deep she managed to implant her Steely Dan. She turned it on when Beth was having her second and third climax— one after the other. Then Beth started moaning about tying Karri up, fucking her into submission, and urinating on "her fat titties." That promise got them off at the same time.

I had to admit that this form of sex seemed to be more liberating and inventive than anything I had experienced before.

After they were done, Karri hung up and asked, "Well, what do you think?"

I said, "It blew my mind. I totally understand why you love it."

She smiled knowingly. "You know, Beth's husband was right next to her and got off watching her fucking herself and listening to us girls hard at play."

"How much do you charge for your phone service?"

She slowly licked her lips and replied, "We are all in this because we love it. There is no money involved, just good, raunchy sex."

I fixed us another drink, putting a serious dent in the bottle of Jack.

Karri asked casually, "Would you like to try it with Kathryn and me?"

I had no idea if Kathryn would be interested, "I'll talk to her tonight about it and if she is, we can all have a go on the phone."

"Why don't you let me call her? I can talk just about anyone into sexual play."

I gulped down my bourbon and went to use the bathroom. It occurred to me that it would be interesting to see if Kathryn would let herself be baited on Karri's sexual hook. It also would show me, one way or another, what she was all about.

When I returned Karri had changed into a sexy black lingerie. Noting my quizzical look, she purred, "I want to watch your cock pulsate as Kathryn undresses me."

Stung, I snapped, "Leave me out of this and see if you can seduce Kathryn without my help!"

Smiling at me, Karri removed a small vibrator from her bag of tricks and placed it in the same position by her side.

I fixed us two drinks with what was left in my bottle and moved to the bed. I wanted to be a little closer to the action on this call.

A little thrill shot through me when I heard Kathryn's familiar voice. Karri told Kathryn she got her number from a friend who felt they both were in the same predicament, with estranged, abusive husbands, and suggested that maybe they could bond and help one another to heal from their pain. I almost started to laugh at such a far-fetched sounding sob story and thought that Kathryn would hang-up, but I was dead wrong. Karri's come-on worked to perfection, and soon all-too-familiar, little choking sounds started to emanate from the phone as Kathryn shared some of her sadness with Karri.

Within minutes Karri had her talking about her need to be fulfilled and before long, to my amazement, she had Kathryn begging her to "lick my hot cunny." My mind recoiled at the thought that someone could seduce a total stranger using only the phone, but my rock hard penis told me otherwise. It was at this point that I realized that I had gone too far in letting this mistress of seduction coax my new lover into wantonness. I quietly got off the bed and walked out the door a dejected man, castigating myself for once again letting my insecurities ruin a potentially wonderful love affair.

I was not in my room more than 20 minutes when my cell phone started to ring. I figured it was Karri wanting a little nightcap, but the voice that came back to me was Kathryn's. Feeling suddenly awkward, I was at a loss for words. My mind ran through all the possible situations that Kathryn had acted out with Karri after I left.

Kathryn must have read my mind, because she said, "Did you enjoy the show?"

I nervously asked, "What show was that?"

"Why, honey, the one you and that depraved bitch had me do."

I was stunned. Fortunately, Kathryn, figuring I had had enough, let me off the hook. It turned out that when she had called me earlier, rather than toggle my cell phone to voice mail, I had inadvertently hit the speaker button, enabling her to hear most of what Karri and I were talking about. She had been pretty pissed off when she heard another woman in my room. But, after a few minutes, she realized that I was more curious than lustful. So, when her phone rang and it was Karri, she already knew what it was about. She decided to get over her anger and give me a little show. Besides, she had always wanted to try something kinky like that.

"But in the future," Kathryn said sternly, "you have to ask me first before committing me to one of your sexual escapades. And never again give my phone number to freaky people!"

I said contritely, "I promise," and figured I'd gotten off easy.

But then Kathryn asked, "Did you have sex with Karri while she and I were talking?"

"No!" I exclaimed. "I felt nothing for her, other than morbid curiosity. Kathryn, it was like watching a bad adult film without popcorn, and the only thing that turned me on was hearing your voice."

The silence at the other end of the phone convinced me I had to go on. I relayed the trust issues I have with women I got close to and admitted that I was putting her through some kind of twisted test. There was another moment of silence.

Then Kathryn startled me with her soft reply, "I believe I am falling in love with you. I would never do anything to hurt you."

I felt both touched and thrilled.

She recovered some of her levity and asked, "Did I do a good job on the phone?"

"I am still turned on!"

"Do you need me to take care of you now?

"Yes."

Day 7

The next morning I awoke with my mind in turmoil. I could not get the image of the child prostitute from Throckmorton out of my thoughts. I fixed myself a cup of coffee and by the time I breathed in the familiar aroma, I'd come to a decision of sorts. Throckmorton was only about 190 miles back east from Brownfield, and I saw no harm in taking a run there to see if I could find the lost child.

I was just finishing checking out of the motel when the clerk handed me an envelope with my name on it. I tore it open and found a business card with the name Karri Blackman and a Los Angeles phone number on it. Printed sideways across the card in purple to give the effect of hand stamp running, were the words *CALL ME—I GIVE GOOD PHONE*. I stuck it in my wallet along with other cards and torn papers covered with names and numbers of people I had long forgotten.

The ride into the rising sun was chilly and uneventful, and by half past 10, I was back in Throckmorton. I figured I would go to the laundromat and do a small load, consisting only of a pair of underpants, a pair of socks, a tee shirt and a sweatshirt. While my clothes were dancing in the machine, I kept looking up, hoping that my lost Lolita would come waltzing through the door in search of someone who'd pay to play.

After an hour and a half I began to think that she would not be stopping by this morning. But as I was about to leave, I saw her mom's van pull into a parking space across the street. A minute later the girl jumped out of the van and started walking across the highway. My heart was racing with nervous anticipation as I watched the little blond waif approach in her cutoff jeans, tennis shoes, and green and white halter-top that hugged her diminutive breasts and drew attention to her small, hard nipples. It was obvious that she was quickly learning the tricks of the trade. I had a flashback of Jodi Foster crossing the street in Martin Scorcese's *Taxi Driver*. I hoped that our movie would not end with the kind of bloody ultra-violence unleashed by Robert De Niro's character, Travis Bickle, when he shot up the brothel.

The girl entered the laundromat cautiously. When her pupils adjusted to the change in light, her blue eyes settled on me and I noticed the beginnings of a smile of recognition.

"So, you are here again. I thought I recognized your motorcycle." Her voice had a more confident ring than yesterday.

Looking deep into her eyes, I said in a fatherly tone, "I have come back to talk to you about changing your life."

"What do you mean, change my life?"

In a more stern voice, I continued, "You need to get the hell away from that bitch in the van and you need to do it soon, or you will end up like her and one day you will be pimping your own daughter for drugs."

She rocked back a bit and replied with a whimper in her voice, "What can I do? I have nowhere to go and no money to live on, even if I had somewhere to stay."

"You told me yesterday that you wished that I were your father. Well, I would like to be your father and take you away from all of this. I don't know what it'll take to raise you; I just know I can."

She started to mist up a bit, inched closer to me, and in a small voice, tinged with fear, said, "I don't know, Mister. If my mom and her boyfriend catch me, they'll beat the shit out of me and might even kill me. Besides, how do I know that you are not like all the others and just want me to spread my legs so you can have some fun?"

I put my hand on her shoulder and said, "I am a good man and would never do anything to hurt you. Whether you come with me or not, I have driven a four-hundred-mile round trip to try and save your ass, and I've never done that for anyone before."

"Mister, you don't even know my name!"

"Well, what is it?"

"Kelly Porter. What's yours?"

"Brett Tempest."

We smiled at each other as she considered that. Then she asked, "How could we get away from Maryanne and Jake?"

"Who are they?"

"My mom and her sleazy boyfriend."

I thought for a moment, then asked, "Do you ever get out on your own?"

She nodded. "They usually let me out around four and I can hang at the *Allsup's* until eight when it's time to go home and see if they want to cruise again."

"Where is that?"

"Just up the street," she said, pointing north.

"I tell you what. I'll be waiting in the convenience store parking lot from 3:30 to 4:30. And don't sneak any clothes out of the house. We can buy what you need on the road."

"Where are we going to go?"

"More than likely back east. But for right now, I think we should head towards California,"

I smiled reassuringly, and Kelly broke into a grin.

As she was leaving the laundromat, she turned around and, with an innocent, but concerned look on her face asked, "Brett, you won't hurt me, will you?"

"No, I won't, Kelly. I only want to protect you and let you know that somebody cares. You will never again have to sell yourself to anyone for any reason. And if you decide that you want to change your life and come with me, then put on long pants and a long-sleeved shirt because the motorcycle ride can blister your arms and legs with sunburn, and you'll be freezing your ass off."

She looked relieved and a small sigh escaped her. Then she turned around and was gone.

I had a lot to do. Rearranging the *Valkyrie* to make room for Kelly was the easy part. I only had to turn the big bag around so it rested on the luggage rack behind the sissy bar and bungee the sleeping bag on top. I needed to buy a helmet for Kelly and some riding gear, but those things could wait. First, I had to get her out of town and into a motel, and then we could find what we needed.

A couple of days earlier Kathryn had asked to take her with me, and I was not prepared to accommodate her wish because it did not suit my plans. How ironic that now, here I was, ready to change my life for a young hooker!

I was at the *Allsup's* by 3:15. Ten minutes later Kelly walked up the street in a long sleeved shirt, jeans and sneakers, looking like a 13-year-old girl, not a 16-year-old prostitute.

By 3:30 we were on U.S. 380 heading west.

Five hours and 300 miles later, I pulled into the Ramada Inn in Roswell, New Mexico. The sun was down, but there was still plenty of light. I stopped the bike under the motel's large portico and asked Kelly if she would like her own room.

She looked nervous as she said, "I want to stay with you, if you don't mind."

I understood how she felt. Had I been in her position, I would have said the same thing.

I booked a suite that had two queen beds and opened out to an enclosed courtyard that surrounded the swimming pool. Kelly helped me unload the *Valkyrie* and bring the bags into the room, something that would become part of her daily routine while we were on the road together.

While she looked around the suite, I ordered a large pizza and a couple of Cokes, since they did not have Dr. Pepper, her "drink of choice."

Over dinner we talked about our situation and what we would have to do to make it work. First and foremost, she could never call her mom or her mom's boyfriend, or any of her friends, for that matter. And from this day forward she would start a new life, completely separate from the last.

I asked her, "Will Maryanne go to the police when she discovers you're missing?"

She laughed and said, "My mom hates the police and they hate her. It'll take her a couple of days until her stash runs out. Then she might be desperate enough to look for me." She added, "My mom only thinks of me as a money machine. Whenever she needs to buy another bag of meth, she marches me out into the street."

I noticed that she was referring to her former trade as if she were still in it, so I said pointedly, "That is over now!" Then I asked, "What about Jake?"

"He is too stoned to give a shit one way or another." She smiled shyly and added, "Besides I have something on him, which guarantees he won't be any trouble."

Before I could ask her to elaborate, she said something that tore at my heart. "I don't have any friends, so you don't have to worry about me calling anybody."

I reached over the table and briefly held her hand. Kelly looked at me and smiled.

So far so good. But I knew that we were just taking the first baby steps on a very long and hard journey. I told her, "First thing after breakfast we'll go and buy you some clothes and personal items. You'll have your own set of leather riding gear."

When she heard that, she lit up like a neon sign. I figured I had a budding "road warrior" on my hands.

Kelly asked all the what, where and why stuff she could think of. But her big question was, "How do you make your money?"

When I said that I was an art dealer, she reacted as if I had told her that I sold real estate on Mars. She had no idea what it meant, so I gave her the dollar tour of the mysterious world of art, artists and art dealers. I finished by telling her that I had houses in North Carolina and Washington, D.C. and was out on the road to complete a photography book about America.

When Kelly realized that we did not have to worry about where our next meal was coming from, her whole body relaxed and she became more like a fun loving kid than a streetwise hustler.

We talked for quite a while about my self-appointed mission of photographing the back roads of the United States. I shared some of my more entertaining road stories and soon had her laughing and asking me if she could help me make photographs. I said that might be possible and, if she really got into it, then she certainly could work herself into being a real part of my photographic venture.

I thought about telling her that she would never have to turn another trick, but I had already promised her that and did not want to raise that subject back in her mind.

I did ask her about school.

Her face darkened when she admitted, "My mom pulled me out of school a year ago to work the streets and I have not been back since."

Sternly, I said "As soon as we get settled, I am putting your young ass back in school."

Kelly nodded, giving me the impression that it was fine with her.

We continued talking until midnight. When it was time to go to sleep, she chose the bed closest to the door for herself and went to take a shower first. I could hear her humming under the pulsating water. She emerged with a large bath towel wrapped around her body and another one around her head in a way that made her look like a very young nun. I gave her one of my tee shirts to sleep in. It draped all the way down to her knees. Twenty minutes later she was sleeping like a kitten in a pile of socks.

Day 8

Kelly didn't open her eyes until 9:15 the next morning. For the first minute or so she had that deer-in-the-headlights look, but when she had all her faculties back, she smiled up at me and said, "I'm hungry."

We found a cozy little restaurant with the cute name of *Mi Cabana* and stuffed ourselves with omelets and pancakes, washing them down with milk on her part and black coffee on mine. After breakfast we found a Target store and bought her a couple of pair of jeans and some tee shirts along with two sweatshirts. One of them had a large Mickey Mouse on the front. I found it pretty ironic—she'd been wearing the Disney rodent on her shirt the day we met, and it would be a good reminder of why we were together. We also added a nice bathing suit, cotton underwear, thermals and travel-size toiletries. At the last minute, Kelly grabbed a small box of tampons.

She also had her eye on a pair of gaudy green and purple shoes, but I said, "We only have enough room for your tennis shoes. Besides, I am going to buy you a pair of good motorcycle boots."

We found a motorcycle store right near our motel and I got her a leather jacket with matching pants, rain gear, a helmet that matched mine and a pair of good boots.

Back in our room, Kelly refused to take off her new leather jacket, which she had put on over her one-piece, pale yellow bathing suit that still had the tags dangling from a strap. She kept walking over to the mirror to check herself out. Watching her prance around reminded me of old Joe the cook wrapped in my heavy jacket with Ester laughing her head off. That North Carolina hash house seemed like a long time ago and in a completely different reality.

Over a late lunch, I told Kelly all about Kathryn and that I needed to call her tonight and spill the beans about what had happened.

Kelly looked a little worried, drew back like a worried kitten, and asked, "What will happen if Kathryn doesn't like me."

I assured her, "I don't think that will happen. And if it does, we will still be together, so don't worry."

Kelly came around to my side of the table and gave me a tight hug and kissed me on the cheek.

I was touched and I asked, "What would you like for dessert?"

"I really love cherry pie, and my second favorite is apple."

I looked at her with new admiration and asked the waitress. "Do you have any homemade fruit pie?"

The matronly woman said matter-of-factly, "Only some chocolate fudge cake and it's really good."

I checked with Kelly, whose face reflected what I was thinking, and said, "We'll take a pass."

We got back on the road our hungers sated, yet unsatisfied.

That night while Kelly sat on the edge of her bed wearing her new motorcycle jacket, I picked up the phone and made what would end up being a life changing call.

At first Kathryn was shocked, but as I laid out Kelly's tale of woe, she began to understand. Before I put Kelly on the phone, I assured Kathryn that this was not another phone sex game.

I poured myself a stiff bourbon on the rocks and nursed it for the duration of the call. The two of them talked for about 20 minutes. Then Kelly handed the phone back to me with a smile on her face.

Kathryn said, "I must be out of my mind, but you can count on my help to do whatever is needed to keep this child off the streets."

I was so excited to hear her say that I blurted out, "I love you and cannot not wait to see you again."

Kathryn said, "I love you, too." Then, in a soft, beseeching voice she added a familiar request, which tied the three of us together in an unusual way. "Brett, you won't hurt me, will you?"

I said with all my heart, "No, I won't Kathryn."

After bidding a warm goodnight to my lover, I noticed that my cup was not as full as when I had left it on the table by the chair. I sighed, realizing that I had a lot of work in front of me.

Before I could call my little motorcycle-jacketed sneak out of the bathroom for a little chat, the phone rang. It was Kathryn again wanting to know what the consequences of kidnapping might be. I spent the next half hour reassuring her it would be all right. I had a plan that would erase all of her worries about getting caught.

"This is not the time to go into details because I have to make a few phone calls to put it in place," I told her.

The explanation seemed to placate her for the moment, but I was sure that this was not the last time I'd get a concerned or anxious phone call from her about it.

I was so involved with Kathryn that I didn't notice Kelly coming back. When I hung up the phone, she was already in bed and fast asleep, with her jacket next to her. Our little talk about booze snitching would have to wait until morning. I turned out the lights, finished my drink in the dark, and fell asleep in the chair.

Day 9

We were both up at the crack of dawn. Over the sparse continental breakfast the motel offered its guests I gave Kelly the rundown on how to settle into the *Valkyrie*. I had noticed yesterday she was fighting the curves with her body, making it hard for me to keep the motorcycle balanced.

When we had finished packing the bike, we returned to the room and dressed for the road. Kelly mimicked my routine of putting on my garments, starting with thermals, adding the sweatshirt and finishing with the leathers and boots. She wasn't sure about the "weird looking" hair protector I made her wear over her freshly braided golden tresses. I gave her some advice on how to put on and remove her new, yellow and black helmet which she was not thrilled to wear. She fancied herself more like one of those "Harley chicks" who rode with their hair flying in back. But I insisted and described what her brains would look like if she had the misfortune to hit the concrete roadway at 70 miles an hour without the helmet.

I mounted the big *Valkyrie* first and steadied it while she hopped on the back. With a touch of the starter the powerful engine roared to life and we were on our way. Kelly followed my suggestions about how to become one with me and the motorcycle, and I didn't think we would have any more balance issues.

After we left Roswell, the highway started to turn lonely. At this time of the morning we pretty much had the road to ourselves. Kelly got into a routine of riding with her right hand on my shoulder, but every now and then she would wrap both of her arms around me and pull herself tight into my back, letting me know that she loved being there.

About 50 miles down the road, we arrived at the town of Hondo, New Mexico where I had to make a choice—keep driving straight on U.S. 380 to Socorro via some outlandish scenery and historic old houses in Lincoln and Capitan, or turn off on U.S. 70. That would detour us up the mountain to Ruidoso, a storybook town crowded with shops and cafés. I chose the detour.

When we got there, Kelly's eyes grew big as a pajama-clad kid's on Christmas morning—the glitz and glimmer of the countless shop windows cast their spell on my West Texas lass. We drove up and down Mechem and Sudderth Streets, passing by more shops than Kelly had ever seen in her young life. When something caught her eye, she tugged on my jacket and we'd pull over to have a gander. We saw everything from jackalopes to a stuffed jackass.

At *Michelle's* I bought Kelly a pair of Lucky brand Jeans and a black tee shirt with the Lucky logo on the front, which she insisted on wearing under her leather jacket right away. One of my plans for Kelly was to expose her to culture wherever I could find it. So it was off to *Studio W*, a gallery that exhibited a variety of paintings and sculptures with a focus on Southwestern art. I figured that cowboys and Indians would be more appealing to start with than Picasso or Miro.

The gallery was a maze of rooms. You never knew what the next space would contain. A large canvas by the artist John Hopkins, which showed a nice rendition of color-infused clouds, fascinated Kelly. I encouraged her to delve into the painting and find what the artist was trying to communicate. I loved watching her giving herself over to the experience. Her facial features transformed from concerned study to child-like joy as she unraveled the painting's meaning. After about two minutes of intense scrutiny, she said that it reminded her of freedom.

Before we left, I had one more lesson for her—in courtesy. We strolled over to the front counter and thanked the gallery owner for allowing us uninterrupted time to enjoy his presentations.

As we walked to the motorcycle, Kelly turned to me and, with the heartfelt emotion only a 13-year-old girl can muster over food, burst out, "I'm hungry."

We drove another mile and a half up the mountain until we came to the *Alto Café* in the village by the same name. If you didn't know how good the food served there was, you would not stop. I was one of the lucky ones who knew.

The *Alto Café* was only open from 6:30 a.m. to 3 p.m. It featured a great buffet for breakfast and lunch, and what Kelly and I planned to gorge ourselves on this afternoon was the Mesquite Smoked Bar-B-Que. Inside, the place was not much to look at—a few tables and chairs scattered about on a gray Formica covered floor. We grabbed a table for four, tossed our jackets and helmets on two of the chairs and sat down.

A silver-haired waitresses, who looked older than the place, approached us with menus and two red plastic glasses, which I assumed contained water. I waved off the menus and told her to just bring us some bar-b-que. She pointed to a small buffet table in the corner that was stacked with smoked meat.

As Kelly headed for the restroom, I watched her navigate through the café and marveled how good she looked in her Lucky shirt and leather pants. Two teenage boys sitting at a small side table with their backs against the wall were checking her out as she maneuvered around the tables.

I certainly could understand their fascination. Kelly was a real Texas beauty. She had not been in the "profession" long enough to acquire the battle scars of seasoned street traders. She still had a fresh, scrubbed look and her large, blue eyes seemed to welcome you with their innocence. She also had a perfectly shaped nose and the lips of a cherub. Her hair was of the color of white gold and came to a couple of inches below her shoulders, although today, with her braid, it rested at the nape of her neck. She was blessed with the magic combination of charm, beauty and innocent curiosity which, in the right mix, leaves people spellbound.

Kelly encountered the same appreciative scrutiny on her trip back to our table, only this time she caught the eye of the greasy looking cook as well. She slipped into her seat just as the boys were leaving. The timing pleased me because I needed to have a little talk with my wayward ward and did not want any teenage flirtations interfering with my message.

Before I could say what was on my mind, Kelly again blurted out with conviction, "I'm hungry."

So we headed over to the steam table to pig out, so to speak. The meat was as succulent as I had remembered, and we made a real dent in the café's stash.

When I felt that she had satisfied her prodigious appetite, I decided it was time to broach the subject of her sneaking a belt of my bourbon while I was on the phone with Kathryn. But as I looked into her eyes, she covered my hand with hers and said, "I know what you are going to say."

"What is that?"

Smiling nervously, she said, "I am sorry that I drank some of your whiskey last night."

I put on a stern expression. "What pissed me off wasn't so much the drinking, but that you were sneaky about it."

Kelly lowered her eyes and looked contrite.

I reached over, gently laid my hand on her arm, and asked, "Can I trust you to never do that again, whether it's sneaking a snort of booze or lifting a few bucks from my wallet?"

Her nervous blush gave way to a look of fear and she asked, "Are you going to punish me?"

I knew right then and there that this child had paid a lot of dues for her natural curiosity. I wondered what her twisted mother and Jake had done to her. One day soon, I needed to find out what was causing the flicker of fear in her eyes.

I shook my head and told her, "I've said what I had to say. I don't make a habit of doling out punishment for simple mistakes." Then I gave her arm a little squeeze and added, "If we are to make it as father and daughter, then we must be able to trust each other with our lives, because all we have is each other."

She seemed to relax a bit and said, "I will never cheat you again. I promise."

Leaving the café, I wanted to lighten things up a bit and asked, "Did you notice the boys looking at you?"

Kelly laughed and said, "I did, but the cook would have been good for fifty bucks."

I gave her a good smack on her leather-clad rear and said, "There will be no more of that!"

She put her arms around me and said, "I love you. Promise you'll never leave me."

I smiled to myself knowing in a few years it would be her leaving me to negotiate the minefield of adulthood.

We left Alto and made our way back down the mountain to join U.S. 380, just east of Carrizozo. This part of the highway is a motorcyclist's dream as it twists and turns over mountainous terrain. The starting point for the curvy portion of the road is the Valley of Fires National Park. I pulled off to the side to give Kelly a chance to see the black lava chunks that covered about 120 square miles of desert terrain. Although the highway view did not give her the full experience that going into the park would have, there were still plenty of lava boulders piled on top of each other to let her know that she was in a different world.

Kelly jumped off the bike and tossed her jacket back at me in a flash, and before I could count to three, she was cavorting among the volcanic boulders. I quickly pulled out the Leica, twisted a 90 mm lens onto the camera and went to work. Kelly's blond, youthful beauty in contrast to the black surroundings was magnified by the lens's telephoto optics. She was a natural model, able to become part of the vision without any self-consciousness as she gave herself up to my direction. She did not strike a stiff pose, she simply existed in the frame of my camera. I fired off about 20 shots and knew I had at least five workable emulsions. I photographed her in black and white but was pretty certain that color would have been just as effective. As I put away my camera, I wondered how she would react once she saw the photographs and realized she was an impressive model. An idea started to formulate in my mind that, maybe, I had just discovered the focal point for a new book.

After we drove on, Kelly developed up a couple of new riding habits. The first was putting her hands inside the pockets of my riding jacket and trying to pinch me through the thick leather. The second was even more personal and comical at the same time. She'd place her hands under my jacket and reach into the back of my pants where the leather bubbled out from the small of my back. Once she managed to get inside she'd insert a finger under the elastic of my underpants, pull it back and then let the rubber snap back into place. She also used this prank as a way to communicate, telling me when she needed a pit stop.

We soon arrived in San Antonio, New Mexico, a small hamlet where U.S. 380 came to an end at Interstate 25. It also had *The Owl Café* which, for my money, served the best green chili cheeseburger in all of New Mexico. We were still topped off from our bar-b-que extravaganza, however, so we didn't stop but headed north to Socorro to spend the night.

We pulled into the Best Western and I booked my usual two queen beds room. The nice thing about this hotel was that it had an indoor pool and hot tub, both adjacent to a full-size sauna. After we settled in, we went to a Chinese buffet restaurant we had passed on our way through town and made two satisfying trips through the chow line.

Back at the motel, Kelly had a quick shower and emerged from the bathroom decked out in her form fitting, pale yellow bathing suit—without tags this time—ready for the swimming pool. I gave her some do's and don'ts about talking with strangers along with her own plastic room key card, which had attached itself to Karri Blackman's purple and black phone sex card while it was in my wallet. As she read the card, a perplexed look crossed her face. Then she handed it back to me and left for the pool. I decided to use the time alone to call Kathryn and my brother Tommy back in Washington, D.C.

Hearing Kathryn's voice once again sent chills through me. She said how much she missed me and that her love for me had grown. Then she giggled.

I asked, "What's up?"

She explained, "I called an old customer whose name is Charles by your name. Not once, mind you, but, Brett honey, I did it to him twice." She added in her wonderful, soft Tennessee drawl, "You have made me blind with love and I am just beside myself."

Southern women have this wonderful ability to go from one subject to the next in the same breath, so she continued without missing a beat, "How is our little traveler doing?"

I told her that I had sent her down to the pool and filled her in on all that had transpired, right down to the excitement of our photo session. Kathryn shared my enthusiasm for starting a photographic chronicle of Kelly. I told Kathryn as much as I could about my plans, but that I was still working out the details and finished with, "I see the book as a surrealistic journey from puberty into adulthood, shot in bizarre settings, and I envision your beautiful body to be part of this photographic voyage as well."

There was a moment of silence at the other end of the line. Then Kathryn said with a highfalutin tone in her voice, "Maybe you should ask me if I would be willing to put the time and effort into doing this?"

I didn't hesitate. "Will you?"

"Yes, I would love to," she responded, giggling again.

While the two of us talked, time seemed to disappear. We must have been at it for about half an hour when Kelly came bursting through the door with her bathing suit still dripping and tears running down her flushed cheeks.

I told Kathryn to hold for a minute and asked, "What's wrong?"

She exclaimed, "Do I have the word whore written on me?"

Shaking my head, I gave her a quizzical look.

She went on, still upset, "I was in the sauna when a middle-aged couple came in and offered me money to go to bed with them. After I said, no, that nasty woman kept touching my breast and running her hands down here." She put her hand between her legs.

"What did they look like?"

"The man was tall and blond with a tattoo of some kind of black bird on the right side of his chest, and the woman had dark hair and was wearing a blue, two-piece bathing suit. She had large titties."

I kissed her wet cheeks and told her to stop crying. Then I picked up the phone from the desktop and asked Kathryn, "Did you hear any of that?"

"All of it."

I held out the phone to Kelly and said, "Talk to Kathryn. I'll be right back."

I was down to the pool in a flash, but nobody was there or in the sauna. I decided not to go to the front desk to complain and returned to the room. I found Kelly still on the phone with Kathryn, laughing about some shared secret. I was glad she had bounced back quickly to her normal self. I went and got Kelly a towel and gently wrapped it around her shoulders. She looked up at me with a warm smile that told me that she was over her shock and went back to chatting with Kathryn.

I interrupted them just long enough to say, "Keep talking. I'll be down at the pool making a call on my cell," and left to reach out to my brother in D.C.

Thomas William Tempest, better known in the clandestine world of espionage as "Tommy Gun Tempest," was two years and three months older than me. We looked roughly the same with me being an inch taller and just about 10 pounds heavier. The major physical difference between us was that Tommy had bluish green eyes, which were cold as ice and piercing as a killer's, hence the reference to the gun in his nickname. I possessed a gentler nature.

Tommy and I had remained close even though we conducted our-lives in very different arenas. His work required him to take care of a lot of bad situations, and he was good at it. As I saw it, kidnapping a young girl was a bad situation. Even though it was late, I took a gamble and called him at Langley and got through to him without too much hassle.

I only had to go through two "secretaries" before I heard a familiar voice, "Hey, little brother, what's shaking in the art world?"

We shot the breeze for a while before he asked what was really on my mind. I asked him to call me back on a safe phone as I needed to get some advice from him.

He asked, laughing, "Is this about pussy?"

I said, "Kind of," and hung up.

Three minutes later he called back and I gave him the rundown on what had happened.

When I had finished with the whole enchilada, he said jokingly, "You ought to send Kelly to D.C. I know some rich Arabs who would pay handsomely for a little Texas tail." When I didn't find that com-ment funny and refused to laugh, he said, "You are crazy as hell to take such a chance for a young whore!"

I kept my mouth shut while Tommy ran down his litany of "loose bitches." I was used to his colorful language and not offended. After the lecture, he agreed to fix Kelly up with a new identity and to check if there was any missing person reports on her. He finished with, "Just sit tight. I'll give you a call when I have something ready for you."

I told him, "Kelly's mom's name is Maryanne. She and her loser boyfriend Jake are out of it and don't give a shit about her. The only problem is getting her a new life."

Tommy snapped back, "Don't you believe it. These fucking junkies have a way of popping up at the most inopportune times." He hesitated for a moment and then asked, "Do I need to 'take care' of the bitch and her druggy boyfriend?" Before I could answer, he added, "I hope the pussy is worth all of this shit."

Then there was a click and he was gone.

My adrenalin started to kick into high gear when I got back and the room was empty. My thoughts started to cartwheel regarding what might have happened to Kelly until I heard the shower running behind the closed bathroom door. I pulled the bottle of Jack Daniels out of my bag, poured myself a stiff shot and called Kathryn to say goodnight.

From her conversation with Kelly she had determined that the girl had "maybe flirted with those assholes in the pool," but it was just a little game and she was not interested in anything they had to offer. She expelling an exasperated breath sighed and said "Brett darling, we sure do have our hands full with that one."

I said, "Don't worry. I have long range plans to turn our little Liza Doolittle into 'my fair lady.'"

Kathryn snickered and said, "That's not the only reason I love you, Brett."

It made me feel good, and I whispered a soft goodnight.

As I turned to hang up the phone, Kelly waltzed into the room stark naked! Looking at her freshly toweled body and her soft curves heralding approaching womanhood, I experienced utter surprise, amused curiosity and a faint wisp of arousal.

"I forgot my panties and your big shirt," Kelly babbled in my direction, while covering her breasts with folded arms.

I replied kindly, sharing one of my core beliefs, "It's only when you use nudity to control others that it becomes a bad thing."

I watched her assimilate what I said. Kelly looked right at me, dropped her hands to her side, turned and walked back into the bathroom to finish getting ready for bed.

When Kelly had slipped under the covers, I sat on the edge of her bed, and softly said, "I'd like to know a little more about your life." She looked up at me and added, "I'm worried you'll stop loving me if I tell you everything."

I took her hand in mine. "That will never happen no matter what happened in your past."

She scooted closer, turned on her side, looked up at me with uncertain eyes and started to talk in a low voice. Her tale of woe was so horrific, so sickening, I had a difficult time maintaining my composure. It made me furious.

It seems that one night while Maryanne and Jake were drinking and smoking crack cocaine they came into her room, a converted pantry off the kitchen. They pulled her out of her tiny bed and led her into their bedroom. Maryanne made her lift her arms and pulled Kelly's nightgown off. She pushed her onto the bed and told her that it was time for her to become a woman. She made Kelly take her jeans off and deflowered her with a large, hard rubber penis. Then she took the crack pipe for herself and watched as Jake took his turn. Kelly had no idea how long it lasted but it felt like it went on forever. Three days later Maryanne fixed her up with their drug dealer for a bag of crystal meth.

Since that night of depravity, Kelly had been with 16 men and two women, not counting the frequent nighttime visits from Jake when he was stoned out of his mind.

Needless to say, the experience had scarred Kelly badly. She'd never had a boyfriend and believed she never would. She thought she would be spending the rest of her life turning tricks.

One night her mom and Jake made her smoke some meth, but she got so sick that she couldn't work the streets for three days. Not wanting another loss of income, they never again forced her to take drugs.

"The other night was my first drink of bourbon," she admitted. "I hated the bitter charcoal flavor and only did it to see what it tasted like."

When she had finished her dreadful story she broke into uncontrollable tears. I held her tenderly in my arms and kept rocking her until she drifted off to what I hoped was a more soothing place.

Day 10

The next morning we went down to the lobby for our "free" continental breakfast. As we entered the room, Kelly extended her right arm and gave the finger to the man and woman sitting in one corner having breakfast. They took one look at me, got up quickly and departed, leaving their unfinished plates behind. Kelly turned to me with a big smile and gave me a hard slapping high five. We never spoke another word about that sex-crazed couple or the lesson learned.

After breakfast we went to a community health center. I wanted Kelly to have a complete physical examination, including a battery of test for sexually transmitted diseases. I gave the hotel as our address and asked if the results could be expedited since we would be staying here for only a few more days. The attending nurse said that they would do everything in their power to accommodate us, but it could be up to three days before all the results came back. That time table worked for me. By then I expected to have the paperwork from Tommy in Washington, D.C. as well.

I thought Kelly might enjoy a little cruise around the area to take her mind off what her medical condition might be, so we took a twisting 30-mile ride to Magdalena. The town is 2000 feet higher up on the Magdalena Mountains, than Socorro. About half-mile from end to end, it has a few cafés and a smattering of artsy shops. We decided on eating before browsing and ended up in *The Magdalena Café*. The food was okay but we struck out once again in our quest for homemade fruit pie.

Then we checked out the *Magdalena Arts Gallery*, a cooperative of local artists to promote their various pots, blankets, beads, chaps, coats and smattering of paintings. It was a small, cozy space, and Kelly was soon captivated by a pair of custom-made chaps by an artist named McCloud, which included an inordinate amount of beadwork on colorful, hand-tooled leather. I found them quite intriguing, too, and could imagine a cowboy catching a lot of bull, so to speak, for wearing a pair of these gaudy eye-dazzlers.

What stopped me in my tracks was the discovery of a museum-grade artist whose work was hibernating in this *tienda* on the mountain. Her name was Ilse Magener and her art was of such quality that I wondered what it was doing in this out-of-the-way place. Why had I not seen it on display in some of the better native galleries? I tried to explain to Kelly the intricacies of Magener's panels and crosses, from her use of color to the way she burnished gold leaf to catch or reflect light. Her work was extremely personal and I felt that only an intuitive viewer would be fortunate enough to discover the visual messages on her wooden surfaces.

After an enjoyable afternoon we left Magdalena and headed into the last vestiges of the sun. In the distance the lights of Socorro were just starting to dance against a dark indigo-blue sky. Kelly wrapped her arms around me and pulled herself tight into my back. She stayed that way until we drove under the portico of our hotel. When she got off the *Valkyrie* and flipped her visor up, I could see tears in her eyes.

"What's wrong?"

"I have never been this happy. I love you so much."

At the front desk, I asked the clerk if she had any recommendations for good Mexican food. She said there was only one place to go—*El Sombrero*—and called for a taxi to pick us up in an hour's time to take us there.

Kelly changed into her Mickey Mouse sweatshirt and Lucky jeans with sneakers. I went with my Zorro look—black sweatshirt, black jeans and my charcoal black motorcycle boots, which I had wiped off with a damp washcloth to remove 1000 miles of dust.

Unfortunately, our outfits were the best things about our outing. The service at *El Sombrero* was slow as molasses, the food was mediocre and the outfits of the strolling Mariachi band had seen better days. The only thing of note was our waitress, who flaunted her recently augmented breasts wherever she went. They were way out of proportion with her small body and would have made a Holstein proud, but they garnered her plenty of attention. The location of our table gave us a view into the back area, where all the other servers were eager to take a look and, occasionally, "give 'em a squeeze."

Kelly turned up her nose and commented disdainfully, "I would never change my body just to make people look at me."

I looked into her dark, ice-blue eyes, and said, "I am really proud to have photographed you. You have the body of an angel and are as beautiful as anyone I've ever shot."

She leaned as far across the table as she could without giving Mickey a taste of the Pico de Gallo and asked, "Is what Kathryn told me true?"

"Just what did Kathryn say?"

"That I was going to be your model and you would be making a book about me growing up to be a lady."

Touching Kelly's cheek, I moved closer to her. "Something to that effect would be nice. What do you think about it?"

She blurted out, "I would love to be your model and become famous!"

"I don't know about becoming famous, because a lot of things have to happen first. But then, with good luck, yes, you could become well known."

Smiling, I placed a salsa-laden chip in her mouth to put an end to the discussion. Kelly went back to attacking her stack of enchiladas with the dedication of a hungry plow horse emptying her feedbag. I had to give this child some lessons on table etiquette or, no matter how famous she became, there would be no dinner invitations sent her way.

By the time we finished we were the only customers in the restaurant. The manager made the universal cut-off gesture by sliding his forefinger under his chin, which changed our smiling Mariachis into a band of ordinary Mexicans eager to get out of the old *Sombrero*. Disappointment registered on Kelly's face at the abrupt end to our enchanting evening. As I got ready to sign the credit card slip for the bill, our taxi signaled its arrival outside with a blast of the horn.

I tried to cheer up my pouting princess by asking, "How much of a 'tit' shall we leave our waitress?"

That little bit of absurdity brought a ghost of a smile back to her glowering, but still beautiful face.

Day 11

We were the only patrons in the hotel's breakfast nook. Kelly poured me a cup of black coffee encased in Styrofoam and two small plastic cups of orange juice for herself. Balancing them precariously in her hands, she brought them over to our table. Before she could sit down, however, the front desk clerk approached us and said she had a letter for Kelly Tempest.

Hearing her new name pronounced by a stranger, Kelly perked up and blurted out, "That would be me, Miss." She took the letter, smiling at the young lady, and uttered a soft "Thank you."

Then she sat down, carefully opened the envelope and pulled out her medical report card. She scanned the document quickly, but as she tried to look at it more closely, her eyes narrowed and she soon put it down in frustration.

I asked, "Do you need help?"

She handed me the document with a quizzical expression and brought her chair around to sit next to me, almost as if she was afraid that I might miss something. It was a big relief that she did not have any of the big three venereal diseases, although the letter mentioned that she had to be tested for HIV again in six months. Unfortunately, her urine indicated the presence of early stage Chlamydia.

Kelly must have been reading the letter along verbatim because she asked, pointing, "What's that word mean?"

I said, "Chlamydia is a sexually transmitted disease that comes from either intercourse or oral sex."

She pulled back from the table and mumbled, "I feel perfectly OK, so they must have made a mistake."

I took her hand gently and said, "There's no mistake. It's rare to feel or see it. The good news is that we can have you cured in no time flat."

She relaxed a bit and moved closer to scrutinize the letter again. Enclosed with the report was a prescription for Doxycycline, which she was to take twice a day for one week. There was a postscript from the clinic instructing her to abstain from sexual activity during the course of her medication, and not to have any sexual contact with the person she contracted the disease from, or she could easily become infected again.

Kelly proclaimed, "I hope whoever gave me this Chlamydia shit dies!" Then she looked at me and said, "Could I have given it to any of the men I had… you know…?"

"Absolutely."

As Kelly thought about that, a smile flitted across her face.

I started to clean off the table when Kelly grabbed the envelope from my hand and said, "This is the first thing with my new name on it and I want to keep it."

Back in our room, I decided to call Tommy and have him send the papers to our next stop. I figured getting on the road would be a good thing to take Kelly's mind off her vaginal problems. But when I suggested it, she begged off.

"I feel sick and want to just hang around here for a day longer, watch TV and veg out," she pleaded.

I considered it, then asked, "Will you be all right on your own if I go out for a while?" I couldn't stay cooped up all day long.

She grinned and said, "Don't be so silly, you big bear. Of course, I'll be all right."

I was uncomfortable leaving her alone because of what had happened in the sauna. But I figured she'd learned a big lesson and she had to be able to handle herself sooner or later.

I gave her 20 bucks for a Domino's pizza and told her, "Stay away from the pool until I get back this evening. You can reach me on my cell phone, if necessary."

Outside I looked at the map and decided to take a ride up to one of my favorite spots in New Mexico. The town of Madrid was a small artists' community tucked away on the Turquoise Trail, which ran from east of Albuquerque to just south of Santa Fe. This historic roadway comprised a good part of the Navajos' "Long Walk," their forced march from Arizona to Fort Sumner, New Mexico. More than 200 Native Americans died during the 300-mile trek. The man in charge of this brutal and unnecessary resettlement was none other than the American folk hero Kit Carson. Nowadays, few travelers have any idea of the human suffering that took place as they happily buy the rugs and pots the Navajo make.

Riding into the village of Madrid was like going back in time, to the beginning of the 20th century when it used to be a booming coal-mining town. The last miners left in 1954 when the Santa Fe Railroad no longer needed their coal, and the place became a ghost town. But in the early 1970s artists arrived and converted the old company stores and boarding houses into studios and galleries. Now this little treasure trove supported over 30 galleries along with a slew of sidewalk food vendors, espresso bars, cafés, and restaurants with full-blown table service.

Cruising past a studio with the appropriate name of *Tiny Town* I noticed a motorcycle perched on top of the second story roof that I hadn't seen on my previous visits. On closer inspection I realized that it was made entirely of bones. Of course, everything the gallery owner, Tammy Lang, produced was made from bones. I wasn't in the mood to view her work this time around, so I motored on into town and visited about a dozen of Madrid's 30 galleries. By the time I was done, I was in ocular overload and in desperate need of some open scenery that did not have a frame around it. My feet were a bit sore from the hard, concrete floors, so I found a vacant bench in front of the Gypsy Plaza and took a load off.

I hadn't rested for more than a minute or two when Kelly's face popped into my mind. I decided this was a perfect time to check on my little friend.

Kelly's first words were, "When are you coming home?"

It was nice to hear her voice on the phone, although through the receiver she sounded more like an adult than a little girl.

I told her, "I'm almost finished and will be back in a couple of hours."

But before I left Madrid, I needed to find a little something for "my girls." I went back to one of the jewelry stores I'd visited before and bought a beautiful turquoise and silver bracelet for Kelly. It was an inch wide and had engraved turtles crawling between the turquoise stones. The necklace I got for Kathryn, made by the same artisan, was a choker with sapphires set between silver nuggets of the same size. I imagined with pleasure the cerulean gem stones playing against the silver metal and the white skin of Kathryn's neck. I was a little concerned the choker would be a bit too tight. I knew Kelly's bangle would fit her perfectly. I had held her hand enough times to know the diameter of her wrist.

I was about to head home when I noticed a place called *Mama Lisa's Ghost Town Kitchen* advertising "homemade everything." I almost stopped to see if that included pies, but my need to get back was greater and I barely slowed as I sped past the eatery and out of town.

Back at the motel I was about to open the door to our room when I heard soft whisperings. My heart sank imagining that Kelly was "at it again." I entered as quietly as I could, made my way to the end of vestibule and peered around the corner into the main suite. To my surprise, there was Kathryn sitting behind Kelly on the bed, pulling a hairbrush through her golden tresses and telling her how beautiful she was.

Looking straight ahead, Kelly asked, "Do you really think I'm pretty enough for Brett's book?"

Before Kathryn could answer, I burst in. "Isn't anybody going to help me with my saddlebags?"

Both women turned around in unison and Kathryn let out a little squeal of joy. She dropped the brush on the floor, rushed over and almost jumped into my arms.

"Baby, I have missed you," she said and let her lips feast on mine.

Looking into her eyes, I felt she was somehow "different" from the woman I had left in Tennessee. I held her at arm's length for a moment. She was as beautiful as ever, just changed somehow.

I glanced at Kelly. "Did you have anything to do with this?"

She giggled and replied, while giving Kathryn an exaggerated wink, "I don't know what you are talking about."

Kathryn slipped out of my embrace, went to my undisturbed bottle of bourbon on the dresser, and poured me a splash on the rocks. Handing me the drink, she said, "Guilty as charged! The two of us put this visit together the night of Kelly's 'little episode.'"

"I see."

Touching my cheek Kathryn asked, "Well, Brett, are you glad to see me or should I head back to Tennessee?"

Before I could answer, Kelly came over, put her arms around us and said to Kathryn, "You aren't going anywhere." Then she announced, "I'm hungry!"

I grinned and asked, "Do you want to go out, or should we get take out and have a nice night here with just the three of us?"

They both voted to stay home, which was my choice as well.

Kathryn grabbed her car keys and went off with Kelly to pick up some dinner for us. I jumped into the shower, washed off the road dirt and changed into a clean set of clothes. Then I carefully removed my little presents from the saddlebag, making sure not to ruin the special wrapping, which had been designed by the artist himself. I placed Kelly's gift under the pillow nearest the door and Kathryn's under the one on the bed she would share with me.

No matter how I jostled our room table about, I could not position it for the three of us to sit comfortably with food and drink, so I called to the front desk, explained my dilemma and asked if we could use the breakfast room. By the time I got there the clerk had unlocked the place and set up a table already for our personal use. I camped out in the lobby and waited for the girls to show up.

Soon Kathryn and Kelly waltzed in carrying three large shopping bags containing our dinner and who knows what else. I diverted them into our private dining room. They were pleased with the accommodations. Kelly started to unload the paper containers while Kathryn replaced the motel table settings with dinner sized paper napkins and three wine glasses. Then they brought out their goodies. It was a Chinese, soup-to-nuts spread with Spanish wine and Alpine mineral water to add an old world touch.

The only thing missing were paper plates, so I teased, "What are we going to eat on?"

Kathryn replied in her sweetest southern accent, tinged with just a hint of sarcasm, "Why out of the cartons, honey. How else does one eat Chinese take-out?"

She withdrew a corkscrew from the back pocket of her jeans, offered it to me along with one of the wine bottles, and with a sweet smile asked, "Would you do the honors?"

It had been a while since I held a wire-encased bottle. As I removed the foil covering the cork, I noticed that it was a reserve from 2001, a wonderful vintage that did not need to breathe.

I popped the cork and handed the open bottle to Kathryn. She poured equal measures of the deep red liquid into the three wine goblets. Then she topped off Kelly's glass with mineral water in the traditional method used for youngsters in Spanish homes.

I remembered Kelly's medicine and was about to grab the glass away from her, but then I figured the watered-down version wouldn't do any harm.

I tipped my goblet towards Kelly and said, "To the newest part of my heart. God has given me the daughter I never had and a photo model to stimulate my creativity. What more could I ask for?"

Turning towards my lover who was standing next to Kelly, holding her hand, I said, "Your radiance came to me in a place out of the past, and now your glow has lit a path into the future." Then I took a step back to frame them both in the same vision and concluded with, "To the women of my life. I drink to our love, honor and respect, for now and until we walk into our sunsets." Putting the wine glass to my lips I let the rich, red liquid seep into my mouth. The taste brought back memories of my time in Spain and on the island of Ibiza.

What I didn't expect was the effect my words would have on Kathryn and Kelly. Both were misty-eyed when they came around the table and into my arms. Kathryn planted a kiss on my right cheek and Kelly did the same on my left.

Then Kelly reminded us what we were really there for, bursting out, "I'm hungry."

We dug into the little white containers with red dragons printed on the sides and talked about everything from which school we might enroll Kelly in, to what she and Kathryn would wear on the photo shoot the next day.

At some point Kelly surprised us by standing up and proposing a simple toast. "To my new mom and dad."

I felt a small lump in my throat and could tell Kathryn was moved, too. We both realized what her words meant and the enormous responsibility they placed on our shoulders.

Before we finished, I asked Kathryn something that had been bothering me throughout the meal, "How did you know that I had lived in Spain?"

She gave me a puzzled look and said, "I had an idea about it, call it more of an intuitive thing."

"Then how did you know to buy Marques de Riscal."

She smiled and said, "Somehow I knew this was the wine that you drank when you lived in Ibiza and besides, I loved the way the bottle was wrapped in chicken wire. More importantly, it was on sale."

As I wondered how she had guessed Ibiza, too, Kelly broke in with a concern of her own. "I have a request and it's very important to me," she said earnestly. "Promise me that I won't have to go to school until after the trip is finished."

It was hard to take her seriously, though, because she had pieces of chocolate cupcake clinging to her mouth. As she snaked her tongue around her lips trying to catch the sticky crumbs, she looked like Gene Simmons from the rock group *Kiss*. Kathryn and I couldn't help laughing.

"It's not funny," she pouted.

"Of course not," I said and, catching Kathryn's eye, continued, "We'll see."

Later, back at the room, I fixed drinks for Kathryn and me while we waited for Kelly to finish her toilette. After a taking sip I asked, "How long can you stay?"

"For at least two more days and maybe longer, if I make a phone call," she whispered. "I want to be with you no matter what."

I held her at arm's length. "Kathryn, how did you know that I lived on the island of Ibiza? I don't recall sharing that with you."

Her puzzled expression returned. "Brett darling, I have no idea how I knew that about you. I just know that I know it."

That answer did nothing to dispel the mystery. In fact, it created more questions in my mind, but I decided to put them on the back burner and get on with loving my woman.

I pulled Kathryn close to me and, placing my lips next to her ear, whispered. "I am hopelessly in love with you."

At that moment Kelly came into the room wearing another one of my large tee shirts. She reached out for Kathryn's hand and pleaded, "Please make my hair beautiful."

I sat back and watched as Kathryn brushed Kelly's hair. I could almost see the oils being released as the bristles passed through her silky tresses and hair came to life and glowed with luster under Kathryn's loving touch. I only hoped Kelly's young soul would come back to life under our caring supervision. I also realized how much I needed these women in my life and what a gift they were to me.

When Kathryn was done, I called her over and asked her to look under her pillow. She giggled when she saw the silk beribboned package and, with eyes sparkling, asked, "Brett, what did you get me?"

"You'll have to open it to find out."

Kelly and I watched as Kathryn gently undid the wrapping and opened the box. She pulled out the beautiful blue and silver necklace and draped it over her outstretched hand. As she turned it to catch the lamp light in different angles, her eyes filled with tears of joy.

"Put it around my neck, Brett," she said huskily.

As I went to her to help her, she pulled off her cotton garment and stood there in a light blue lace bra. In her dark blue, slim-fit jeans, she looked like a fashion model changing outfits. I stepped behind her and locked the clasp into place. When the choker came to rest around her neck, I was pleased to see that it fit her perfectly and looked stunning.

Kelly whistled and said, "That necklace is the prettiest thing I have ever seen." She came over, draped her youthful arms over Kathryn's shoulders and whispered, "I love you, Kathryn Baily, and think that you are the most beautiful woman in the world."

While the two shared this joyful moment, I took out my camera and snapped a picture that I hoped would be my own hallowed memento. Then, acting befuddled, I said, "Kelly, how come you haven't looked under your pillow yet?"

I didn't have to prompt her twice. She dashed to her bed, tossed the pillow aside and grabbed her beautiful box. When she tore it open like a hungry lioness attacking a gazelle, it dawned on me that this was the first present anybody had ever given to her.

Kelly's eyes devoured the heavy silver bracelet. She turned to me and said with a quiver in her voice, "This is the happiest I have ever been in my life."

Then she walked over to the long, vertical mirror to do a little casual modeling, trying her new bangle on both wrists before settling on her right arm.

Kathryn put on a black silk blouse that could be unbuttoned to display her necklace to its fullest advantage.

I told Kelly, "We're going to sit by the pool a while. Try to get some sleep. I want you to be pretty as a picture for our first photo session."

She turned away from the magic mirror, put her arms around my neck, gave me a moist kiss on the cheek and murmured softly, "Thank you."

Before we left, Kathryn and I tucked her into the covers with whispered good nights.

I found us a table in the corner of the pool and spa area and we discussed what fate had delivered us into this complicated triangle. At some point she took my hand between both of hers. "Brett Tempest, make an honest woman out of me," she pleaded in a soft, sensual voice.

I looked intently into her green eyes and said, "I can't do that Kathryn, because you are still married."

She left her chair and maneuvered herself onto my lap. "I won't be in ten days. Then will you marry me?"

I replied seriously, "Kathryn, you are the missing piece that I have been looking for the better part of my life. I want to spend the rest of my life with you. Will you come to Washington and live with me in my home and help me raise this child? If after one year you still want to, I will marry you once a month for the rest of our lives!"

She kissed me and said, "Brett, I love you right out of my socks. When can I move in?" Then, without taking a breath, she continued, "You never said that you had a house in D.C."

"You never asked," I said, smiling.

Back in our room, we completed our engagement with the softest and most silent lovemaking I had ever experienced. Kelly was sound asleep with her dreams while Kathryn surrendered herself to me in a consummation of shared love. Our culmination seemed to go on and on—my soul had finally found its mate.

Day 12

There was an air of excitement around the breakfast table as Kathryn and Kelly bantered about their big day in front of the camera. I had told both of them to dress down and not bother with make-up because this shoot would be more of an exploratory session to see how they looked together on film. Kathryn wore jeans and a dark blue cotton shirt and sneakers. Kelly had borrowed one of her formfitting, silk tee shirts, also in dark blue, and wore them with her Lucky jeans and tennis shoes. Both women had their hair tied back with the ribbons they had saved from the wrapping material of their new presents and went bra-less upon by my request.

I wanted a casual, "laid-back" look for this first photo session. The scenario I gave them was that they were the only two people left in a destitute world after the apocalypse. My explanation raised their eyebrows, but they soon started to get the concept and any apprehension they might have felt was soon replaced with unbridled excitement. After we finished our continental breakfast, the three of us loaded Kathryn's rented silver Mustang with my camera equipment, munchies, and enough water for us to swim in.

They both were anxious to know where we were going. I shared the sense of excitement I had felt three years earlier, when I had been driving down U.S. 60 from Springerville, Arizona. Just across the New Mexico border past the town of Datil, I had found an incredible old Union Pacific freight car. Somebody must have bought it, then towed it out to the middle of nowhere, and simply abandoned it. Time and the elements had turned the railway relic into a collage of pale colors and peeling paint.

"Now, If my memory serves me well, that old boxcar will make a perfect background for photographing my newest models," I said with an exaggerated wink. "The decaying paint will be a perfect contrast to the human body."

It was a 90-minute drive and, to our joy and amazement, we found the old railway car about a half mile off of U.S. 60, sitting alone in a field of blowing desert grass. It looked pretty much how I remembered it.

We had a bouncy ride on the remnants of a dirt road leading to the old freight hauler. *At times like this*, I mused, *it's a good thing to be driving a rental car.* We piled out of the Mustang and while the women got used to their new surroundings, I adjusted the film setting to the right splay of light to illuminate this location.

I gathered my models and explained that I was looking for a desolate look. I needed Kelly to be the ultimate "lost child" who was forced to become a woman to survive. Kathryn would be her mentor in life and had to wrap her in the protective warmth of her presence without dominating Kelly's frailty. I knew that Kathryn would be ready to become one with my intention, but I was not so sure about Kelly. So I decided to do some singles work with her first and let her warm up to what I wanted from her.

I lifted her into the partially open door of the boxcar and had her hide half her body inside, exposing the other half to daylight. I asked her to fix her eyes on an imaginary horizon. Five frames into the shoot, I realized that we had to get rid of her clothes. They took away from a vision of purity. Kathryn readily agreed with me and we had Kelly toss her clothes down to us. I reset the shot exactly as before and after five more frames, she came alive and started to become part of the reality I was creating.

The image that seemed to work best was when Kelly gave her ribbonless hair a disheveled look and gazed hauntingly into the distance.

A pale yellow and white paint chip from the wall of the boxcar had attached itself to the swell of her adolescent breast, incorporating the organic whiteness of her unblemished skin into the inorganic plane of peeling paint. The combination emphasized my vision of a lost child's despondency in this hopeless world.

As I released the Hasselblad's shutter, Kathryn, who was standing directly behind me, expelled a loud breath. "Wow," she said, "I'm experiencing exactly what you are creating."

I told her to disrobe and join Kelly. Standing behind her, Kathryn loosened the ribbon in her own hair and let it tumble onto Kelly's shoulder while molding her body snugly against the young girl's back.

The image I saw through my lens was two women with only half of their bodies exposed. Kathryn's more mature figure with her womanly breast and sensuous flair of her hip was all about softness in contrast with Kelly's firm, budding breast and newly defined line of the waist and thigh. Their hair melted into each other's in a kaleidoscope of golden, russet color. The image of an adolescent girl transforming into a mature woman became a celebration of womanhood.

We continued to create stimulating images right up until five o'clock, not even stopping to eat. I photographed my models in the most suggestive situations. For the final shots I climbed the ladder to the top of the old freight car and stuck my camera through a hole in the roof. This last series was perhaps the most provocative, with both women lying flat on their back, their hands extended over their heads, just touching each other's fingertips. It looked as if they were bound to the wooden floor by an unseen restraint. Adding to the illusion was a full day's worth of dirt that had settled on their skin. A feeling of hopelessness pervaded that final image, as if posing the question: *Was there a way out of this claustrophobic world?*

The ride back to Socorro was a feast of potato chips, pretzels and nuts interspersed with excited chatter. Neither Kelly nor Kathryn could stop talking about what we were going to show the art world.

By starting to create their own characters, in just one day they had completely embraced and understood a very complex idea. Becoming part of a photographer's vision was the hardest part of creative modeling, and they had succeeded better than any of the professionals I had worked in my career.

When we got back to the hotel, Kathryn decided she and Kelly needed a good scrubbing. They showered together to wash the grime off of each other's backs and, I suspected, to build on the camaraderie they'd established. Meanwhile, I called *Pizza Pro* for a large pie and a bottle of Coke for Kelly, in lieu of Dr. Pepper. Kathryn and I would uncork the second bottle of Marques de Riscal.

As I hung up the house phone, I heard the muffled ringing of my cell phone. I managed to locate it under Kelly's box of tampons in my small, now cluttered tank bag. It was my brother, Tommy. He hurriedly informed me that he had no time to talk but that I should expect a FedEx envelope at the motel tomorrow morning. Then he was gone, leaving me to wonder if he ever had time to slow down.

I fixed myself a splash of bourbon with one ice cube, sat down on the small sofa and listened to the laughter emanating from the bathroom. My thoughts drifted from the beauty of the female form to what to do tomorrow. Perhaps we would drive up to Albuquerque to have the film developed, replenish my supplies with fresh film stock, and do a little Bling & Things shopping with my girls.

There was a knock at the door and when I opened it, a buxom 20-something pizza delivery girl stood there with a dazzling smile on her cute face.

"Would you come in and put the pizza and Coke on the desktop?" I said.

As she complied, she noticed my cameras sitting on the bed. She turned around, casually pulled her Pizza Pro uniform blouse tight to her body, accentuating her rather large bosoms, and asked, "Are you a professional photographer?"

"Yes, I have sold quite a number of my pictures."

Slowly running her tongue over her lips, she tugged her company shirt even tighter. "I do a little modeling on the side whenever I need money."

I decided to encourage her. "Would that be the case now?"

She flashed me a bleached smile and asked, "Would you like me to come back after I get off work to do some special poses?"

Before I could reply, the bathroom door burst open and my two models came waltzing into the room *au naturale*, looking for their clothes.

The pizza girl's eyes became larger than the pie she had brought.

I said, "I will not be needing your services tonight, as I just hired these two from McDonald's, not more than fifteen minutes ago."

She was so discombobulated that she hightailed out of our room without collecting money for the pizza and Coke!

Kathryn asked, "What in the hell was that all about?"

"I believe that I just got propositioned by the pizza delivery girl."

Kelly perked up and asked, "What did that little bitch want to charge you?"

I answered, laughing, "We did not get to talking price before we were interrupted by you two, but I am sure that I could have gotten a good deal from her."

Kelly looked at me and muttered, "I hate whores."

After we enjoyed our free pizza dinner, Kelly headed to the laundry room to run a load, and Kathryn and I went to the pool for a little aquatic recreation. Our bodies still wet from swimming we went to the sauna and had just settled when Kelly poked her head in the door. She cautiously looked for us in the dark heat and shouted loud enough to let the world know, "That is some fucking laundry room!"

The way she delivered her news reminded me of the circumstances in which I first met her, and I replied jokingly, "Such language! I hope the only things taking a tumble in there are your clothes."

Looking at me, she proclaimed sarcastically, "I only was able to get a handful of quarters for the hand job I gave to the motel's janitor."

Shocked, I exclaimed, "Where did you do that?"

"While he sat on top of the washer."

"Where are the quarters now?"

"Sorry Brett, I used them for the dryer."

Sticking her tongue out at me, while winking at Kathryn, Kelly left the heat of the sauna and headed to the pool, laughing like she had just got away with stealing the emperor's clothes.

Day 13

I gently pulled open the drapes to encounter a morning sky that was swollen with dark clouds. I put on a pot of coffee, checked on my sleeping beauties and hopped into the shower. Letting the water run over me, I started to think about what to do about our living situation and where it would be best to raise Kelly. At first I considered Washington, D.C., for that city would give Kelly all of the culture that had escaped her in Throckmorton. I had recently renovated my three-story, turn-of-the-century brick house on Capitol Hill. From there she could walk to the Library of Congress, great art galleries and the Smithsonian Museum. The other benefit was that Lydia Gordon, my personal assistant, lived there in a basement apartment. She had full access to the upstairs and would be able to keep an eye on Kelly when I was gone.

The North Carolina house, a one-story, Rambler-like structure, was right in downtown Durham, the home of Duke University. Because it was in the middle of the research triangle area of Raleigh, Durham, and Chapel Hill, it would offer a diverse academic culture. Washington had more private schools, but Durham boasted one of the better private schools in the South, the Durham Academy.

While these alternatives were spinning around in my head, the shower curtain slid open and Kathryn joined me under the pulsating water. Taking the sudsy washcloth from my hand, she started to lather me all over, turning me into her "soap suds man."

I felt a rush of air as the bathroom door was being pushed open. Peeking out of the curtain, I saw Kelly's face through a cloud of warm mist.

She smiled at me and said, "I'm hungry."

Unfortunately, the continental breakfast was so unappetizing that I worried I would have a full-blown mutiny on my hands. The orange juice was watery and the bagels were so hard they could have been used as tennis balls. We gulped down what we could manage and got ready for our day's outing in record time.

The ride to Albuquerque on Interstate 25 was wet and visually boring. I found the photo lab I'd looked up in the Yellow Pages without any problems and dropped off two weeks' worth of color and black and white film. When I asked how long the processing and proof-making would take on a rush basis, I was pleased to hear that everything could be done in just four hours. That gave us plenty of time to cruise down Menaul Boulevard to the Coronado Center, have lunch and do a little shopping.

Kelly started to pout a bit when I reminded her, "We only have space on the *Valkyrie* for the processed film and maybe a tee shirt or two."

I placated her by making her the lead dog on our restaurant hunt and when I said, "You'll get a vote on choosing a ring for Kathryn," she rewarded me with a smile.

Kathryn's face wavered between joy and concern. Regaining her composure she drawled, "Why, Brett darling, you never mentioned to me that you planned to encircle my finger with your love. Did I tell you yet how much I love being yours?"

We entered the mega mall and its 140 plus shops much like three kids walking into a candy store.

Amazed, Kelly grabbed hold of my hand and said, "This place is bigger than all of Throckmorton put together, and I ain't never seen anything like it."

Kathryn put her arm around Kelly and said, "Honey child, you just wait until you see where you are going. Your ride is just beginning. And don't say 'ain't' because it's not ladylike."

Much to my surprise Kelly didn't bristle, as she would have if I had said that. I doubted we would be hearing the "ain't" word anytime soon.

Our first stop was *Crabtree & Evelyn* which, according to Kathryn, was "one of the necessities of life." As we walked inside, she said, "Kelly honey, a women's skin is a sacred covering that tells the outside world what's going on inside, so you must take special care of it and never use junk lotions on it."

I tagged along and did my best to look interested.

As Kathryn purchased some exotic potions for herself and Kelly, she told me, "Find room in those old saddlebags for this jar of magic."

She also bought Kelly a container of body cream made from mango and grapefruit extracts and insisted Kelly use it on our upcoming rides. "You don't want to end up looking like one of those old windblown broads whose faces looks like a road map," she warned.

We must have gone through 10 stores before Kelly's eyes yielded to her stomach and she uttered her familiar mantra, "I'm hungry."

We found a store directory and let Kelly make her choice of dining location. She started laughing and put her finger on one of the restaurant listings. "What kind of a name is that?" she asked in her best Texas accent.

I moved her finger out of the way and had a laugh myself, knowing where her mind had taken her. I turned to Kathryn and said," It's *Fuddruckers* for lunch."

Bloated on butter burgers, fries and Dr. Pepper, we finally made it to my primary objective, *Helzberg Diamonds*.

The salesman soon had both of my women in his pocket by pointing to Kathryn's necklace and saying, "That is one of the most stunning pieces I have ever encountered!

When Kathryn told him that it was handmade, he nodded knowingly like a seasoned sales pro. As I looked at the different black felt cases filled with engagement rings, Kelly kept thrusting her bangle-laden arm across the counter in a provocative way to alert the salesman to her new bracelet. I caught his eye and he got the message.

He oohed and aahed appropriately and told Kelly, "You have impeccable sophistication in your choice of jewelry, Miss. You are blessed with fine taste."

Kelly beamed and I rewarded his flattery handsomely by spending 10 grand on a white gold, solitaire, 1.1 carat diamond ring that had the highest quality, color and clarity rating of the store's entire inventory.

Kathryn was beside herself and could not hold back her tears. "It's such an elegant ring and I am already in love with it," she said. "Brett, are you sure about this? It's a whole lot of money and maybe we could get something a little less expensive?"

"Kathryn, it's only money," I reassured her. "The superiority of this diamond will remain long after the cost has left your mind; besides, did you really want something of lesser quality?"

Smiling, she lowered her head a bit and shook her head, no. Moving close I wiped away a tear on her cheek and gently touched her lips with mine.

Then Kathryn turned to Kelly. "Thank you, sweetie, for helping make this one of the happiest days of my life." As Kelly responded with an "aw, shucks" look, she continued, "We have one more stop to make before we pick up the film."

Kelly asked, "Where's that?"

Ignoring her question, Kathryn led us directly to the entrance of *Victoria's Secret* and gave me a special, but unmistakable you-can-find-the-space-on-the-motorcycle look.

Smiling wryly, I acquiesced. "Kelly, baby, we have just enough room in the bags for something from this store, so you and Kathryn go and have some fun."

The drive back to Socorro was a rollicking "Show and Tell" with Kelly and Kathryn alternating wearing and displaying the luminous diamond ring, and oohing over Kelly's new lingerie. The pale blue bra and matching panties came in pure Turkish silk and were gorgeously sexy.

Both women badgered me to open the package of prints from the photo lab, but I refused to drive while looking at the proofs. I told them, "We will be back at the motel in less time than it takes to work that aromatic grapefruit and mango cream into your hands."

When arrived at the motel, the women went up ahead to the room. I stopped at the reception desk where Tommy's FedEx envelope was waiting for me. I sat in one of the lobby chairs and investigated the contents.

A hand written note from Tommy was attached to the manila envelope inside. It was short and simple: *This should get you started, but I need up-to-date photographs asap. Call me on my cell in three or four days.*

I knew the last bit meant that something was brewing but that he'd be out of reach till then.

The inner envelope contained a Certificate of Baptism from The Cathedral of Saint Helena in Helena, Montana, and a Certificate of Birth from St. Peters Hospital in the same town. According to the false documents, Kelly Michelle Tempest was 15 years old with a birthday coming up on December 17. There also was a District of Columbia Library Card issued to Kelly Tempest at my Third Street address. It seemed that Tommy had picked our family address for us.

I was tempted to open the envelope that contained the photographs and quickly browse through them, but I knew it would be better as a shared experience.

Entering our room, I tossed the envelopes on the table. While I fixed myself a drink, I could hear whispers coming from the bathroom and wondered what "the girls" were up to. I didn't have to wait long as the bathroom door opened and out walked Kelly wearing her new lingerie. She looked beautiful with her hair brushed back from her face and held in place by Kathryn's gem-encrusted barrette. I could have sworn that she had grown larger breasts in the week or so that I had been with her, but I knew that it must have been the effect of the new silk brassiere, one of those "push 'em ups" which were all the rage.

After complimenting her, I asked Kelly, "What is your middle name?

"I don't have one."

"You do now."

She got a funny look on her face and asked, "What do you mean?"

Walking casually over to the table, I fished out her new birth and baptism certificates and in my best master-of-ceremony voice said, "Young lady, your new name is Kelly Michelle Tempest and you are now fifteen, soon to turn sixteen, and you live in D.C."

This news rendered her speechless but not immobile. She bounded towards me and grabbed the official-looking documents in such a rush I thought she would tear them.

Kathryn drawled, "Brett darling, can you get me something like that which will make me ten years younger? I am just so thrilled for our little Kelly I could just pee."

When Kelly looked up from the documents, her body started to tremble uncontrollably and tears flowed down her cheeks. I had seen her cry tears of joy and sorrow before, but this was something completely different, as if all of her sins were being erased and she could walk free of guilt. When she looked at the library card, it brought on a new wave of tears. I walked over to her and held her until her body stopped shaking.

She stood up on her tiptoes, placed her moist cheek next to mine and holding me tight asked, "Does this mean that I am now really your daughter?"

"You have been from the day in front of the *Allsup's* when you got on the back of the *Valkyrie*. But now you are officially mine."

Kathryn burst out, "No, Brett, she is officially ours."

She came over and joined us in a long, emotional hug.

When we finally disengaged, I took the proof prints and quickly organized them into a chronological sequence starting with the "out of time" shots of Kathryn. As I laid them on the table, I noticed things looked a bit different from how I remembered the shoot. It was almost as if the negatives were flipped and then printed in reverse.

Although the lighting wasn't the best, I was able to pull two prints out that I felt were spot on and put the weaker ones away. The ones I'd chosen came from near the end of the shoot when Kathryn was no longer posing. Her passion had taken over her intellect, conveying the essence of pure lust.

Placing the photos in front of the two women, I said, "Look at the photographs as if you were looking at total strangers and not at what you think are flattering or not-so-flattering depictions of yourselves."

Kelly picked up one of the proofs and said, "She looks hot, like she's staring at someone who had just paid for her."

Kathryn, seeming a little rattled, glanced at me and asked. "Do you think that's true?"

I replied honestly, "For me, the look was of wantonness and not quite what Kelly has in mind. I think she picked up on the rawness of emotion coming through in the photograph, which was exactly what I was looking for."

Skipping the "Shave Ice" photos from Mississippi, I went right to Kelly's poses on the black rocks of New Mexico. Because the clothes were wrong for the setting, there was nothing that could end up on someone's wall. But it was clear that Kelly was the real McCoy when it came to being photogenic. One or two pictures would also make good headshots, and I made a mental note to mail them off to Tommy in the morning.

Next up were five photographs from the "Datil Derailment" portfolio. The test shoot turned out to be what I felt were the first images for our new book! Both Kathryn and Kelly were surprised how well these images told the story I had laid out to them that day in the desert.

As Kathryn hunched over the table to look at them more closely, Kelly walked behind her, leaning into her back and said with admiration, "Wow, we really are good, aren't we?"

Kathryn turned, kissed Kelly on the forehead and pronounced, "Kelly, I love how Brett used us both in this pictorial narrative. But one day soon, little girl, you're going to be famous throughout the world all on your own; and have I told you today just how much I love you, my little peach."

I laid out the next few pictures without any editorial comment. They were of the girls on the night they opened their presents. Kathryn gave Kelly and me a minute to examine them before scooping them up and putting them in her suitcase.

Seeing our questioning faces, she explained, "Don't worry, guys, I am going to start our new family scrapbook with these little jewels."

The dinner that night at the *Ranchers Steak House* was nothing special, but we celebrated Kelly's new legal status nonetheless. We determined that Kathryn would go back to Tennessee in the morning and then fly to Washington over the weekend to start to get our new house in order. Later I gave Kathryn a key to my house along with the phone number there and my private assistant's cell phone number and, most importantly, the alarm code. I also warned her that Lydia, my girl Friday, could be a bit on the frosty side.

Since we were only a three-day, easy ride from the Pacific Ocean, our natural turnaround point, I told Kathryn to expect us in no more than two weeks' time, no matter what. With her 9:30 a.m. flight, I figured a 5:30 wakeup call would get her to the airport in plenty of time, but it meant going early to bed.

Kelly said, "I want to take some of the pictures I haven't seen down to the lobby to look at them more closely. I'll be back in an hour."

Walking out of the door, she winked at me.

The instant the door closed behind her, Kathryn was unbuttoning her blouse and urged me to hurry out of my clothes. "The clock is ticking and I am dripping with desire for my man," she cooed.

Our lovemaking ran the gamut from driving desperation to the softness of angels' kisses. After we exhausted each other, I held Kathryn close and felt her heart beating through her chest. She whispered loving endearments into my ear and told me that her happiness was greater at this moment than at any other time in her life. Her words aroused me again and, as she felt my hardness, she rolled on top of me and gently rocked us to ecstasy.

We weren't in the shower more than a few minutes before Kelly popped her head into our steamy reverie and declared, "I'm back."

Day 14

It was awkward leaning down to kiss Kathryn through the open window of the rental car. I didn't really want her to leave. My heart was full of affection. The sorrow I felt at parting confirmed what I already knew: she was the love of my life and I, of hers.

In her soft and most feminine southern accent Kathryn whispered, "Now baby, I don't want you to be sad because I will love you until the moon leaves the sky." She must have seen my despondent look because she continued, "Brett honey, when you get lonely, think of me in our kitchen baking you and our Kelly a welcome-home fruit pie. Now don't forget to call me tonight."

Then Kathryn looked once more into my eyes and drove off.

Kelly had our bags packed and ready to go by the time I returned to the room.

I imagine she felt my sadness because she came over to me, wrapped her arms around my neck and kissed me softly on my cheek.

She whispered, "I love you more than anyone in the world and I will take away your sadness."

I thanked her by kissing her on the head and decided to let go of my melancholy mood. "All right, Kelly Michelle Tempest, you are now in charge of supplying the beauty and charm around here. So that the new job title doesn't go to your head, get your ass in gear and load up our motorcycle."

Tossing me one of her most beautiful smiles, she saluted and said, "I'll get right on it, boss man, especially the part about being pretty."

After packing the motorcycle we came back upstairs, put on our leathers and, after a final look around the room, closed the door on our Socorro encounter.

Straddling the *Valkyrie* brought back the excitement and anticipatory exhilaration of heading out on the open road again. Kelly tapped my shoulder to let me know she was set to ride. The big engine roared awake, letting me know that the *Valkyrie* was ready to fly.

Driving west on U.S. 60 just past Datil, I saw our colorful Union Pacific boxcar off in the distance. Kelly must have noticed it at the same time because I felt the rapid snapping of my underpants' elastic band against my back, her highway Morse code message for me to pull over. When the bike came to a rest, Kelly's gaze fell onto the old boxcar as if she were taking her own photograph of the place of her liberation. A moment later we were back on the road.

Twenty-five miles further down the highway, we came to the outskirts of a place called Pie Town. It looked like we were about to meet the Holy Grail of baked goods. When Kelly saw the name of this New Mexico mountain settlement, she started to play the band of my shorts like a banjo, and I pulled over so we could forge a plan of attack to put an end to my quest for homemade fruit pie.

I felt like an excited teenager telling Kelly, "We just needed to cruise this town slowly until we find the right place."

It turned out that the only eatery in this "blink-and-you'll-miss it" town, was a restaurant with the promising name of *The Daily Pie*. But as we got close, something seemed not right. There was not one vehicle in the parking lot.

We hopped off the *Valkyrie* and marched to the front door to find a hand written note taped to the glass pane: *The Daily Pie will be closed today for the funeral of Sally Meacham and will reopen at 6 am tomorrow.*

Kelly simply said, "Well, shit."

That obscenity expressed my disappointment as well. I could not believe that I had spent more than 13 and a half days out on the road and still had not satisfied my craving for a slice of homemade fruit pie.

On the map the closest place to eat and refresh ourselves for our afternoon run was Springerville, Arizona, less than an hour's ride west.

When we got there, the first place we spotted was a Mexican establishment by the name of *Los Dos Molinas*. Since we had eaten Mexican for breakfast and there was a better than average chance they wouldn't have any fruit pie, we whizzed by and kept searching. I spotted what looked like the perfect place—a little cream colored cottage trimmed in grayish lavender, sitting by itself behind a shabby-chic picket fence. It smacked of homemade food.

Springerville was far enough away from Pie Town that I doubted *The Bluebird Cafe* would be closed for Mrs. Meacham's interment. Yet it turned out to be another exercise in frustration. It was permanently shut. But, hallelujah, there was an additional message on the notice taped to the door that mentioned a "legendary" place called the *Bear Wallow Café* only 25 miles up the mountain in Alpine, Arizona.

I asked Kelly, "Can you hold on a little longer?

In reply, she grinned and licked her lips melodramatically. I took that to be a big yes. So we drove up the mountain to Alpine, population 300 on a good day. Finding the *Bear Wallow Café* without difficulty was a piece of cake, so to speak, as there were only five viable commercial eateries.

At the far outside corner of the *Café*'s property stood a giant bear. It looked to me like he was taking a piss. Next to this 10-foot behemoth was a weather vane tower with a metal bear on top. It was a foot or two higher than its wooden cousin. Hanging over the outside rail was a white on black Viet Nam era POW flag adjacent to an American flag of the same size. They gave the place the appearance of a log cabin war memorial. Just as I was about to pull open the screen door, a sign dangling from a hook in horizontal spacer bar attached caught my attention: *No firearms in the building—Thanks!*

Entering the restaurant I felt like we were walking into a Salvador Dali painting. The place was nothing like a bear's wallow, but more a cemetery for elk. Standing in the doorway, Kelly held tightly onto my hand, while she took in the surfeit of antlers greeting us. There must have been 30 mammoth head ornaments on the walls, looking for revenge.

To Kelly's relief, one of the owners, a lovely woman with a characterful, wrinkled face, looked reassuring. She introduced herself as Veda and sat us in a booth just across from a 10-seat counter and took our drink order, a large Dr. Pepper for Kelly and an ice tea for myself.

"My daughter Talia will be back with your drinks in a jiffy, and she'll be you waitress," she said.

Our seats gave me a perfect view of the back counter which had a raised, plastic covered, round tray that should have displayed a treasure trove of baked wonders. But lo and behold, it was empty.

Talia, a tall, striking blonde, appeared at our table with two large, red plastic containers and a couple of menus. As she placed them on the table, I asked, "Do you have any homemade fruit pies?"

With a knowing smile and a sparkle in her blue eyes, she turned over her order pad. On the back was a list of seven different fruit pies. "They were baked by my sister Taani this morning," she assured me.

Talia seemed to sense the traumas that Kelly and I had endured lusting for our favorite dessert, and what she said next put us further at ease. "Why don't you just order a nice lunch and I guarantee that the pies will be here when you are ready for them."

I told her to give us a few minutes, as this was our first time here. But, before she left, I just had to ask, "What is your her favorite item on the menu?"

She answered predictably, "Everything is good," then added, "but for me, the honey-dipped chicken rings my bell. You two have a look at the menu and I'll be right back."

Talia disappeared into the inner sanctum of the *Bear Wallow Café*. Looking over the menu, I found a quote on the bottom that got my attention: *A good horse, like a good man, had a good mother.* Now that old saw had absolutely nothing to do with good cooking, but I figured it all but guaranteed that we were going to be served an excellent meal.

Kelly decided to go with Talia's recommendation. I ordered the 16-ounce Rib Eye steak, cooked rare, with French fries on the side.

The food came out hot and in a timely manner and was by far the best meal that I had eaten in two weeks on the road. My dinner companion felt the same. We spent at least 45 minutes eating and talking, discussing everything from out photo shoots to how beautiful Kathryn's ring was.

At some point Kelly asked, "Do you think that maybe one day I will wear something that expensive?"

I replied, "I am sure you will wear something beautiful on your third finger, but you should never weigh love by how much something costs."

When it was time for some homemade fruit pie, Talia returned to our table empty-handed and without the sparkle in her blue eyes. In a low voice she said, "I'm so sorry, but unbeknownst to me someone in the kitchen sent the remaining pies to the Alpine fire station."

I was disappointed but shrugged it off. I thought of my mother who was a great baker and responsible for my addiction to baked pies. I wondered if she knew that at times it was as difficult to find good pies as ascending Mount Everest in a wheelchair.

Kelly looked across the table at me regretfully and said, "I imagine that anyone who bakes good fruit pie must have a line of men waiting at her back door."

I smiled at her. "Now that is the right way to think."

I asked one of the passing waitresses, where the town post office was. She said it was just a half block back on U.S. 191 and up a few feet on the right.

Leaving Kelly on her own to finish off her Dr. Pepper, I went out to the bike and retrieved a couple of usable photographs of Kelly Michelle Tempest and walked up to the post office to send them to Tommy.

When I returned to the restaurant, Kelly was nowhere to be seen, causing an instant spike in my blood pressure. Veda, seeing the look of concern on my face, smiled and pointed to the ladies room.

I paid the check and left a tip while telling her, "I'll be waiting for my daughter outside on the bench."

She replied with a crinkly smile, "You sure have a pretty one there."

At that moment Kelly reappeared from the restroom, causing a bit of a stir amongst the group of hunters sitting in the main dining room surrounded by elk horns. It's funny, but I hadn't noticed them before, maybe because of all the camouflage they were wearing. For a brief instant, Kelly's beauty stopped this pack of predators from talking about killing and had them thinking about reproducing. I reflected on my gender and mused: *When it comes to pussy, all the camouflage in the world can't hide what men are thinking.*

Outside, the sun was starting to dip west, leaving quite a chill in the air. I felt that it was time to drop down to a lower altitude and decided to head straight south on U.S. 191 toward Safford, Arizona. Kelly finally broke out her thick pair of gloves and I wondered if they would put an end to the snapping of my underpants.

We were smack in the middle of the Apache-Sitgreaves National Forest and 50 miles from anything in any direction, when I knew we had to stop and "rough it" for the night. I found a little pull-off that had an old wooden picnic table accompanied by a fire pit and enough of a clearing for us to camp. Kelly was in a state of total confusion, happy that this would be her first night camping and at the same time, worried that bears would eat us and we didn't even have a tent to sleep in. I told her not to worry about the bears, because they wanted nothing to do with us. We did have an issue regarding where and how we would sleep, but I was confident that I could solve that problem with a little ingenuity.

Finding a spot close to a big pine tree, I rolled the *Valkyrie* over and removed all the bags. Then I sent Kelly to scavenge some kindling and old fallen branches, figuring it would occupy her mind and help dissipate her fears of the unknown. She did a great job gathering and came back several times with a pile of sticks in her arms.

I had her gather some of the fat pine cones, too, telling her, "They're like rocket fuel when starting a fire."

I built a small pyre and lit the crumpled up paper I had torn from my notebook. Once the flames caught and the crackling of the pine cones slowed to an occasional pop, the fire acted like a tranquilizer for both of us and, before long, we snuggled together watching the light show provided by Mother Nature.

When Kelly was good and relaxed, I went off to put together our makeshift shelter. I started out by tying the canvas tarp, which the sleeping bag was rolled up in, between the tree and the motorcycle handlebars. Then I extended the other end to its fullest point and secured it to the ground with some boulders. We now had a kind of lean-to shelter with the open side facing the fire, which would keep us warm through the night.

Kelly, seeing the makeshift structure come to life, began to lose all her fears and started to have a little fun. "You're pretty good with this camping thing," she said, laughing. "You must be Daniel Boone's great-grandson, with all your tricks of the woods."

"We'll be as snug as a bug in rug," I promised.

Happy that I didn't have to worry about cheering her up anymore, I continued to work. I laid the yellow rain suits on the ground inside our shelter and spread out all our spare clothes over them. Then I placed the sleeping bag on top. We now had a mattress that would cushion some of the hardness of the ground.

Next I made a pillow by wrapping our underwear inside the sweatshirt that I'd been wearing over my long johns and rolling it into a tube shape. The motorcycle jackets and pants would act as our blankets. I felt proud of my inventiveness and knew that we would have a good night.

Finished with our sleeping quarters, I placed a big log on the fire, fetched the bottle of bourbon and took a long, slow swig.

Kelly looked at me shyly and inquired, "I hear that stuff really warms a person up."

After a brief debate with myself, I passed the bottle over to her, holding up one finger. She took a tentative swallow of the amber liquid and handed the bottle back to me, muttering, "There must be another way to get warm."

All seemed right with the world, except my cell phone was useless out in this neck of the woods, so Kathryn would have to wait until morning for her call. Night came quickly and brought with it another 15-degree drop in temperature. It was fortunate that we did not have to worry about firewood. There was an abundance of it within a 20-yard circle of our camp. I added a few thick branches to the pyre. Then I found a nice log for sitting and rolled it close. We both plopped down on it and watched the dance of the flames and occasional sparks as the fire slowly consumed the wood.

Looking up I noticed a strange flickering light coming through the trees, which seemed to grow in intensity. Kelly saw it too and grabbed my hand, a worried expression on her face. Soon we heard a car passing by and we relaxed. I mused how odd it was the only one in over two and a half hours. We were far from humanity in the solitude of the night.

Kelly started fidgeting when she needed to go and relieve herself. I fetched my blue Maglite and some Kleenex from the tank bag and handed them to her for the journey into the forest. When she returned, the light beam breaking up and spreading through the trees reminded me of carnival lights viewed from a distance.

Yawning, Kelly asked, "Can we go to bed now?"

I told her, "Take off your leathers. We can use them as extra covers."

She sleepily removed her Mickey Mouse sweatshirt along with the leathers and boots, leaving her clad in long johns and wool socks, the perfect sleeping attire for this neck of the woods.

I got her tucked into the far corner of our sleeping cocoon. I would take the open end because I needed to be able to get in and out to tend the fire. I figured there would be just enough room for the two of us inside the down sleeping bag. With our leather riding gear spread on top we should be as warm as toast.

After giving Kelly a little smooch, I went back over to the sitting log, had another slug of bourbon and became mesmerized looking into the fandango of flames.

After about 20 minutes, Kelly's voice brought me back to a different reality. "Please come to bed," she pleaded.

Reluctantly I removed my boots and leathers and slipped gingerly into the down nest.

I was lying on my side facing the fire when Kelly gently pulled my shoulder. When I turned onto my back, she let her free arm rest across my body. We both looked out at the stars, which seemed to fill the chilly sky from end to end.

Kelly asked me, "Do you think anybody is living out there?"

"Absolutely!" I answered. "What you are looking at is only one galaxy of millions, possibly billions. The odds of Earth-like duplication are astronomically in favor of other life and, anyway, I have seen a space vessel on a night very similar to this in Colorado."

She propped herself up on her elbow and pleaded, "Tell me more."

So I shared what had happened to me on night when I was camping out in the Colorado wilderness some years ago. "I was sleeping in the back of my Volvo station wagon and got up to pee when, suddenly, this incredible translucent spacecraft passed silently right over my head. It had to be a mile long and as wide as a football field. Although I couldn't make out its walls, it seemed to have solid structure and integrity. Inside it was filled with warm red and yellow lights that were softly pulsating, but not in a science fiction way. It was as if a living force was holding the energy inside. The translucent vessel took about two to three minutes to slowly pass over me. There was no doubt about what

I had seen and, for my money, it was proof positive of extraterrestrial life. No technology on this Earth could have produced that."

Kelly drew closer to me extending her leg and laying it on top of mine and asked, "Where do we go when we die?"

"Honey bunch, that is the big question of life and before I tell you about my experience with death, I need to pee. Where did you put the flashlight?

"Back in the tank bag. Where else would I have put it, silly?"

Fumbling around I finally located the flashlight after emptying most of the contents on the picnic table. When I turned on the powerful beam and started to repack the bag, I came across the unopened box of tampons that Kelly had been lugging around ever since we bought them in Roswell. While I relieved myself, I thought about it. I swore I could feel eyes watching me and wondered what nighttime creatures were stalking me.

Getting back into the sleeping bag, I asked Kelly, "Why are you hauling the tampons around? Have you started your period yet?

"I started getting it over two years ago and never had any trouble," she said. "But I'm over a month and a half late and don't know why."

"Do you feel funny in any way?"

"My titties are a little sore," she confessed.

I was reluctant to ask her a question that might bring back her memories of the bad times of Throckmorton, but I had to know. "Kelly, when you were 'working' for Maryanne did the men use any protection?"

"Everybody except Jake who never used anything."

I put my hand on her stomach and said, "There is a good chance that you are pregnant."

I saw her face sag in the flickering light from the fire.

"That would mean all of my dreams are over and you and Kathryn will hate me for what I have done and will throw me out on the street, doesn't it?" she whimpered.

"Nobody is going to throw anybody out on the street and, besides, we are not sure that you are pregnant, are we?"

She answered with a tear-muffled, no. I could feel all the confidence she had mustered over the past few days leaving her as fast as air leaves a pierced balloon.

We finally dropped off to sleep, but at some point in the middle of this anxious night I had a distressing dream. I saw Kelly and myself in a lover's embrace and, try as I might, could not shake this vision. I was feeling alarmed, aroused and trapped at the same time. At some point I grasped that I was having a nightmare, but I was helpless to leave its thrall. Desperate to escape I finally willed myself awake only to realize that Kelly had hold of my penis and was trying to bring me to orgasm.

She moved her lips close to mine and whispered seductively, "I wish with all my heart that this baby was yours and then nobody could take you away from me." Then she slid her tongue into my mouth in a kind of lover's kiss.

Fully conscious now, I moved my head to dislodge her lips and reached down and removed her constricting fingers from my swollen loins. Then I placed her despondent hand on my chest and held it there.

Looking as deeply as I could into the hidden sanctuary of her soul, I told Kelly, "You should never want me to be the father of your baby because then I could never be the father you have always wanted." When I didn't see any reaction, I pushed the point harder, perhaps more brutally than I intended, by saying, "You don't have to fuck me to make me love you. You only have to be my little girl and I will love you with all my heart."

I kissed away her tears and fears and held her hand until she sank back into her dreams. As for myself, I had trouble getting back to sleep, for a problem of giant proportions had just surfaced. To put it crudely: How in the hell could I drive an old whore out of a young girl?

Day 15

The crack of dawn is not an easy time to deal with a distressed youngster. I was still half asleep when I became aware of Kelly shaking with fear and uncertainty. I drew her to me and felt her dread dissipate like morning dew in sunlight. But I knew we had to deal with the real reason for her jitters.

I sat up and made sure she was paying attention. Then I said, "Your mother warped your ideas about sex. Last night, you tried to steal distorted love when pure love already made a home in your heart, I know that as a fact, for I placed it there. Kelly, sexual attraction should be shared between two people as a mutual gift."

Her face showed signs of bewilderment and she was unable to look at me. I knew I was merely planting a seed at best—it was a lot for her to take in. So I decided to lighten the mood a bit and said, "Okay, now get your ass out of this sleeping bag and help me get ready for the road."

Forty-five minutes later we drove along the magnificent Coronado Trail. When we reached the giant Morenci Copper Mine, an eyesore of gargantuan proportions and a testament to the human exploitation of the Earth, there was nothing for us to stop and admire, so we endured 20 minutes of ugliness before we emerged on the other side. We passed through the old mining town of Clifton and stopped for breakfast half an hour later in Safford, Arizona.

I called Kathryn and told her about our mountain adventures far from civilization. She was excited and worried at the same time.

"I can't believe you actually slept where bears and mountain lions roamed," she said.

I thought it better not to tell her about Kelly's promiscuity or the possibility of her pregnancy quite yet.

Kathryn continued, "I'm having trouble with that funny talking housekeeper of yours. She told me she had no bloody idea who in the hell I was!"

I couldn't help smile at the vision her complaint conjured up: Lydia Gordon, a slight woman with soft, blond hair and steel blue eyes, giving Kathryn the old British one-two.

"My next call will be to her," I promised.

Before I could hang-up, Kelly wanted to say hello. She kept the conversation short and sweet. "Kathryn, I love you no matter what and I can't wait to see you again." Then, "Is everybody just crazy about your beautiful ring?"

I could not hear the answer but, from how long it took, I had a pretty good idea what it was.

When I called Lydia, she picked up after the first ring. I always loved hearing her British accent. She was amazing with my clients. In fact, most of them preferred dealing with her on logistics, rather than me. A whiz at organizing, she had become my right-hand woman and lent an air of class to my operation.

Lydia was not thrilled to hear about two strange women invading her domain. She considered the little basement apartment where she lived, along with the rest of my house, her sphere of influence. It took 10 minutes of gentle persuasion to lower her blood pressure enough to become a tad more tolerant of the idea of us living with two more "bitches." Lydia could be as salty as any man when she wanted to be.

She ended our conversation snickering sarcastically and said, "That damned willy of yours has sure done a fine job of it this time."

On our way out of Safford, I stopped at a Walgreen's and I bought an e.p.t. pregnancy testing kit. Oddly enough, it fit perfectly in the space left by the unused tampon box, which I moved into the large bag behind Kelly's seat, hoping she'd have to retrieve them soon.

Heading dead west on U.S. 70 towards the Pinal Mountains was like riding into a painting. The eastern sun daubed the dusty mountains with a palette of golden colors that highlighted the glory of the burnished pinnacles.

The stretch of open road was seductively lonely and made for easy cruising with long straight-a-ways and elongated lazy curves. Around 75 miles an hour the *Valkyrie* settled into a purring drone that had my passenger holding on tight to me and placing her helmet clad head sideways against my shoulder. I could sense her tiredness and figured Kelly would not make it much further than Globe, Arizona, which was 35 miles ahead.

The first place we stopped in the old mining town was decent enough for us to secure a room. Kelly unpacked in what felt like record time and had the bath water running for what I was sure would be an hour long soak.

I wasn't ready to call it a day yet. "I'm going to scout out the town for images," I called into the bathroom and received an affirmative murmur.

I was no more than five miles west of Globe when I spotted what I thought would make a great photograph. On the left side of the highway was a small, stone encased street grotto. The parking lot next to it was empty. I dismounted the *Valkyrie* and I walked into the roadside shrine. The grotto was filled with candles, some lit, some waiting for a match and prayerful offering. In the center stood a statue of the Virgin Mary. As I got closer to the painted plaster figure, I was shocked to discover that it bore an uncanny resemblance to Kathryn Bailey. A sparkling glow, emanating from the right side of the head, resembled her jeweled barrette.

I shook my head and looked around. Pasted onto the grotto's interior walls were a multitude of photographs and snapshots of the less fortunate, along with various bits and scraps of paper with hand written notes. All the annotations were in broken English or Spanish. Venturing deeper inside was like walking into a dark void, even though the shrine was open to the parking area and street beyond. I felt like I was the last soul on the planet. The place was so eerie it raised goose bumps on my upper torso and arms.

I started to feel nauseous and light headed. For an instant, everything went black. Suddenly I was surrounded by hundreds of slow moving, colored lights like the reflections from a turning disco ball. But these lights were not generated by any visible apparatus and seemed to be curiously alive and dimensional.

It felt that the lights were real and I was a fabrication.

The colorful specks of radiance started passing through me as if I were a cosmic sieve. Multitudes of swirling bits seemed to freeze time and reality. At the height of their luminous dance, a resonant, overpowering voice filled me. It came from everywhere and nowhere and spoke to me not in any language I knew, yet I understood it clearly. It surrounded my world and shook me to the very core.

I started to shake uncontrollably, but the swirling lights seemed to support me. Then a rushing sound, like a freight train passing close by, encompassed me from head to toe and the lights finally stopped swirling and melted into nothing. Suddenly, without the benefit of my ears, I heard a voice so powerful it brought me out of dizziness and to full attention. It ordered me in no uncertain terms to bring Kelly to this place at daybreak.

I staggered outside, back into the world of passing cars and trucks, and slowly came back to a more familiar reality. I tried to figure out what had happened to me. My mind and intellect gushed with questions, but I had no answers. All I knew was that I had returned from a very strange place, where a commanding presence, not of this universe, called for Kelly and me for some purpose, although it did not say what.

I arrived back at the motel, feeling unsettled and confused. When I entered the lobby, I somehow knew that Kelly had used up all of our allotted towels, so I stopped at the front desk to pick up some more.

The cute Chicano girl who had checked us in earlier and could not have been older than Kelly, smiled and said, "Yes, sir, I'll get some for you right away." But in my mind it registered as: *These fucking gringos always want more stuff than they can use.* I was startled by the clarity of her thoughts but knew that I had "heard" them accurately.

Walking down the hallway toward our room, I dismissed the notion that I could now read people's thoughts and decided not to tell Kelly what had happened to me.

I found her sitting up in bed, wrapped in an abundance of towels.

"You hungry?" I asked.

"Sort of, yeah. But let's do the test first."

"It needs a strong flow of urine."

"I've been slamming down water since you left. I could piss out a fire," she retorted and headed towards the bathroom.

A few minutes later she burst from the bathroom naked, grinning like a Cheshire cat, and announced, "I'm not pregnant, isn't that great?"

When I asked, "Are you sure of the results," she approached me and stuck out the test stick. The minus sign on it clearly indicated that she was not pregnant!

There were two test sticks left in the box, so I asked her, "Could you do another test tonight?"

Smiling like a little girl, Kelly inched closer to me with her hands behind her back and said, "Sure, but aren't you happy about this?"

I kissed her on the nose and replied, "I love you, Kelly Michelle. Now get some clothes on that pretty body of yours before you freeze and turn into a marble sculpture."

Hearing that, Kelly smiled at me and let fly with, "That would be all right by me, boss man. And didn't you tell me it was a good thing to be proud of my body."

I replied, "I sure did say that, little one, and I am proud of you for taking it to heart. Kelly, darling, you just taught the teacher a good lesson about practicing what he preaches. Thank you."

A funny look appeared on her face, causing her to stare at me blankly for a second or two. Then she turned and marched into the bathroom. A few moments later she returned with the same negative result as before. Two out of two was good enough for me.

I yawned and said, "We have to be at a special place for sunrise, so we both need a good night's sleep."

I was grateful that Kelly didn't ask any questions, but cuddled up in her bed. Watching her sink deeper and deeper into sleep, I wondered if my afternoon's experience had been a true encounter with the supernatural or a hallucinogenic breakdown signaling worse to come.

Day 16

We made it to the grotto a good 15 minutes before sunrise. I was as nervous as a cat in a dog show. My mood must have affected Kelly because she wasn't her usual, adventurous self either.

"There is something funny about this place," she said.

At this early hour only two of the red-glass encased votive candles were lit. They sat on the top row and flickered softly, near the end of their lives. Below on seven descending rows sat hundreds more in darkness.

Holding tight onto each other's hand Kelly and I ventured a bit deeper into the grotto. As the sun started to rise, the magical lights returned and embraced us in a cocoon of colored luminescence, swirling and circling around and through us at will. Their energized intensity cast no shadow. Kelly was covered in a glow of pinkish hues that bathed her from head to toe.

I started to shake uncontrollably and watched my spirit leave the confines of my body and float in front of me. Although unable to move, I was not frightened. My petrified state allowed me to observe and concentrate on my translucent being. Emanating from a small core in the center of my ethereal form, a spinning nucleus of purple energy sent concentrated beams of light towards Kelly and fanned out to encircle her entire body.

Immobile, I watched as my soul dissolved into Kelly's body. When its energy became one with her spirit, the globes of light increased in intensity to the brightness of a million suns and her aura changed from a pulsating, soft magenta to a solid, opaque, purple blush. Building to a brilliant apex, the swirling lights fused into a single, magnificent white radiance whose luminescence defied description or comprehension.

A deep, resonating sound, like the bellow of a ship's foghorn, emerged from the luminous presence. The reverberations captivated our consciousness and left us in a trance-like state. A nonverbal understanding of what this was all about flooded my being.

My mind's eye was filled with an ancient utterance: *In the beginning there was the word, and the word was made whole.*

As soon as I feelingly understood those old and forgotten words, my soul left Kelly's being and returned to me, and she slowly folded like a ribbon and sank to the ground in a fetal position.

There was a rushing sound, vaguely familiar, and the world of light and mystery disappeared into nothingness, as if it had been sucked away. We were left in empty silence.

I started to pick up my ghostly pale companion and was about to ask her if she was all right when Kelly looked into my eyes and softly murmured, "I am now."

As we made our way outside, we kept turning back for another look at the place of miracles. Our last vision was most remarkable. Upon first entering, we had seen only two flickering candles. Now every candle was blazing in a dazzling conflagration of orange, gold, red and blue. Suddenly, the flames left their paraffin hosts and danced disembodied in the air. And then there was nothing.

We stood motionless with our mouths agape. I reached into my pocket and pulled out my gold watch to check the time, hoping the mundane activity would calm my jangled nerves. It didn't and only added to the mystery. When I flipped open my old timekeeper, which always keep perfect time, it read 2:23.

I turned to Kelly, showed her the watch face and exclaimed, "We've been in this place for over six hours!"

Back at the motel, I immediately removed my clothes and took a shower. While the hot water cascaded over my body, I wondered how Kelly was handling her encounter with the miraculous. Did someone her age have enough life experience to understand what is beyond our comprehension? I wasn't sure I did. The mystery left me with an unanswerable question: Why we had been chosen to have contact with the Light.

Suddenly, the shower curtain slid back and Kelly stepped into the pulsing spray, letting the hot water splash onto her skin. After what we had just gone through together, our nakedness bore no disgrace; our bodies slid against each other as naturally as a cat rubbing against its owner's legs.

Kelly was no longer the child of yesterday and seemed to have aged about five to six years. I let my eyes travel over her wet body. The woman in front of me had grown into fertile maturity. At the same time, my mind was filled with all there was to know about her. Why I was given this knowledge was beyond me, but Kelly now occupied a corner in my brain, which gave me a window into her being. I now had the ability to look into her thoughts and experience her feelings. I also knew that she could do the same with mine. We had become one and, for better or worse, were woven together for eternity. Our fate sealed, we allowed ourselves to bask in the glory of the moment.

Kelly took hold of my soapy hand, placed it on the entrance of her womb and whispered at the same time, "You and I are one, and soon our baby will make the world whole."

Silently I withdrew my hand from the comfort of her womb, wondering why this astonishing event had happened to us, and who and what we had become.

Day 17

When we checked out the next morning, the cute Chicano girl was still behind the front desk. Her wishing us "happy trails" seemed genuine, but Kelly leaned into me and whispered, "Despite that phony smile on her face, that chick really doesn't like gringos very much."

I was surprised to realize that she, too, was able to read other people's thoughts.

Before our descent down the mountain, we made a final stop at the grotto. We looked for any signs or remnants of yesterday's mysterious occurrence but there were none. All that remained were a collection of unlit candles, faded photographs and handwritten notes and letters. Disappointed that there were no more clues for us, we drove off.

I was eager to get to California, so we rode U.S. 60 into Phoenix, joined Interstate 10, and followed that busy thoroughfare all the way to Blythe across the Arizona state line. I think we were afraid to stop until we absolutely had to. The droning hours on the road allowed us to put physical and mental distance between us and our inexplicable experience.

Blythe, California, a high desert border town, is not known for its restaurants. But we found, sandwiched, so to speak, between a *Long John Silver's* and a defunct rock shop, a Chinese restaurant where we spent a good hour talking about what to do regarding out encounter with the unknown.

I felt we had to go on despite the weirdness and see what was waiting for us at the end of the road.

Kelly, however, wanted to turn around and head for Washington right away. "I want to start to take care of myself and nurture our unborn baby," she insisted.

I knew that if I didn't stop her line of thinking, I would be in a whole lot of trouble when Kathryn reentered the picture.

Taking both her hands in mine, I began, "What happened was not of this world and we do not know the significance of the message, or even if there was one. But you have to stop with this nonsense about being pregnant. You tested negative twice and if, by some one-in-a-thousand chance, the test was wrong, then it wouldn't be my child in any event."

Looking straight into my eyes, Kelly responded with words that surprised me with their maturity. She didn't sound like a brash, young girl. "Your quintessence made me pregnant with your child, just like Mary conceived Jesus. Nobody has been able to comprehend that spiritual conception and they have had two thousand years to think about it. All the naysayers will not understand or empathize with us either."

Reaching across the table with my napkin, I wiped a bit of duck sauce from the corner of her mouth and tried once more to snap her back into reality. "Why, honey, that is just a young girl's wishful thinking. There is no way any sexual stuff happened to you on my part in that prayer cave. And don't you think I might be aware of impregnating you?"

Kelly abruptly pulled her hands from mine, and banged her fist on the table top. "You will see who is right and who is wrong. And this is not a fucking fairytale."

She left the table in such a rush that she almost ran into a waiter on her way to the restroom.

While she was gone, I tried to get hold of Kathryn at work, but the person picking up said that she was with a customer and to try back later.

After 10 minutes Kelly returned, considerably more composed then when she stormed off.

We got back on the motorcycle and traveled in silence, keeping our thoughts to ourselves. Six hours later we stopped at a motel in Palm Springs. By then we were ravenous, so we picked up some pizza to share in our room. Between noisy mouthfuls of her second slice, Kelly asked, "Does Kathryn know about our blessing?" When I shook my head, no, she started to rotate her right hand in a slow circle around her belly. Then she said, "I'm not sure it would be a smart idea to inform her of all that has transpired between us."

I could not believe that I was looking at a 13-year-old girl. She appeared to be a well-educated young woman in her early 20s. I walked into the bathroom wondering for the umpteenth time if this was some kind of hypnotic dream. I looked into the mirror to see if I could find any clues to what was happening to me.

I didn't realize Kelly had come up behind me until she proclaimed, as if she was reading my mind, "This is not a dream, Brett. We are real and alive, just like the light-spirit who made us. I don't know why we were brought together. All I know is we were meant to be together. I was soulless until your spirit swirled into me. Now, through a miracle I am with child, and because you breathed new life into me, I will be with you forever."

I noticed that her penetrating eyes were flashing with a new found intelligence and answered cautiously, "Until we are sure of what this is, we tell no one about what happened to us up on that mountain. We will soon know truth from hallucination. We will find out if what you claim is true or a child's wish. You can't be pregnant by all known physical laws. But I admit, your physical transformation is as strange as it is real." I let my eyes travel up and down her mature body and said, "You are no longer the little girl who asked me in a dusty Texas laundry if I wanted to buy some pussy."

Smiling, she looked straight at me. "Well, do you?"

I was considering how to best answer her challenge when the muffled, staccato ringtone of my cell phone in one of my saddlebags interrupted us. It was Tommy and he seemed to be in a heightened state of excitement. "Are you alone?" he asked. "Can you talk 'free of ears'?"

"Yes, I'll step out into the hallway."

The instant I closed the door behind me, Tommy started in excitedly, "You are not going to believe this, but Maryanne and that jackass boyfriend of hers were found dead this morning in their van. Apparently they got hold of some bad heroin and checked out before they knew what hit them."

I wasn't shocked at the news although the coincidental turn of events was surprising.

Tommy continued in more measured tones, "I was able to have all the records erased that there ever was a Kelly Porter. So now you are on your own with Kelly Michelle Tempest. I will let you know in a day or two when her other identifications are ready. By the way, little brother, you owe me really big this time." And then the phone went dead.

When I let myself back in the room, Kelly stood by the dresser fixing a drink. She handed it to me with a sardonic expression on her face and said, "They got what they deserved and now that chapter of my book is finished."

Taking a sip of the slow, burning bourbon, I sank into the one armchair in the room. I felt worn out, so much so that I didn't bother to ask Kelly how she knew what Tommy had just told me. I sat quietly with my thoughts, bewildered by everything that was happening.

Without a word Kelly marched past me into the bathroom and closed the door firmly behind her. When she came out a few minutes later, she was wearing my white, oversized tee shirt. It gave her the appearance of a funny ghost. She flounced towards me and plopped down next to me. She took my hand in hers and started to babble on about going to D.C.

I stopped her cold. "Tell you what, if you test pregnant with the last tester, I will call Kathryn and see if she can meet us in L.A., and the two of you could go home together."

Smiling like she just won an Olympic Gold Medal, Kelly extended an arm, turned her palm upward and opened her fist. The e.p.t test stick showed a "+" on the read-out pane, clearly indicating that Kelly was indeed pregnant!

I got off the bed, fixed myself a fresh drink to steady my shaking nerves, picked up the phone and called Kathryn's number even though it was past midnight back in Tennessee. I got a busy signal and tried again with the same result. By then I started to feel flames of jealousy lapping at my judgment. I called once more—still busy.

Putting the phone down, I sat on the bed. Kelly started to softly rub my back and said, "Kathryn is having phone sex with a woman by the name of Karri Blackman, and she seems to be really enjoying it."

I was flabbergasted. How did Kelly even know about Karri, and how could she know that my Kathryn was on the phone with her at this very moment? I got my wallet and found the card with Karri's number on it. As I pushed the buttons on the phone, my heart beat in anxious anticipation. After the fourth ring Karri's recorded voice came on, "I'm having a little fun on the line right now. Leave me a message and we will hook up a little later."

I ended the call and took a swig of bourbon. Then I confronted Kelly. "How do you know about Karri?"

She smiled and said, "The same way you knew about what that Chicano girl was thinking."

"You mean to tell me that you not only hear what people are thinking, like that motel clerk back in Globe, but you also know the names of the people in your telepathic encounters, as well?"

"Yes, in my mind I heard Kathryn talking to Karri about me, telling that bitch she now had a new 'little' step daughter to play with. Kathryn craves young girls and wants to have me all to herself, like with Ray Ann. But she got caught in bed with her and that is why her husband sued her for divorce. Kathryn Bailey is a perverted bitch and has big plans to take your money and my pussy."

I was rendered speechless. If this child was right, and it sure looked like she had not picked Karri's name out of thin air, then what kind of choices had I made? And how could I put this mess back into some semblance of sanity?

"Are you sure of what you are saying?" I asked, but before Kelly could answer, I put my hand over her mouth to stop any words from escaping. I already knew the answer.

I finally got through to Kathryn. She sounded tired. After apologizing for the late call, I hurriedly told her about our change of plans; that I needed for her to fly out to Los Angeles right way. Money was not an issue. I would take care of all her expenses.

Kathryn kept asking "Is something wrong?"

"On the contrary, everything is great," I assured her. "Kelly misses you and wants to know if you are divorced yet?"

"I will be by the time I get out there."

"Book a one-way ticket so you and Kelly can fly to D.C. together."

"I will." Then she blurted out, "Brett honey, every time we talk on the phone, I am reminded of that Karri woman."

I caught my breath and swallowed my hurt. In a soft voice I asked, "Do you still love our little girl?"

"More than you know," she breathed into the phone and then clicked off.

I turned to look at Kelly. She was livid. "How can she be so cruel to let you buy that beautiful ring for her? I can't wait for you to take it off her finger and put it on my hand. Then the whole world will know that I am yours."

When I slowly shook my head, her eyes flashed cat-like and she insisted, "Brett, can't you see that God has put us together to raise this child? You don't have to worry, I will be a good mother to our child and a soft woman for you."

Although my heart was not in it, I was wounded by Kelly's revelation about Kathryn's lack of morality and pressed on, "Kelly, you have to back off and stop hammering me when I am down. I want you to stop all of this bullshit right here and now!"

Chastened, she withdrew and pouted on the bed.

I had an inkling that everything would be resolved when we got to the California coast. I called to make a reservation at my favorite inn, the Malibu Waves, which overlooks the cliffs of Point Dume. Twenty minutes later I had a five-day hold on the only room left. There had been a cancellation and we were fortunate to get one of only two ocean view suites.

Soon after Kathryn rang back with an update, sounding less tired. "Brett honey, I will be arriving at LAX at 9:15 p.m., and I'm so excited to see you both that I could just pass out. I've booked a car, too, and will drive out to wherever you are. Now, don't worry, honey, I'll map quest the directions and will be there in plenty of time for a midnight flute of bubbly champagne."

I gave her the address of the Malibu Waves Inn. By the time we ended the call, I was exhausted and almost stumbled into bed.

But deep into the night in the middle of a dream, I awoke with a start. In the dreamscape, I had watched a plastic keycard falling from Kelly's fingers and dropping to the carpet. When she bent down to pick up the keycard she noticed the purple and black business card that had attached itself to the back when I put it in my wallet. Her eyes narrowed as she read the message written on the card: *KARRI BLACK-MAN—I GIVE GOOD PHONE SEX.*

As I tried to go back to sleep, my mind would not let go of the fact that Kelly must have known about Karri days ago in Soccorro, and all because of a simple twist of fate. She had used the opportunity to smear Kathryn by creating a vision of swirling impropriety. Grudgingly, sleep won the battle over tumbling thoughts and I slowly drifted off knowing I was about to wade deep into the waters of mystery and revelation.

Day 18

The next morning the sky was clear as glass. I decided to treat Kelly to breakfast at *Sherman's Deli*. I had first discovered it 20 years earlier and it had become a must stop whenever I was in the Palm Springs area. For my money, *Sherman's Deli* served the best New York style delicatessen fare in Southern California. We were lucky that the place wasn't too crowded and walked straight to an unoccupied patio table.

It looked like Kelly was really coming into her own. Every male in the room kept ogling her, and a surprising number of female patrons as well. I didn't think it was her cool Mickey Mouse sweatshirt or Sherman's sticky rolls that brought her the attention of all those roving eyes. My money was on the promise of what lay beneath the happy Disney rodent.

When we were finished, I suggested we go for another photo shoot. The day before we had passed some interesting looking deserted buildings in Desert Center that might provide a great setting. Kelly was eager and excited for another opportunity in front of the camera. We did not have to be in Malibu for the start of our five-day mini vacation until the next day, so backtracking 60 miles was no big deal.

When we got there an hour later, I was pleased. The location was good and we quickly found a place tailor made for my new vision. The building had been abandoned decades ago and every window in the place had been shattered from outside in, leaving a profusion of glass shards scattered across the old wooden floor inside. They acted like mini prisms, catching the sunlight pouring in through the open window frames, and creating a carpet of small rainbows across the floor.

While I was thinking how lucky we were to have discovered this place, Kelly shed her clothes and tip-toed to the center of the room. As if reading my mind, she carefully lay down on one side among the glinting shards and turned her head back towards me. We got to work and became so involved in what we were doing that we didn't notice the time passing.

At some point I did register that the angle of the light had changed. I was about to suggest we take a break when a pair of yellow and black snakes came from under the house through a broken floorboard and slithered across the glass and dirt encrusted floor to curl up in a circle of sunlight near Kelly lying in repose. She saw them and made no move.

My first instinct was to grab a loose brick and smash their heads but Kelly, reading my mind, whispered, "Wait. I can feel them. I will calm them and coax them into my world."

She slowly rolled on her back next to the pair of desert vipers and within minutes they had slithered onto her chest, enjoying the warmth. One of the snakes curled around Kelly's breast while its mate found her belly captivating. I shot pictures with three different cameras while the reptiles slowly slid across her dusty body. The image I felt would become a global phenomenon had one of the serpents between Kelly's swarthy thighs, nestled at such an angle that it looked as if it was emerging from her womb, while the other snake lay on her stomach facing its mate. Kelly was still on her back with her dust encrusted, yellow hair splayed out over shards of broken glass. A drop of saliva escaped from the side of her partly open mouth as if she were totally engrossed in an orgasmic frenzy of forbidden lust. It was perhaps the most dramatic and brutally beautiful shots I had ever taken.

At some point the reptiles slinked back into their hiding place and we decided to call it a day. It was sunset by the time we packed up all the gear and counted up the exposed rolls of film. I was shocked to discover that I had taken over 200 photos!

Motoring away from that place of dark wonder I was so enraptured by the shoot and the surreal atmosphere that I didn't see the west-bound train ahead until a loud whoosh brought me back to reality and I squeezed the brake lever just in time. With freight cars whizzing by, I fell forward against the handlebars with the realization of how close we'd come to crashing. I wondered from where I'd gotten the power to stop the *Valkyrie*.

We rode west for about an hour until we reached the concrete oasis of Indio where we found a motel. As soon as we got to our room, we both collapsed onto the bed, dead to the world.

Day 19

I awoke to find Kelly resting her head on one elbow, looking down at me and whispering a hypnotic greeting that sent chills running down to my toes, "I have loved you from the beginning of time and will love you until the end of us. Brett, there is no place to run and nowhere to hide. Breathe into me, my beloved, so we can make this baby whole."

Mustering strength from the deepest regions of my moral center, I gently turned from her descending lips and said, "Wait until we reach the place where the mountains meet the sea."

Knowing we were getting close to our destination, we rode all morning and most of the afternoon before entering the Lincoln Street Tunnel that marks the beginning and ending of Interstate 10. Entering the darkness with only moving red taillights visible ahead was an otherworldly feeling, fraught with anxiety. It was a pleasurable relief to finally exit at the other end, driving into the sun along sandy beaches and the sea. Leaning comfortably on the *Valkyrie*, we swept into a slow right curve and arrived at the start of California's famed Pacific Coast Highway.

We rode north towards Malibu, passing some of the most exquisite and expensive real estate in the United States. It occurred to me that the wealthy homeowners put up precarious structures not only in disregard of the delicate ecology of this ocean paradise, but also in willful ignorance of the vengeful perils of Mother Nature. No matter how often this storied highway had been ravaged by mudslides and forest fires, they rebuilt, gambling once again on borrowed time. Ultimately, no amount of money would save them when the celestial cards finally signaled total destruction via an earthquake or other extreme natural disaster.

As the sun made its descent towards the ocean, I pulled over to the side of the highway to take in the spectacular view. Standing on a bluff with the waves crashing on the rocks below, we watched a dance as old as time, as the golden globe seemed to hover above the dark waters.

We were reluctant to break the magical atmosphere and rejoin the busy highway. But we finally did, and 15 minutes later made it to the *Malibu Waves Inn*. After a routine check-in and bite to eat at the hotel's *Grunion Café*, Kelly and I quickly changed in our room and made a mad dash to the heated pool. Somebody in management must have had a sense of whimsy and creativity, because strings of twinkle lights crisis-crossed the pool into the surrounding trees. We sipped champagne while floating in the color bathed waters, listening to the crashing surf and gazing at the lights reflected in the warm pool surface.

It was under these circumstances that I enticed a promise from Kelly to keep news of the pregnancy between us during Kathryn's visit; we would work it all out in Washington. Grudgingly, she agreed to keep mum about "our child" and give Kathryn the benefit of doubt regarding any recent visions of impropriety.

I gently said, "We are a family and not mortal enemies."

Kelly laughed and changed the subject. "Where are we all going to sleep?"

"In that giant king-sized bed," I replied.

"In that case, I get dibs in the middle!"

"Kelly, what we have is what we got, which should be pretty cozy. If not, you can always sleep in the tub."

I couldn't help laughing when she scrunched up her face in reply.

A large group of guests celebrating a young man's Bar Mitzvah arrived and dove into the pool en masse. Splashing loudly they destroyed our relaxed reveries. It was time to leave.

On the way back to the room, Kelly wanted to know, "What in tarnation is a Bar Mitzvah?"

I explained that it was the Jewish tradition's initiation ritual of a boy's coming of age, but I had to say it in several different ways before I was reasonably certain that Kelly got it. I finished with, "It's the archway a boy passes through on his way to becoming a man, a signpost or marker on his journey through life."

Kelly snickered and said, "That shit sounds weird. Seems to me that a good whore would do the trick just as well."

Once again I was so shocked I had no reply for her outrageous repartee.

I had noticed while we were frolicking in the pool that my ability to "read" the thoughts of strangers was rapidly departing, and I suspected the same thing was happening to Kelly.

To make sure, I asked as we were lying in bed in our room, "Have you felt or heard any thoughts of others out in the pool area?

"No," she acknowledged. "The last voice that I heard inside my mind was back in the desert."

I caught myself unconsciously twirling her hair around my fingers. But when I started to pull my hand from its golden entanglement, Kelly grabbed hold of it and pleaded, "Don't stop."

I watched her for what seemed like an hour as she gradually fell asleep. Only then did I remove my hand from her soft tresses. Although we had had a long day on the road, I wasn't ready to go to sleep, so I slipped out of bed, fixed myself a drink, and sent a text message to Tommy, advising him of what hotel we were in. Then I quietly left the room to take a walk on the beach just below the hotel.

The night sky was cloudless and filled with bright stars and a half moon, which promised just enough light for an extended stroll. I shed my shoes at the edge of the beach, walked barefoot through the cool sand to the waterline and headed towards Point Dume. With swirling energy currents, both from sea and space, it was a spiritual place. The

Chumash Indians who lived there before we ousted them used it as a conduit to the world of dancing spirits.

I found a good spot among a smattering of sand dunes and sat down to do some quiet thinking. The beach was deserted and before long I drifted into a state of meditation. I was in that tranquil mode for some time when a hauntingly familiar, disembodied "Voice" entered my being.

Without hearing specific words it informed me that I was about to start a journey into the miraculous. I would acquire keys to unlock the gates of mystery and, in a short time, would gain a complete understanding of why I had been chosen.

The voice left me with a proclamation that felt like a command, "Do not be afraid of the crossing, as you have taken this journey many times before."

A cold, salty wind brought me back to the reality of my body, and I shivered as much from what I had just experienced as from the cool breeze. I got up slowly and headed back to the warmth of the hotel, prickling with excitement and anticipation, even though I had no idea where I was headed and what I would do when I arrived.

Day 20

I was having a wonderful dream of consuming a large country breakfast of Eggs Benedict sitting on thick sliced bacon, home fried potatoes, freshly brewed coffee and orange juice. Before long this culinary apparition was replaced by the sound of voices in my room, but the aroma lingered on. I instinctively reached over for Kelly and felt nothing but cold sheets.

My eyelids fluttered open with the sound of the door of our room closing. I forced myself into awareness and looked around. Everything I had dreamt about was on the linen covered table except for the orange juice, which had been replaced with Mimosas in champagne flutes.

Kelly, standing behind the table like a hostess, blew me a kiss and asked, "Is anybody up for a little breakfast?"

I was out of bed in an instant and slipped into jeans and a tee shirt, ready to join her. Because of the total surprise, this morning feast was one of the all-time, greatest meals I have had the pleasure to enjoy. There is something to be said about awakening and feasting on a dream.

Finishing my last swallow of coffee I looked at Kelly and asked, "What would my little princess like to do today?"

"If you don't mind, I want to find something nice to wear tonight and also a little something for when Kathryn and I fly back."

I knew just the place. "We'll go to the Malibu Country Mart. It has plenty of little shops that will fit the bill."

Kelly left her chair in a flash and was in my lap, covering my face with little butterfly kisses and telling me how much she loved me.

We drove down Pacific Coast Highway to Cross Creek Road, made a left and headed for *Marie's Place*. Unfortunately, despite all my fond memories of Marie, it was now called *Rachel's Place*. We walked to the *Planet Blue* boutique, where I left Kelly to her own devices and went in search of one of my area favorite shops. *Tops* is known for its fanciful gifts and what-nots. Unable to find it, I was totally befuddled, standing in front of where I thought it used to be. What could have happened to this old Malibu landmark?

It turned out that the place was now an upscale clothing boutique nouveau. Wealthy shoppers issued from its sliding doors, toting more fancy looking shopping bags than a thief would want to carry. What used to be a laidback, fun area had turned into Rodeo Drive by the Sea.

Disappointed, I walked back to *Planet Blue* and found Kelly waiting for me at the register. She had picked out a nice, soft pink and blue dress, Mary Jane type shoes, and a couple of other items that were folded and ready to go into the waiting shopping bag. I couldn't wait to see Kelly Michelle in her new clothes. I just knew they would look great on her.

We roared away from that den of conspicuous consumption and drove a mile or so north, just beyond Pepperdine University, to the most unpretentious place that I could think of to have lunch. *Malibu Fish and Seafood* is a small, whitewashed wooden structure on the landside of the PCH, which has a four-table, outdoor café adjacent to the fish market. I was relieved to see that some Beverly Hills developer had not yet replaced this old landmark with an unattractive, high-class joint that had no character. We had a quick lunch of fish and fries and headed back to our retreat by the sea.

When we arrived back at the inn, Kelly asked, "Why are you so despondent?"

"When I used to live here it was a paradise and I figured that was still the case when I booked our room," I explained. "That Malibu was enjoyed by the rich and famous as well as by ordinary mortals.

Everybody walked around on equal terms and people were relaxed and friendly. This new breed of self-indulgent glitterati with their snobbish attitudes and money have ruined the place."

While Kelly changed I fixed myself an early afternoon drink. I wasn't more than two sips into my bourbon when she strolled provocatively into the room, the new dress clinging to her body as if it were another layer of skin. With the silken fabric emphasizing every curve and swell of her lithe figure, she was a vision of feminine sensuality!

Kelly did a slow turn to show me the way the back of the dress highlighted her body. I was so impressed with her transformation that I wanted to show her beauty to the world.

Picking up the phone, I said, "I'm going to call *Beau Rivage* and make a dinner reservation for tonight."

But Kelly put her hand on mine to stop me and said, "Brett, I wish you wouldn't. With Kathryn coming to take me to Washington, this might be our last night together and I don't want to share you with anyone else."

I replaced the receiver in its cradle and had a swig of whiskey, all the while marveling at the new maturity of the adolescent beauty standing in front of me. I figured since we were not going out to eat we would bring the outside in. I wanted to create an environment in our own room, which would closely resemble a fine restaurant. When I called the *Grunion Café* to order our meal, I made sure that the dinner would come with the best china and cutlery along with candles in silver holders.

Thirty minutes later there was a knock on the door. I sent Kelly to the bathroom so that I could prepare my surprise.

She readily agreed. "I want to change anyway. Wouldn't want to get any stains on my new dress."

The meal I had ordered consisted of an appetizer of shrimp and scallop feuillet, New York steak au poivre with a serving of wild mushroom risotto as our main feast, and two bottles of Fess Parker's vintage

Syrah wine; and for dessert, one piece of an orange liquor brownie, to be shared. I arranged everything on the table, poured the wine, lit the candles and ignited the fireplace. Then I turned off the room lights and opened the curtains to allow the glow from the patio lights to mingle with the glimmering candlelight.

Kelly emerged from the bathroom wearing nothing but her pale blue silk bra and panties. Looking around the suite she said, "This is even more than I prayed for. You have made this night into a fairytale and I love you so much for doing this for me."

I was taken aback by her choice of attire but had to admit that she looked stunning in the soft light. Maybe this was the way to eat—al fresco indoors. I felt a bit odd in my jeans and tee shirt, but the first sip of wine dispelled any awkwardness. I did not bother to water down Kelly's wine. She had sipped at the champagne in the pool the evening before, never allowing herself to overindulge on that wonderful nectar. I explained that the wine she was drinking came from the vineyards of Fess Parker who some years back had starred on TV as Davy Crockett and Daniel Boone. Kelly found that mildly amusing, but she had never seen any of his shows and wanted to know if he still was an actor? I shook my head and told her that he was no longer alive.

We took our time eating, using our fingers to put succulent morsels of steak into each other's mouths. We laughed and drank the deep red Syrah until the candles flickered close to the end of their life.

The spell lingered on. When we had consumed the last piece of dessert, Kelly stood up. Her wispy blue lingerie slid to the floor. Slithering around the table to my side, she pulled me out of the chair and led me to the bed. I was like a puppet on a string, completely immersed in her passion and offered no resistance. My clothes fell in a heap by my feet. My heart was racing so fast that I thought it was going to jump out of my chest.

Kelly lay on the bed with her arms open, beckoning to me. Slowly I put my knee onto the mattress and crawled into her waiting arms.

Her hand found my rock hard penis as our lips opened to receive each other's tongues. She whispered words of love and endearment between warm kisses. With unstoppable passion riding roughshod over the last vestiges of my moral code, I enclosed one of her hard nipples between my lips and fed like a newborn baby. The sweat poured from our raging bodies onto each other's flaming skin.

Kelly grabbed the hair on the back of my head with her free hand, pulling my lips off her throbbing bosom, and brought my mouth back to the warmth of hers. I broke the kiss momentarily to give her room to throw her legs up and secured them in place by wrapping her eager hands around her wide-open thighs. I entered her in one stroke and thrust deep into her. Our eyes locked onto one another while we bucked insanely until I was close to climaxing. Feeling a change in the throbbing of my shaft, Kelly stretched her legs even wider while screaming her tortured love at me.

Just as I was about to splash into her womb, I heard the sound of knuckles tapping a familiar beat on the door. I instantly knew that it was Kathryn!

I tried frantically and with all of my might to prevent my semen from bursting out, but to no avail. Kelly, hearing the sound at the door, dug her nails into my buttocks and pulled me even deeper inside her. I exploded in a spray of lust into Kelly's begging vagina.

At the instant of inception, I heard a mammoth boom and felt my heart explode like a bursting glass vessel, the red shards burrowing themselves inside my chest.

My world turned into a fragmented slideshow of events from my past lives, which were being projected onto Kelly's frantic face. I saw good things, bad things and chaotic moments, all twisted into grotesque images through Kelly's teary cries for help. It was over in seconds but felt like eternity.

With the scent of burnt passion dominating the room, my consciousness eased away from my death and floated to the furthest corner of the room, just above the doorway. From that vantage, I saw Kelly run to the open door and watched the shocked expression on her and Kathryn's faces as their eyes took in my corpse. I observed the two most important people from my earlier existence pound and lament over what used to be Brett Tempest.

I knew that I had to leave this room soon to start a new journey, so I tried to project my thoughts onto the women who were mourning my passing. As close as we had become, I was not able to raise a blink or sign of recognition that they registered any of them.

Soon, others arrived and removed my corpse from the tear-filled room. It seemed all too soon that the images of Kathryn and Kelly started to fade in and out like old black and white pictures from a 1950s television. And then they were no more.

I existed in another dimension, yet felt more alive than when shackled to the restraints of my earth-bound body.

A whooshing sound, identical to the one I had ingested in the Grotto of Wishes, encircled my consciousness, and I knew that I was about to fulfill my preordained destiny. The sound intensified and became one with an emerging luminosity. Pulsating together they created a vortex of colored lights that started to rapidly spin around me. Their blurring speed and sound became overwhelming and felt like they issued from eternity. I watched this maelstrom of life spin into blackness while the whirling sound hissed into an absolute silence, leaving me suspended in a world beyond light, sound or time. My consciousness focused on opaque darkness until a vision of myself manifested in front of me. I was now looking at myself looking at myself.

Then I started to speak and listen to my own story, told to me by my cosmic balance in total rapture:

We existed in non-existence for a million years or a millionth of a second, for time did not exist in this dimension. Our emptiness was complete!

Out of this blissful void, emerging from emptiness and crawling into my realm of existence, a speck of life at the far edge of comprehension signified the start of a new reality.

I came to the realization that I was no longer stationary or alone. My consciousness moved through a translucent tunnel, a kind of wormhole that connects parallel universes, and I instinctively knew that only pure consciousness was buoyant enough to be propelled through it.

I became aware of other vibrations. It was as if unseen voices were crying out to me in dialects and word shapes. They were foreign to my last life, but I'd known them in eons past and I completely understood the sorrow they conveyed.

Dark, wraithlike spirits started to emerge, wrapping themselves around the invisible convex walls of the cosmic tube in which I traveled. It was as if they were trying to break through the walls, not to harm me, but to join me on my journey towards the Light.

I started to experience intense torment and dread, not mine—theirs. Unable to join me, they conveyed an agony so excruciating, a sorrow so deep, it became a universe of its own. The indiscernible walls of the wormhole kept my light intact and prevented the creatures of darkness from extracting the radiance of my being. I felt safe as a baby in his mother's belly.

My understanding was so complete that I did not need to analyze the situation any further. I knew I was passing through the gates of what I used to call Hell. Soon the beings of agony started to disappear as the luminosity became more intense. In an instant the brilliant Light took over everything and permeated my being, overwhelming me with a feeling of peace, wellbeing and profound knowledge. Serenity replaced all feelings of discord. The Light became everything. I was no longer in the tunnel; I was now part of a new and glorious world of radiance! I stopped thinking in the singular and became part of all thoughts that make up the cosmos. I stopped being insular and melted into the consciousness of life.

I finally understood what the meaning of God really was. God is not a being, or similar to humans in any way shape or form. He is all that and everything else in the universe, for God is pure energy. The Creator of all is simply all, a hub of everything, held together by simple desire.

I realized that everything I had experienced was a lesson in balance. In the light there is only ecstasy and a total understanding of all that was and all that will be. Birth and death are nonexistent, for there is no time and they have no meaning in the luminosity of the Supreme. Since we see and feel through all matter, the blood of earth has no consequence. There is no fear in the brilliance of the everlasting. We occupy billions of suns and trillions of worlds all at the same time and watch for an opportunity to bond with the righteous few who are working their way to ecstasy.

I experienced worlds made up of airy beings. I inhabited trees and plants in countless worlds and watched the cycle of life happen a billion times a second. I saw the earth grow old and change into a barren waste-land, being pulled into its own exploding sun. I saw celestial bodies spew-ing their matter into supernova that, in turn, ejaculated new life and new worlds that offered more life and death, only to repeat the cycle countless times over.

All that mattered was the Light, for it never changed it only existed.

Experiencing a new level of awareness, I entered into a place in another dimension where I found myself in a black room, devoid of light. Soon a fig-ure appeared out of the darkness and floated in front of me. It was Kathryn Bailey. Her form was in a process of materializing right in front of me, yet I knew that I could not mentally or physically touch her, as she was a manifes-tation from another plane and time. She was unclothed and wearing in her hair the bejeweled barrette that I had admired in my last material world. The image before me soon dissipated into the emptiness of black.

Another form appeared and this manifestation of Kathryn was almost an exact duplicate of the first, but with one slight change—the jeweled barrette was now on the left side of her head.

I was experiencing two versions of the same soul.

Then the most amazing thing happened: the first image reappeared alongside the second iteration. The two Kathryns turned to face each other, formed one image, turned towards me and smiled. At that very instant, the jeweled barrette dropped from her head. I was mesmerized watching it tumble, catching unseen light, until it faded into an explosion of pure color and disappeared from my reality.

When I looked up, Kathryn had disappeared.

I floated alone with the knowledge of understanding death as life. I also came to realize in this dark room of enlightenment that I chose my lifetimes.

As that thought faded, my gold pocket watch suddenly appeared out of nowhere, slowly spinning in front of me. I watched, frozen in time, as the golden metal cover flipped open on its own. But instead of its normal analog dial, the number 223 appeared in red and lifted off the blank face of the timepiece. The red numerals started pulsating in waves of searing Light.

Day 30

The intensity of light flooding over me was so bright it pierced my closed eye lids. I found it interesting that this light clearly had a source, whereas the light I had just experienced seemed omnipresent.

When I managed to open my eyelids, I saw solid bodied beings hovering over me and moving in slow motion around me. They were shrouded in white and blue garb with small, rectangular openings at the head from which human eyes peered down at me. I knew that I was in a body of some kind because I became aware of my awakening senses and felt, for the first time in a while, a sense of heaviness.

As my mind slowly cleared, I figured I was either in a hospital or in an interrogation room.

And then I heard soft voices and felt them vibrating inside my ears: "He's coming back to us…" "Oh my God, I thought we lost him…" "I already marked the time of death at 2:23…."

I was relieved that these beings turned out to be doctors and nurses who were trying to revive me. As I continued to come back to my more familiar being, I realized that none of them knew that I had already healed myself when I reentered my body. Using the knowledge I had gained on my recent crossing, I had projected strong, remedial energy into the damaged areas of my body. By rearranging and recharging stagnant atoms I had recuperated and returned to life and a fully cognizant state.

The first coherent words that tumbled out of my mouth were, "What hospital am I in, and how long have I been dead?"

One of the attending doctors replied, "I don't know about being dead, but you have been in a coma for ten days. While we were treating you for a pretty nasty infection with doxycycline, a type of penicillin, you developed an allergic reaction that sent you into anaphylactic shock. Your lungs filled with liquid and your heart gave out. We thought we had lost you several times and were about to throw in the towel when you just opened your eyes."

While the doctor further explained what had happened to me, a kind nurse wiped my brow with a cool cloth and smiled down at me like a mother adoring her new baby. I could read the name "Madelyn" on the tag she wore above her left breast. Her breath was soft and fresh with an aroma of cloves and mint.

Bending closer, she whispered, "You are my personal miracle. As long as you are here in Christus Saint Michael Hospital, I will be your guardian angel and will not let anything hurt you again."

Bewildered, I asked, "Is Christus Saint Michael a new hospital in Malibu? I haven't heard of it before."

The nurse said, "We are not in Malibu, we are in Texarkana, Texas. This is where they brought you after that nasty motorcycle accident you had ten days ago. Lucky for you it happened right in front of our hospital. In fact, the side mirror from your motorcycle, wrapped itself right around mile marker 223. Those numbers add up to the lucky number 7, and you were the beneficiary."

How odd that a nurse was into numerology. I was curious to hear more and was pleased when she continued.

"I know all of those details because a woman came by to check on you and told us exactly how your accident happened. She has visited you every day since. In fact, she just left fifteen minutes before you came back to us. According to her, your motorcycle went into a slide on the wet and oily pavement. What saved you from certain death was that you flew off your bike and landed in a large, overstuffed chair that, by the grace of God, just happened to be on the shoulder of the road.

You and the chair slid for about a two hundred feet. By the time you came to a stop, it had all but disintegrated and most of your leathers were torn to almost nothing. Your motorcycle was totally destroyed. All that remained was one saddlebag, which we have put away for you. You are truly blessed and one of the luckiest persons I have ever met. Anybody else would have been dead two times over."

I looked deep into Madelyn's hazel eyes and whispered, "I was dead."

She was startled and gave me a puzzled look.

I suddenly felt a wave of exhaustion flood over me. I felt so done in I closed my eyes, slipping into darkness, and did not open them until the following morning.

Day 31

I started off the day wrapped in good cheer and hope. When my attending physician looked in, he told me that I was "improving faster than computer technology" and would be out of the hospital "in no time." He left me to ponder his upbeat prognosis.

At some point the door to my room opened and a young, attractive woman came in. She looked to be in her early 30s, but her beauty was tarnished by the sorrow in her deep blue eyes. She hovered by the door, holding a large bouquet of purple, pink and yellow flowers.

I looked at her and asked, "What has made a beautiful woman like yourself so upset?"

Coming closer, she said, "I am the one who ran you off the highway. When it happened I just knew I had killed you. You have no idea how sorry I am. At the same time I am relieved to see you alive and doing so well. Quite frankly, it all has been so overwhelming that it has made me an emotional wreck."

She came over to my bed, placed the flowers across my legs, leaned down and kissed my forehead. Then she started to cry. Her weeping escalated into heaves and convulsions. Her shoulders and breasts shook so hard that I thought I might have to ring the nurses' call button.

I reached out and put my hand on her lily-white face and held it there. As her tears subsided I said, "Everything is all right. What happened was supposed to happen. I should really thank you. Without you, I wouldn't have gotten the chance to meet the absolute in the absolute!"

The sorrow in her eyes changed to relief and she smiled for the first time. Holding my free hand in both of hers she asked, "Did you really meet God?"

I squeezed the hand on top of mine and replied, "I did, indeed, and want you to know that the Creator is aware of everything that you think, do or say. But you are just part of the grand plan and, believe it or not, you had no control over what happened out on that highway." When I saw her relax even further I went on, "So tell me, lovely lady, what is your name, and can I count on you for a ride out of this place when I need to go since my motorcycle is kaput?"

"My name is Kelly Porter and I will drive you to the end of the earth, if you want."

I wasn't sure I heard right. "Did you say that your name is Kelly Porter?"

"Yes, that is my name and has been for the past thirty-one years."

Stunned, I pushed on. "Kelly, by any chance are you from Throckmorton, Texas?"

"No, I was born and raised in Vincennes, Indiana and only moved to Texarkana two weeks ago."

I said cautiously, "Kelly, do not let this next question offend you, but on my journey into the Light I met a Kelly Porter who was as real as you. So I must ask you. 'Have you ever been a prostitute? Are you now?'"

At first she looked shocked. She pulled her hands away and replied with a chilly edge in her voice, "No, I have never been a prostitute. In fact, I am a virgin and hope to remain so until my wedding night."

Looking at her, I found it hard to believe. This Kelly was sexy and good looking. She had large, indigo eyes and lustrous brown hair. Her nose was so perfect you'd think she'd had surgery done. Her lips were soft and full and added to the allure of her dimpled chin. Her breasts, unrestrained under her beige blouse, promised further softness. I wondered how someone blessed with such beauty had managed to keep the hawks away for so long.

I asked, "What are you doing in Texarkana?"

"I came here to take care of my sick aunt. Sadly, she passed away two days after I arrived. Since then, just as in Indiana, I've been working with runaways and pregnant teens."

The last statement set off an internal light in me. So I continued, "Well, Kelly, my dear, would you mind working with someone a little older and not pregnant by helping me to get my life back in order and bringing me some clothes and other things I might need to get out of this place?"

She laughed, exposing perfect teeth, and said, "I thought you'd never ask. Of course I will. And I promise this time I'll drive better." Then she clasped my hand again and beseeched me, "Please tell me more about your miraculous experiences."

When I next looked at the clock on the wall, I was amazed. An hour and 40 minutes had passed while I had tried to describe the indescribable to her. When I reached the end of my saga, Kelly cried tears of joy. I wiped them from her face and brought her close to me.

With her lips against my cheek, Kelly said, "You must be an envoy from God. I feel a strong inner urge to protect you from harm."

"I'm not sure what I have done to deserve this, but you are the second person today who wants to protect me. Earlier my nurse, Madelyn, conveyed to me those exact sentiments."

At that point an orderly interrupted us. He brought a telephone, plugged it into a wall outlet and placed it on my bedside table. I figured with me hovering on death's door the hospital staff had not seen fit to have one in my room.

Kelly gave me a brief kiss on the lips and said, "I'm sure you have a lot of people to inform about your miracle. I'll see you in the morning."

As she was leaving, I noticed a gold ring on the third finger of her left hand and wondered why a virgin would wear a wedding band.

I desperately wanted to call Kathryn, but her number was in my cell phone, which had been utterly destroyed in my accident. I called

Tommy, whose numbers I knew by heart, to help me hear her soft voice again.

His reaction was as expected. "When are you going to stay off of those fucking bikes?" he fulminated. "Next time you'll break your fucking neck."

I had to laugh. Here was a man, who had prowled the jungles of Columbia with a team of counterinsurgents, worrying about me riding a motorcycle. But he agreed to get all the telephone numbers for Kathryn Bailey in a few minutes.

My next call was to Lydia. She had been worried when, uncharacteristically, I hadn't communicated with her for over a week. When I told her about my accident, she uttered a tortured cry. I didn't repeat the whole chronicle of my cosmic trip to her. I wanted to do that in person.

When her emotions were back in check, Lydia told me that Bernie Cornfield from Malibu had called the day before yesterday. He loved the picture of the Chagall drawing that I had offered him a few weeks back. He wanted the "real McCoy" shipped to the Malibu Jewish Center & Synagogue as soon as possible because he needed it as a tax deduction. I told Lydia to arrange a wire transfer and then to express ship the drawing to the synagogue.

After we completed our business, Lydia said something that was becoming a pattern with the women in my life, "Brett, I feel a strong need to nurture you and make sure that nobody can harm you. I know that's a weird emotion to feel, but it is as strong in me as the Tower of London." Then she returned to her professional demeanor. "I'll take care of everything and have a new set of credit cards and cell phone sent out to you as fast as possible. How long do you think you'll be incapacitated in that funny sounding town in Texas?"

I replied, "Lydia, I'm in Texarkana, Arkansas, not Texas, and I would walk out of here today if I could."

Then I mentioned that I might be able to hole up for a day or two at Kelly Porter's house. That led to a rather lengthy discussion, but finally Lydia agreed that it would be OK for me to stay with "that crazy driving hag."

I had no sooner hung up than Tommy called back with Kathryn's numbers, some of which were completely new to me. Mercifully, he didn't regale me with more exasperated advice this time.

After we hung up, I was just about to call Kathryn when Madelyn came into the room carrying a bowl of ice cream. As she handed me the dish she dropped the spoon on the floor. When she bent down to retrieve it, her white nurse's uniform hiked up, exposing a tattoo of a snake wrapped around her thigh. I couldn't see the serpent's head, which was hidden farther up under the nylon dress. When Madelyn left to fetch me a new spoon, I realized that I had seen that snake before while sipping hot chocolate in a café in New Boston, Texas. It seemed like a lifetime ago and left me feeling somewhat disoriented and out of place, as if I were the unwilling hub of a cosmic carousel.

I dialed Kathryn's number and heard her melodic "Hello." But when I told her who was calling, she hung up without saying a word.

I waited 10 minutes and called back, reaching her voice mail. I left a brief account of my motorcycle accident and the hospital phone number, hoping she would return my call.

When Madelyn returned I asked her to find me a phone number of a motorcycle store in Plano, Texas where I could get a new bike. I was greatly torn about purchasing another motorcycle because the accident had occurred so quickly and I still couldn't quite believe that it had really happened! Thinking about it gave me shivers. But I had always been told that if you have a bad motorcycle accident, you have to get right back on a bike or you would never want to ride again, and I wasn't prepared to give up that freedom. Besides, I was convinced that everything was happening according to a grand plan.

There was an Italian motorcycle that I had had my eye on for over a year now, a Ducati Multistrada 1100 S—a combination of sport, street and dirt road bike with a lot of cachet, and great looking to boot. I was leaning towards the Ducati because its sporty performance wouldn't require me to bend over the tank while riding and it had a reputation for reliability. But I desired it most of all for its top-of-the-line cornering and first-rate acceleration. I just hoped it would have the *Valkyrie's* wings.

Now all I needed to find out was which saddlebag had survived the smash up. I hoped it was the one with my cameras, not my clothes.

I called the nurses station and five minutes later Madelyn appeared with a beat-up looking leather bag. She also handed me a Post-it with the phone number for *European Cycle Sports* in Plano, Texas.

My prayers were answered when I opened the tattered bag and found most of my camera equipment intact! Madelyn agreed to over-night it all to Lydia. Next I called my assistant to give her a heads-up and asked her to take the film to *Chrome Imaging* in Georgetown and have it processed. I wanted to know as soon as possible if "Shave-Ice" was everything I thought it was going to be.

I felt so good about my camera gear surviving that it gave me the confidence to call the Ducati dealer. I told him what I wanted and gave him Lydia's number to call and work out the financial arrangements in advance.

He laughed and said, "This is the easiest sale I have ever made."

I had to laugh myself as I replied, "For me, this is the hardest buy I have ever contemplated, because an accident has made me a bit gun shy." He lost his jolliness, when I added, "I'm calling you from a hos-pital bed."

Madelyn brought me two pills in a paper cup and watched me swallow them. Then she tucked me in, leaned over and kissed me goodnight. As she left, I mused that it was my lucky day. It felt so good to know that these special women had been assigned to watch over me. Now, if I could just figure out what I was supposed to do with them. I knew one thing for sure: Kathryn Bailey was as real as a Tennessee sunset and would be in my future whether she liked it or not!

I was just starting to fall asleep when the phone rang. I wondered why Kathryn had waited so long to return my call, but I was glad she did. I answered with what I felt was my best sounding, heart-felt "Hello."

But it wasn't her. Instead I heard, "Hello, Brett, this is Kelly Porter. I just wanted to let you know that I'd like you to stay with me for a few days. That way I can watch over you and take care of your needs."

Overwhelmed by her generosity, I replied, "I am very happy to accept your kind offer. Would you mind picking up some clothes for me, so I can leave the hospital?"

"Not at all."

We continued to chat. Before we broke off our conversation, I asked, "Why is someone as special as you not married?"

She laughed and said in a soft, sexy voice, "You already know the answer to that question. Goodnight, Brett."

My sleep was filled with images of a world being infused by a new consciousness based on love and fearlessness. In one sequence the whole world morphed into a subway platform, conveying the sense that this life was only a way station from which to catch the train of luminosity to the next existence.

My dreams made it clear that a new king would rule the world, not from a base of temporal power or sovereign countries, but from a global stage that had no use for tired old dogma and what it represented. His symbolic talisman would be an open circle of purple light.

Day 32

I awoke to the sound of the telephone ringing. I groped for the receiver and managed to find it by the fourth ring. I grunted a groggy "Hello" into the mouthpiece.

The voice at the other end came back with a familiar and welcome drawl, "Brett Tempest, this is Kathryn Bailey. You old poop, what have you gone and done to yourself?"

I cleared my throat and explained, "Kathryn, darling, I didn't even know that I was in an accident, or in a coma for that matter, until a couple of days ago."

She laughed and said, "That's no excuse for not calling me. You know, I was worried sick about you. I guess, I'm just going to have to come out there and take you home with me. You are going to need a lot of TLC to get you better."

"Thank you, Kathryn, but I feel better already and I'm about to leave this hospital, so you stay put and I will come to you for a little visit. What do you think of that?"

"Brett, how will you get here?"

Hesitantly, I told her, "I am buying a new motorcycle and would like to ride it to your house. That will be the perfect way for me to get back my road confidence. If it is snowing up your way, I will take the southernmost route back to North Carolina. When I get there, I will try to talk you into coming to meet me there or up in D.C."

"Well, honey, right now the weather is beautiful here and we are enjoying a kind of Indian summer, so if you left today or tomorrow,

I would say come on by. Are you sure you want another motorcycle? They really scare me now."

"Yes, Kathryn, it's my escape from the reality of this world. But I have to do a 500-mile break-in period on the new Ducati, which will keep me in Texas for another day or two."

She snickered and asked, "What in the hell is a Ducati? It sounds like an Italian pastry." Then she added in a slower, more provocative tone, "I suppose it's something you wrap your legs around and ride, isn't it?"

"Yes, it's an Italian motorcycle."

Bored with motorcycles Kathryn switched to a topic more to her liking. "Now tell me everything that happened to you and what will I have to fix when we get together. Speaking of which, how long do you want us to stay with each other?"

I had an inspiration. "We should stay with each other as long as it takes to keep you happy." I could see her smiling at that from 1000 miles away and continued, "When we get together, I have a truly wondrous story to tell you. It's about my encounter with the miraculous, and you're part of it—you are deeply involved with a grand, cosmic plan."

She took it better than I had expected. "Why, honey, I want to hear all about it. I guess we have a lot to share. I've had a pretty fantastic dream myself."

I could tell neither of us was ready to talk about our mystical experiences on the phone. So we made some small talk, exchanged vows of endearment, and whispered emotional good-byes. After I hung up, I lay there for a while wondering what had happened to her.

An hour after lunch, Kelly Porter showed up toting two large shopping bags from Dillard's department store.

Smiling from ear to ear, she said, "This is the first time I've had carte blanche to dress a man, and it made me feel kind of powerful!"

"As long as you didn't buy me pink pants, it'll probably be all right."

She laughed with delight and emptied the bags, spilling shirts and pants across my legs. Then she held them up one by one for me to see.

As far as I could tell, Kelly was right on the money with my taste and size. The first items she showed me were two extra-large tee shirts, one black and one light blue. Then she modeled a pale yellow and blue, long sleeved Ralph Lauren shirt. It was woven in cotton and had a tan twill collar. The rest of the stash consisted of a pair of Ralph Lauren classic jeans, a dark blue Cole Haan belt, and a Daniel Cremieux leather jacket. She had matched the soft tan leather with a wallet of the same color. There were three sets of undergarments and three pairs of socks in black, blue and gray. The final item in her shopping extravaganza was a pair of imported, dark burgundy leather shoes by Bacco Bucci.

When Kelly noticed that I was fascinated by the cross strapping device, she said, "Brett, I didn't want you to have to mess having to tie your shoes. Besides, these are just about the coolest shoes I have ever seen."

I was thrilled with everything she had bought for me. My eyes kept wandering back to my new apparel and I kept saying to myself that, had it been up to me, I would surely have bought the same garments and shoes. I hoped that our shared taste in clothes would carry over to other things, like food and drink.

When I asked her how much she had spent, she said, "Don't worry about it."

I kept pestering her and she finally pleaded, "I owe you this, Brett."

I insisted, "I am fully insured, Kelly. Besides, what will people think if I have a woman I had just met buy me a ton of clothes and pay for it?"

That got her laughing. She said, "OK," and handed me the bill for $1,185. Then she added, "But while you're staying with me, all the dinners are on me."

In answer I pulled her to me for a nice hug, which felt very good.

When I mentioned that she would have to wait a day or two before I could reimburse her, she smiled and said, "None of that matters to me, but I would like another hug."

I opened my arms wide and welcomed her into my world. She snuggled contentedly and we lay on the bed together for a while, tight and secure.

At some point I told her, "I figure I will be leaving the hospital tomorrow."

Untangling herself, she smiled and said, "I'll come by in the morning and take you and your new clothes home."

As she turned to leave I could not restrain myself and gave Kelly a little love tap on her backside. She grinned and said, "I knew you were a naughty boy the first time I laid eyes on you," and sashayed from the room.

I called the nurses station and asked to speak with Madelyn. She was not scheduled to work until nine that evening, but my attending physician was on his way to see me.

Dr. Robert Brawley, a rather handsome man in his early 50s, wanted to do one more scan to reassure himself that I was good to go. He said, "The orderlies will pick you up in a few minutes. In the meantime, I'll send in a nurse to help you dig out from under the pile of clothes that must be weighing you down."

I replied, "I'm getting used to it. Yesterday, I was pinned under a mountain of flowers."

He laughed and said, "Somebody sure loves you."

The scan took no more than a half hour and when I got back to my room, a FedEx envelope and box was waiting for me.

The envelope contained a checkbook and cashier checks in the amount of $3,000, a copy of my insurance information, a driver's permit, and a note from Lydia telling me that my credit cards would be delivered by 10 the next morning. Also included was a rather nice picture of her, which I had taken three months earlier. She'd written at the bottom, "Brett, in case you get lonely on the road, just know that I will be thinking about you always. Love Lydia."

I took a long look at the photograph. I had never thought of Lydia in more than a professional way before. She always dressed impeccably, as if she had just walked out of a Bond Street ladies' tailor shop. Now, I saw her in a different light. Lydia really was quite beautiful with sharply chiseled features and stylish blonde hair. The realization of how much I liked her washed over me as I continued to gaze at her picture. Suddenly, I felt a jolt of recognition. Lydia very much resembled Kelly Michelle Tempest from the other dimension I had experienced. I didn't know what to make of that, but I silently thanked her for sending me her photograph.

I turned my attention to the other box, which contained a Blackberry 9530. It was a new model for me and would provide me with a road computer and phone. But it also meant a lot of time reading the manual. Sighing, I started on page one and didn't stop until the English section finished and the Spanish version started, but even with all that information, I didn't have a clue how to work this computer/phone.

Fortunately, Madelyn came into the room with some great news. "Dr. Brawley says that you have a clean bill of health and that you can go home tomorrow. What do you think about that?"

"I was hoping that's the case. As nice as everybody is here at Christus St. Michael, I need to hit the road and find some answers."

Madelyn furrowed her brow. "What kind of answers are you looking for?"

"Well, for starters," I asked with a grin, "what do you feed that black, red and yellow, thigh snake of yours?"

She was taken aback, but only for an instant. Then she retorted with a great answer. "Well, Brett, if you must know, he lives on an endless supply of French pea soup." Winking at me she continued, "After a good feeding he loves to be petted on his head. Care to give him a stroke?"

"Madelyn, the shape I'm in, I am afraid if I did that, it might give me a stroke."

She looked mildly disappointed "Would you like a nice dish of ice cream instead?

"Only if you drop the spoon again, so that I can have a little peek at that wonderful, pea soup-loving pit viper of yours."

She left shaking her head and soon returned with a cup of vanilla and chocolate ice cream. As she handed it to me she said, "I'll be back a little later to clean you up."

The ice cream was almost as good as homemade fruit pie, and I relished every bite and even licked the bowl. I tried to watch TV, but there was nothing on that interested me. Turning off the set I thought I would try to get some sleep, but I felt too fidgety in anticipation of leaving in the morning. As I scooted over on my side, Madelyn came into the room, pulling the door shut behind her. She proceeded to wash me and did not miss an inch of my body. And then she was gone.

I had a peaceful sleep but I kept seeing an old nun in my dreams, watching over me. Once I opened my eyes and thought I saw the back of her habit as she was leaving the room. I went back to sleep and thought no more about it.

Day 33

I awoke feeling refreshed and eager to continue on the journey of discovering my destiny.

Dr. Brawley came into the room and listened to my heart and lungs, shone his pin light into my eyes and said, "Mr. Tempest, I do not believe that a miracle happened to you, as the nuns and nurses are claiming. All I know is that by any standard, you should be six feet in the ground. Since your accident happened so close to us, I went and looked at the remains of your motorcycle and that old chair before they were carted away, and there was pretty much nothing left of either of them.

He shook his head and continued, "On the medical front, your coma must have been a shielding mechanism by which you protected yourself from the trauma of what happened. The fact that you do not remember the accident is not unusual—another defensive measure your body has employed to cushion the mental shock. I can't be 100 percent certain of the validity of my explanation, but it is as good as any. What I don't understand at all is how your body repaired itself so completely. You should, by all accounts, be one broken man. Maybe the nurses and nuns are right that you are a walking miracle and we are all witnesses through you of God's greatness. I am happy to say that you may go home today. There is nothing more I can do for you here."

He shook my hand and left the room before I could utter a word of thanks or ask any questions. I already knew the reason why I was alive and I imagined Dr. Brawley was himself starting to walk beyond the confines of medical science because of what he had witnessed with me.

It felt great to be dressed in civilian clothes again after the flimsy hospital gown. Checking myself out in the mirror I was happy to see that everything Kelly had chosen for me fit to a tee and complemented the new me.

I had just finished brushing my hair when Kelly walked into the room. She took one look at me and said, "Brett, you sure are one sexy dude. I think I did good picking out your clothes. What do you think?"

"Kelly Porter, I could not have done better myself. I just might have to hire you as my fashion coordinator."

As we were about to leave the room, the second FedEx package arrived with my new credit cards. I sat on the bed and was transferring them to my new wallet when I noticed a small white card lying on my nightstand. I felt a little chill crawling up my spine when I read the name "Madelyn Karri" and a local phone number on it, along with a hand written notation: *Call me.*

Kelly asked, "What's wrong?"

I replied, "Nothing really, just a weird coincidence," and slipped the card into the wallet.

Checking out of Christus Saint Michael Hospital turned out to be a breeze because Lydia had taken care of everything over the phone. All I had to do was sign my name on a few forms.

As I was finishing up, an older woman in a nun's habit appeared. Her face was etched with a myriad of wrinkles, but her brown eyes were sharp and clear. She took hold of my hand, and said, "I'm Sister Mary Alice. I have something for you."

Then she slipped two pieces of paper into my hand—a small yellow Post-it with a phone number and a folded, letter-sized sheet of paper.

"Read the letter when you have a moment of peace," she explained. "You can call me at that number when you need to."

When she made the sign of the cross with her right hand, I noticed that she wore a metallic looking ring in the shape of a circle on her index finger. It was odd. I had never encountered either the metal or the circular shape before, yet both seemed vaguely familiar. The old nun turned abruptly and left me standing in the hotel lobby in a bit of a daze, wondering where I had seen her before.

Parked at the curb outside, Kelly's car turned out to be a true classic. It was a 1967 Cadillac El Dorado, highlighted in two shades of blue paint and in mint condition. I did not recall her driving it on the day of my accident.

When Kelly saw me admiring the car, she said, "This was my aunt's pride and joy, and now it is mine."

"What were you driving the day fate brought us together?"

"It was a rental car, a Chevy Malibu, I believe."

The Cadillac was as nice inside as on the outside and I stretched out my 6' 1" frame in the front seat. Kelly drove expertly to a pleasant suburban neighborhood on the Arkansas side of town with tall trees and ample shrubbery. She pulled into a paver driveway that led up to a well-kept 1980s Rambler home.

As we entered I noted with pleasure that the interior was a prime example of classic 1950s and early 60s décor. I counted no less than six chairs designed by Charles and Ray Eames. All of the furnishings were genuine first editions with not a single knock-off among them. The art on the walls was also vintage 50s—Turners and Bernards displayed in period frames. Some even featured the then popular, tiny mosaic mirror pieces embedded into the off-white, wooden frames. Everything was in mint condition.

I felt like I had walked into a time warp and asked Kelly, "What was your aunt's story? She clearly had immaculate taste."

"Aunt June was one of the first female geologists with the Standard Oil Company. She invested her money well until her death and left me comfortably off for the rest of my life."

"Why did she choose to live in Texarkana? With her money she could have moved to a more exotic place."

Kelly laughed and said, "She was in love with a man she met at work who was born and raised in this town. He built this house for her. When he died seven years ago, she could not bear to leave his memorial."

"So, am I talking to the world's newest oil baroness?"

"No, Brett, just a defrocked nun who has a little bit of money with which to start her new life."

I was taken aback. "What do you mean by defrocked nun? I thought you worked with runaways and unwed mothers."

"That is precisely what I did in the order, but I felt that I needed to find out more about the spiritual mysteries than we were allowed to study, so the sisterhood and I had a parting of the ways."

Kelly found some corn chips in a kitchen cupboard and a container of what looked like salsa in the refrigerator. She put them in a large bowl and a small dish and took them to the living room. Placing them on a low table, she said, "I hope you like salsa. I made it myself."

We sat in two chairs close to each other. I took a chip and sampled the salsa. It was spicy but not too hot. Nodding appreciatively, I asked, "How long were you a nun?"

"About three and a half years, but I was a novitiate for a year and a half before taking my final vows."

Helping myself to more chips, I said, "That explains why you're a virgin and wearing a wedding ring! You must have been the prettiest nun in that convent. I am glad you left that vocation so we could meet. Where will you go from here? Or will you stay in this house for a while longer?"

"I can't answer that right now. My mind has been centered on you ever since the accident. It's funny, Brett, but you seem to have been assigned to me by a much higher power and, in fact, I had quite a dream about us last night."

I said excitedly, "Kelly, I'm all ears. Please tell me what it was about."

She looked at me uncertainly and said, "I really don't know where to start, but I can tell you that it was not the first time I had this dream. I saw you swirling around the heavens in a translucent body that was filled with light. Near your loins appeared a circle of the most intense purple light, and within that circle were three women. Suddenly I saw myself materialize from among them and join with your spirit. I felt that we were making love and were in the throes of creating a new spirit. Then, at the point of what I thought of as conception, we were surrounded by hundreds of colored lights which elevated us past the stars and into a place of brilliant Light."

Her face had a radiance of its own when she continued, "I also think that the paper Sister Mary Alice handed you has something to do with my dream vision. Would you mind if we took a look at the letter?"

"No of course not."

I extracted the piece of paper from my back pocket and read out loud what the old nun had written:

Dear Mr. Tempest,

I am writing this missive after a revelation I had about you. I don't know if you were aware that we found you wrapped around a mile marker post? That marker was number 223 and after prying your hands loose from it, we brought you to the emergency room. I am not sure if you realize that the accident happened right in front of Christus Saint Michael Hospital, so we could get you medical help right away. While you were in a coma I was told by an unseen voice to open my bible to Luke 2:23 and then to watch over you during your stay with us. Here is what I read and interpreted from that reading: "As it is written in the Law of the Lord, 'Every firstborn male that opens the womb shall be called holy to the Lord.

This passage is about the birth of Christ, and I feel that you are anointed by God to exercise stewardship over the Second Coming. And then the Two shall become One! May God watch over you and give you the grace to persevere.

In Jesus' name, I am sincerely yours.

Sister Mary Alice.

Kelly came over to where I was sitting, put her hand gently on my cheek and in a voice choking with emotion said, "I saw you more than five years ago in a dream and you were with me again last night in heavenly propagation. Brett Tempest, I offer you my body and soul for the salvation of mankind."

I laughed nervously at her earnest offer and said, "Boy, if I had a dollar for every time I heard that line before."

She ignored my feeble attempt at humor and continued, "I know in my mind and spirit that you are meant to procreate with me, and it is time for us to produce this child of heaven."

Her purity was evident in her eyes and in the softness of her touch. Even the tone of her voice conveyed wholesomeness.

I was in a quandary. My love was with Kathryn Bailey, although we would have no children together unless it was by immaculate conception. But here in front of me stood a lovely woman beseeching me to father a child with her. Should I try to get her pregnant because of her dream and what the old nun had written in her letter? How responsible would that be? Was this Kelly Porter part of my mission? And what about the other Kelly Porter and the experience I had with her in the grotto? Did she exist somewhere else, on another cosmic plane?

I wondered what Kathryn would have to say about this latest turn of events. Just before I left the Light I was told that I would know what course to take, but right now I was as confused as I had ever been.

Suddenly I felt dead tired and asked Kelly, "Would it be all right if I took a hot bath?"

She nodded and said, "That is a good idea." Then she laughed and added, "You'll get a real kick out of Auntie June's tub."

I had one more favor to ask. "Do you have any bourbon in the house?"

Kelly laughed again and said, "That is the only liquor that June ever drank. Go ahead and get your bath running. I'll bring you a nice glass of whiskey. I take it you drink it like my aunt—on the rocks?"

I nodded and she pointed the way. The bathroom off the master bedroom looked fit for an aquatic Roman orgy. The huge tub, lined with lavender and pale yellow tiles, was a bathing pool sunken into the floor and surrounded by mirrors on three sides. It was large enough to accommodate six people. I counted at least 50 candles of various heights and thickness all over the room. A stack of fluffy, lavender towels sat next to a selection of bottles. I figured they contained bath oils and crystals. Aunt June certainly knew how to live in style.

Kelly entered carrying a large tumbler of bourbon and wearing a plush lavender robe. Embroidered on her left breast pocket was a four-inch-tall oil well, framed on the sides with the initials J and P.

I asked, "Do the letters stand for June Porter?"

"No, June and Paul, my aunt's boyfriend," she explained, handing me the glass of bourbon. "Would you like some company for a little while?"

Before I could answer, she opened her robe and exposed her body. It took my breath away. Her breasts were the size of small, firm cantaloupes with ruby red, erect nipples. Her delicate skin was white as a Chinese porcelain doll and radiated sensuality. There were no tan lines anywhere. Her pubic hair was like a mound of light brown, silken thread. I was mesmerized.

Kelly watched me looking at her and asked, "Well, Brett, when can I look at you? I have a sensation running through me that tells me that you are everything that I have ever dreamt of."

I slipped out of my clothes and placed them carefully on a chaise lounge that was also wrapped in lavender and yellow. Kelly walked over to me, placed her arms around my neck and kissed me so deeply that I almost lost my balance. When her tongue had explored my mouth to her satisfaction, she slowly broke the kiss. She bent down and adjusted the water spewing from two large spouts and added scented oils from the bottles by the towels. Then she lit the host of candles making the bath look like an aquatic heaven.

Holding on to my bourbon carefully, I let my body slip into the hot water. I felt I was entering an immense womb. Surely, no Roman emperor experienced greater extravagance. The residue taste of Kelly Porter in my mouth heightened my sense of being in another time and place.

I watched as in a trance as this elegant creature completely immersed her sleek body in the oil soft water. When she emerged, her hair clung tight to her face, forming a frame that further enhanced her beauty.

She glided over to me, took my bourbon, placed it on the tile floor next to the pool and then molded her body to mine. As our genitals meshed into each other, her hardened nipples thrust against my chest. I pulled her to me and kissed her as deeply as she had kissed me moments before.

Exploring her mouth with my tongue and her wet and oily breasts with my hands, I knew that I was ready to take this virgin and give her the gift of life she craved. But after we broke from our second kiss, I asked. "Are you sure this is what you were put on this Earth for?"

She answered with another kiss that told me everything I already knew and said, "Brett, I can't stop my desire for you. It's like a huge magnet that keeps pulling me to you. I want our souls to dance in the Light as badly as I want you to impale me with your passion. I know whom I will be carrying in my womb and what an honor it is. Our destiny implores me to accomplish this act of love with you, my most holy one."

We frolicked in the warm scented water for the better part of an hour, slowly cleansing each other in preparation for our lovemaking.

At some point Kelly told me, "I have no fear of losing my virginity. I have kept it intact for just over three decades waiting for this moment."

I replied, "I finally feel comfortable giving you my life seed." Smiling, I added, "Engaging in this act together almost feels like a 'command performance.'"

She nodded in agreement and covered my mouth with yet another soul rousing kiss.

As large as the Roman bathing pool was, the bed matched it in opulence and size. It had four steel posts, one at each corner, about five feet tall. The odd thing was that the tops of the steel spikes had rings attached to them. While I was trying to figure out the purpose of those metal rods, Kelly produced a purple satin covered box, tied with a black silk ribbon. She slowly undid the knot and lifted the cover. Inside was a stack of photographs.

The first was a portrait of her Aunt June, who had an uncanny resemblance to Kelly, both in body shape and facial structure. The rest showed June naked, and tied up in various ways. The common denominator was the large bed with the four steel posts, June helplessly restrained, and a man looming over her in a head-to-toe rubber body suit—I figured it was Paul. The outfit had holes for his eyes, mouth and erect member.

I found these photos surprisingly stimulating, as did Kelly. I could tell by the goose bumps that covered her naked body.

She said, "I found this box of photographs under the bed and have been browsing through them for a few days now." She handed me one of the pictures with June trussed, lying naked on her back. "I want our first time together to be like this."

Producing four chains attached to metal cuffs, she said, "I want you to tie me to the bed."

I was bewildered. This was strange behavior for a nun who had only recently left the convent. I didn't think this sort of stuff went on behind cloistered walls and said, "I don't feel comfortable restraining you like that."

Kelly beseeched me, "Don't worry. We will enjoy it and it will be like a spiritual experience for me."

I reluctantly agreed, locked the cuffs on her wrists and ankles, and chained her arms and legs to the four metal spikes. She had me tighten the restraints until her arms were completely stretched out and her vagina spread wide open, forming a heart-shaped tunnel into her womb.

Just before I entered her I had a vision of the other Kelly with the snake-haired head of Medusa sitting next to her. She also was totally restrained and an angel masturbated fire out of me onto her exposed body. I caught my breath and decided not to ejaculate inside Kelly at this time. Something was not quite right.

But I broke through her hymen and plunged all the way into her. Kelly screamed with delight with each long thrust. When I felt that I was nearing climax, I started to pull back, but as I withdrew, there was a tugging on my penis. I knew it could not be Kelly's doing, as she was completely restrained.

I was dismayed. An invisible force pumped my penis and squeezed it so intensely that it felt like I was on fire. I was a full five inches out of Kelly's vagina when an enormous stream of semen left me and traveled directly into her wide-open cervix. I watched as the thick liquid was sucked into her and completely disappeared, leaving only small drops of virginal blood on her throbbing vulva.

The moment the sperm entered her, Kelly started to climax with a series of convulsions and moans. I knew they were echoes from eons ago in another reality. Her contorted visage melted into a vision of spinning faces, whirling as if on giant roulette wheel. When it finally stopped it came to rest on a face I knew very well, and it chilled me to the bone: Kathryn Bailey!

By the time my mind calmed enough and I drew myself up on my knees, Kelly smiled up at me speechless. At that instant, I knew why the spinning wheel of faces stopped on my mistress of light: We were all one and the same in the Circle of Light.

I released Kelly's restraints, ankles first. As soon as her arms were free, she used them to pull me on top of her. Despite everything that just happened I felt myself become rock hard again with desire.

Pushing her mouth away from mine, she rolled me onto my back. Then she guided my penis into her mouth and loved me with her lips and tongue until I climaxed deep into her throat.

Afterwards we slept, satiated, our bodies glued to each other, until shafts of morning light pierced our dreams and coaxed us awake into a new day.

Day 34

When I looked at Kelly in the morning sunlight pouring through the windows, I was stunned. Before she had looked like a young girl, despite her age, and while she didn't seem older, she was different somehow. It was as if she had gone to a plastic surgeon and he had given her a new look. Figuring that she would be back to normal after breakfast, I asked, "Would you mind if I make some coffee in the kitchen?"

She said, "There is some already made. I'll go and fetch us a couple of cups."

The coffee was dark and rich, just the way I liked it, and it quickly brought me to full awareness. I stole a glance at Kelly. The youthful, innocent glitter of her eyes had been replaced by self-awareness. Her demeanor had matured, too. She now exuded confidence. She still was every bit as sexy and enticing, but now she seemed more mellow, as a soon-to-be mother should be.

Noticing me inspect her from head to toe, Kelly smiled and said, "I am sure I have conceived. I had been ovulating. Anyway, I can feel that I am with child."

Later, while we were still lounging in June's mammoth bed, I asked, "Would you mind giving me a lift to Plano to the Ducati dealer?"

"As long as you promise that you will come right back to me. I will be more than happy to drive you there, but I won't set foot in that place."

"I'll have to take the motorcycle on a five-hundred-mile mini trip to break it in. After that, the dealer will change out the partially synthetic oil with fresh, all synthetic oil, and I'll be ready to go."

"How long will it take to go five hundred miles?"

"In about two days I should be right back on your doorstep."

"OK. When would you like to go?"

I hopped out of bed and said, "How about right now?"

Kelly's smile was tight-lipped. She said, "Well, Brett, do you think that you might want to get dressed first?"

Three and a half hours later I was looking at a brand new, diamond black Ducati 1100S. She was a gorgeous machine and had all the accessories I would need already installed. While examining this beauty with joyful anticipation, a flash of yellow light caught my eye. A gleaming, yellow and black *Valkyrie* sat alone in the far display window. The dealer had placed it there to attract passersbys. When I walked over and placed the palm of my right hand on the saddle, I felt her vibration and instantly knew she was made for me.

The dealer was flabbergasted, but the money was about the same. So it was good-bye to a stunning Ducati and hello again to an old and trusted friend.

The dealer gave me a final out. "I was doing a friend a favor when I ordered this bike 10 days ago and, dagnabbit, he up and died on me the day before yesterday. Out of respect for the dead, I didn't put her in the window until this morning."

I didn't feel discouraged. I approached the motorcycle as if she were a familiar spear maiden from Norse mythology and I a fallen hero who'd gotten a temporary reprieve and was not quite ready yet for Valhalla. One thing was certain—we would ride together again! Twenty minutes later, the paperwork was done. I owned her and was lining up new leathers for my ride.

Then I went outside and changed my clothes in Kelly's car and moved the rest from the two shopping bags into the leather side bags mounted on my new *Valkyrie*. I was pleasantly surprised when I found an unopened bottle of Blanton's Bourbon under one of my folded shirts.

When I looked at Kelly with curiosity, she smiled and said, "Just a little something for the lonely road. This was Auntie June's all-time favorite whiskey and I wanted you to have it."

I packed the oval shaped bottle with its distinctive pewter horse-and-jockey stopper carefully in the side bag. Then I started the motorcycle, and Kelly and I both admired the patented six-cylinder whine of the engine. I let it run a few minutes to warm the oil. When I was ready to get rolling, I gave Kelly a long good-bye kiss, to the delight of the three salesmen watching us through the showroom window.

Kelly asked, "Where are you going?"

I didn't want to reveal my destination and said, "I think I'll head northwest for a couple of hundred miles, spend the night somewhere, and go back to the dealer for the new oil in the morning. I'll be at your place later that evening or the following morning at the latest."

Putting on my helmet I watched her walk calmly to the Cadillac and drive away without looking back.

I left the dealer's parking lot and rode U.S. 75 north for about 15 miles before heading west on U.S. 380 towards Throckmorton. I wanted to see if I could reconcile the two realties in which I seemed to exist and I thought Throckmorton, Texas was as good a place as any to start!

U.S. 380 offered no surprises. I had traversed it many times before and knew it as well as my own driveway. The day was perfect for riding and I was starting to settle into my new *Valkyrie*. I amused myself by constructing a metaphysical tale for my new metal maiden: In one vision I was a heroic, fallen warrior gliding over the battlefield with a yellow and black winged goddess who had rescued me to confer on me my true status as a king. In the second I was that newly resurrected king, riding to victory with my sword held high on a sleek black and yellow stallion.

By 4:30 in the afternoon I reached the outskirts of Throckmorton and pulled into *Allsup's Convenience Store* to fuel up. It seemed strangely familiar, yet also completely new.

I rode aimlessly around town hoping to spot the laundromat or the blond Kelly of my other reality, but I had no luck with either quest. After an hour of cruising, I checked into the *Double J Lodge* across the street from the *Allsup's*.

When I asked the woman behind the front desk for a place to eat, she said, "Folks around here either go to *Cook's Restaurant* or, if you like Tex-Mex, then it's *Escalon*."

The Mexican place had a familiar ring to it, so I asked, "Which one can I walk to from here?"

"*Escalon* is just one block north of here, across the 380."

I exchanged my riding suit and boots for my Ralph Lauren duds and headed for a little refried Tex-Mex. Walking into *Escalon* was like entering a small, empty bingo hall with long tables covered with plastic tablecloths. Fortunately, the food made up for the décor. It was good and spicy, just the way I liked it. I was hungry and could have wolfed down the meal in 20 minutes, but I took my time, hoping for a sign, an anchor of some kind to my recent past, but to no avail.

Walking back towards the motel, I stopped at *Allsup's* and bought a bag of gummy bears and some ice for the whiskey. I figured I would call Kathryn tonight and wanted something sweet while we talked.

As I was leaving the convenience store, a husky voice behind me whispered, "Hey mister, you want to buy some pussy?"

Hearing the familiar words of enticement, I felt a jolt. I was afraid to turn around for fear of being disappointed. When I did, I saw a beat-up looking woman in her late 40s. She grinned at me with a set of tobacco stained teeth and raised her eyebrows suggestively.

I said, "I don't think so."

Her smile widened and she said, "Don't turn this down. You will never find something this sweet in all your life."

She held out a tattered photograph of a young blond girl who had pulled up her sweater to expose rather large, and what looked like surgically enhanced tits.

The picture had been taken in one of those cheap supermarket photo booths, but the girl looked like she could be Kelly Michelle. My throat was tight when I asked, "How much would a night with this girl cost me?"

"A hundred bucks will buy you a whole night with my little angel."

"I don't have that much cash on me. Will you take fifty?"

I could see her calculate quickly before she said, "Yes. Are you staying in town?"

I replied, "Across the street at the *Double J*," and pulled out my key to check the room number.

She licked her sallow lips and said, "I'll have that money now."

"I'll pay you when she comes to my room."

She hesitated, then nodded. I headed across the street figuring that, if this was just a strange coincidence, I'd only be out 50 bucks. I had no intention of sleeping with the young whore, but seeing her might settle matters for me and put an end to this bizarre chapter of my life.

Back in my room, I cracked the seal of the bottle of Blanton's and pulled out the metal stopper. The cork sliding out from the glass neck of the bottle made a soft "pop." I threw a few ice cubes into a glass, poured two fingers worth of bourbon over them and took a long sip. The Kentucky mash was by far the best I had ever had.

Before I could enjoy my third sip there was a harsh knock on my door. When I opened it, the ratty looking woman stood there and next to her, a young girl. She was sucking on a straw that protruded from a large plastic cup with the words "Dr. Pepper" printed on it.

The girl was pretty enough, but she didn't look anything like the Kelly of my memories. She was 16 or 17 and two inches taller. Her tired face had a few blemishes. Kelly's skin had been flawless.

I handed the old bag her 50 bucks and invited the young hooker into my room. By the time I had shut the door and turned around, she was halfway out of her clothes already. I held up my hands and shook my head.

She gave me a funny look and said, "Nobody has ever stopped me from getting naked before."

I poured myself half a glass of straight bourbon, sat down on the bed, and said, "I want to tell you a story," and launched into the saga of all that had happened to me.

When I got to the part where I met Kathryn in the antique mall, she asked, "Could you pour a shot of that stuff into my Dr. Pepper?"

As I gave her a little blast of the Blanton's, I found it amusing that it was probably the first time this great whiskey had been mixed with Dr. Pepper. The girl stirred the bourbon around the cup with her straw while I continued my tale. When I got to the part about Kelly in Throckmorton, she pulled her chair a little closer and became more attentive. Her eyes grew wide in wonder as I described my mystical encounters.

By the time I finished my story she was rapt with attention and asked, "Do you think that I am that same Kelly person?"

I said, "I don't know. But I find it very intriguing that there are so many similarities between the supernatural and natural versions. I want to discover the truth!"

Out of the blue, the girl asked, "What's your name?"

"Brett Tempest."

She started to laugh in a strange way, like a person who knows she's in trouble.

"What's so funny?" I asked, a bit vexed.

"Did you say your last name is Tempest?"

"Yes, that is my name. Why? Do you think that is an odd name?"

"No mister, it's only funny because my name is Tempest Storm. My mother thought it was cute to name me after an old stripper that my granddaddy used to fuck." She continued, "The really weird part is, like your Kelly, I'm also used by that old bitch and her boyfriend to get them money for drugs."

"Was that drugged-out pimp your mother?" I asked?

"No, my mother died of a drug overdose when I was three and that woman is my Aunt Ray Ann. She's raised me for most of my life."

"How old are you?"

"I'll be seventeen on December 17." She wrinkled her nose and continued, "I want to get the hell out of this town and try to start a new life, but I have no idea how to do that shit without a lot of money."

I took a deep breath and said, "Sit quietly for a while. I have to make an important phone call."

She asked, "Could I take a bath while you make your call?"

I nodded yes and watched her slink to the bathroom. When she had closed the door, I pulled out my phone and called the one person I felt could help me make sense of this and give me honest advice about what I should do—Sister Mary Alice from the hospital.

Luckily it was still early in the evening and she picked up right away. I told her about all the strange happenings in my life. She made me repeat the grotto story three times before she let me continue and stopped me again when I got to my journey into the Light. Once again she made me repeat the particulars.

I told her what had happened the other night with Kelly Porter, how I had ejaculated into her against my will and seen Kathryn's image. Then I shared my present predicament—that I was now in Throck-morton with a young hooker, hoping to find out more—and ended by saying, "But I really feel lost right now."

Sister Mary Alice responded in a calm, clear voice, "Everything in the universe has an action and a reaction. Trust that you are part of a greater plan. As for the sex with Kelly, don't feel guilty. Everything is as it should be. Just take special care of her." She paused for a moment and added, "If you can't do that, I will take care of her in a convent."

I said, "That won't be necessary. I believe that Kathryn Bailey is assigned that task."

"That makes good sense."

"I guess so."

She heard the doubt and trepidation in my voice and tried to reassure me, "Do not worry. Kelly is, indeed, carrying the Child of Light. Everything has happened and is happening according to God's plan."

After we hung up, I fixed another drink and mulled over what she told me and waited for Tempest to emerge from her bath.

When another 20 minutes passed, I knocked on the bathroom door. There was no answer, so I went inside. Tempest lay in the tub with her eyes rolled halfway up into her head. She was starting to turn purple.

Then I saw the hypodermic needle lazily floating in the water over her stomach.

I immediately turned on the cold shower water, ran into the other room, and grabbed the bag of ice. I rubbed it over her chest while slapping her face.

In desperation, I shouted, "Don't you dare checkout on me, you dumb-ass bitch."

Just when I thought that I had lost this battle with death, her eyes fluttered a little. I kept slapping her and let the cold shower rain down on her until she started to show signs of recognizing me. I pulled her out of the tub, wrapped every towel that I could find around her, and marched her around the room until I felt that she was going to stay awake. Then I sat her down on the bed and made my second call of the night.

Kelly answered the phone on the first ring.

Before she could say anything, I blurted out, "Do you have any experience with detoxifying people?"

"Yes, but why do you want to know? What is happening?"

"I'll tell you later."

She sounded distant as she said, "I have walked a lot of young women through the 'getting clean' process and I can tell you that it's no fun."

I started to tell her that I was trying to help someone who'd overdosed, when the girl interrupted me by waving her arms.

"I shot up with methamphetamine," she mouthed.

I repeated the information to Kelly.

Kelly said sternly, "Proceed with caution and hide your wallet and any other valuables." In a kinder voice, she added, "Come back soon. I can't wait to see you," and hung up.

After I got Kelly dressed I took her for a walk on Minter Avenue. I figured the cold air would keep her awake. I kept marching up and down the sidewalk with her for a good half hour until I was certain she had recovered. Then we stopped in *Allsup's* for a large Dr. Pepper and an even bigger bag of potato chips.

Back in my room, Tempest munched and slurped the food and drank like a hungry hyena.

I took a deep breath and asked, "Do you want to leave this town, get yourself straight, and make something of your life?"

She looked at me as if I were from Mars and said, "Brett, you are one crazy son of a bitch. I wouldn't go anywhere with you. You do-gooder, old fucks think you can save the world by buying your way into somebody's life. You think that you are so superior and believe there's no way anyone would ever turn you down. Why don't you go and fuck yourself?"

She grabbed the bag of chips and her Dr. Pepper and stalked out the door, slamming it behind her.

I called Kelly back. "Well, she just high-tailed it out of here."

Kelly replied matter-of-factly, "That's pretty typical behavior for that kind of addict."

I filled her in on how I had spent my day in Throckmorton and my disappointing lack of discoveries. She asked some questions and I replied as best I could. I was coming down from the adrenalin rush and the cold outside.

Perhaps Kelly heard it in my voice and said gently, "I have to go to sleep, Brett. You can tell me more about it when you come home."

I went to bed, too. Although I was exhausted I slept restlessly.

My dreams were filled with visions of pitch black rivers running in opposite directions from their normal flow. I had no arms and was helplessly trapped in their swirling eddies. I kept drowning, only to have the sinister waters regurgitate me. And then the cycle started over, again and again.

Day 35

I awoke with my tee shirt drenched in sweat. When I rolled out of bed and staggered to the bathroom for a hot shower, I almost stepped on the needle Tempest had left behind. I felt bad for the girl, knowing her life would be brief and end in tragedy.

I packed quickly and was on the road by 6 a.m. The morning was overcast, and I made it back to Plano in good time. The dealer performed an oil change and gave my new *Valkyrie* a quick once over and flashed me the thumbs up sign. I was good to go.

As I headed further east, there was some nasty looking weather ahead. I steadied my mind and drove on toward a squall line of dark gray clouds. As I got closer I could see the sheets of deadly rain and knew it was time to face my fears regarding what happened to me before. Steadying my hand, I cranked back the throttle in small increments before twisting the speed control to its maximum. The *Valkyrie* roared and screamed like a banshee and took off. Before long the speedometer's needle topped the 100-miles-an-hour mark. Suddenly all my trepidations left me like a startled flock of birds exploding into the sky and dissipated in the jet stream in my wake. I was free to ride!

It didn't take long before the first large raindrops started to bounce off my visor. Within seconds I was in the vortex of the storm and it was the power of nature against man-made energy as the big bike and I slammed into the winds and sheets of rain. I was in a Zen-like zone, letting my mind's eye guide the *Valkyrie* through pools of debris that had washed across the road. We raced through rain-slogged traffic, motoring past drivers who were not aware of us. The bike and I surged as one, all the way past the signpost at mile 223.

Exiting at the next interchange, I looped around to approach that death marker from the other direction. I was now speeding towards the last barrier in my quest for redemption. The signpost was still bent down at the corner, but the lifesaving chair had disappeared. Cranking back on the throttle, I whizzed past the spot of my past disaster and flew into the future. When the highway cleared a bit, I lifted my hands from the chrome steering bar and raised both arms in triumph. At that instant the *Valkyrie* and I consummated our marriage.

I was so excited about breaking through my barrier of fear that I quickly pulled off to a side road and called Kelly to crow with pride.

In a low and sultry voice she said, "There will be three of us for diner and drinks at Auntie June's 'hacienda.'" She continued with an odd statement, "I hope you enjoy rain," and, laughing, clicked off before I even got a word out.

I didn't get the cryptic humor of Kelly's remark until I made it back to her house and she introduced me to Rain Clouser, one of the young women she was helping recover from drug abuse. Rain was slight of stature. Her freckle covered face was surrounded by red hair. She could have been as old as 35, but I figured she was in her mid-20s. She had the look of a terrified rabbit caught in the mouth of a racing greyhound.

I offered to do the cooking but Kelly brushed me off, saying, "I love cooking, that's my job. Yours, Brett Tempest, is to take my car and find us some good wine to go with my Porterhouse steaks."

Leaving Kelly and Rain to their own devices, I started on a wine and baguette hunt by thumbing through Aunt June's five-year-old phone book until I found what look like a promising place.

Compared to my *Valkyrie*, Kelly's Cadillac convertible was spacious as the Space Shuttle and for the mile or so drive I felt like General Patton riding through Paris in an open tank. At the liquor store I found two bottles of a nice Columbia Valley red that would go well with the Porterhouse cuts of beef. The proprietor gave me directions to a little bakery. I found it without too much trouble, grabbed a couple of fresh French baguettes, and headed back.

Kelly and Rain were in the kitchen with a pile of chopped, mostly green stuff on the counter, chatting away like two old schoolgirl chums. They interrupted their conversation when I asked for a corkscrew. Kelly pointed to the middle drawer and kept talking to Rain about some sort of mango and grapefruit cream from *Crabtree & Evelyn* she wanted her to try. I opened the two bottles of wine to give them time to breathe and left the women to their own devices. I fetched my bottle of Blanton's from the leather saddlebag in the bedroom and settled on June's bed for some much needed phone time.

My first call was to Lydia to let her know my whereabouts and to check on the Chagall shipment. She told me that the drawing had been sent out late yesterday and my bank account had been credited with $168,000. It turned out that the client was also interested in one of my suites of Picasso etchings and Lydia had already sent out the *catalogue raisonne* that registered each of the 100 etchings.

I had a good laugh when I heard Lydia's account. I had purchased Picasso's "Voillard Suite" of rare etchings more than 20 years ago. Selling them even slightly below today's market price would fetch me over a $1 million in profit. I took another sip of whiskey. The sale should keep me in bouillon and Blanton's for quite a few years.

Then I asked, "Did you get the salvaged film back from *Chrome* yet?"

"It should be ready by the end of the week."

"If 'Shave-Ice' is what I think it is, then I am close to wrapping up the America project."

Lydia's voice took on an earnest tone. "Brett, I just want you to know how proud I am of your dedication to that project. It's impressive that, with all the money you have made over the last two decades, you stayed the course. I don't know of anyone else who would spend over 30 years chasing a dream." Changing the subject she asked, "When will you be back in Washington?"

"Soon Lydia, very soon."

I didn't realize there was another reason for the question until Lydia added with some concern, "Brett, darling, I was very worried about that wonderful Jag of yours sitting in the garage for so long, so I gave it a little spin around Rock Creek Park. I hope you don't mind me doing that?" Before I could answer, she burst out, "Riding with the top down in that car got me more attention than the Queen of England arriving at Ascot."

I laughed and said, "Thank you for taking care of my baby. That Jaguar was designed for beautiful English women like you. No wonder you got those stuffed shirts riding around in Washington in their black limousines to look at something other than the Congressional Record."

I could almost hear Lydia blushing.

She said, "You must have those Texas women hoping to hop off of their horses and on to your steel steed. I know I would if I saw you on your exotic motorcycle."

Now Lydia had me blushing, so I took another sip of whiskey and told her, "I will call you in a day or two, I promise," and hung up.

Next I dialed Kathryn's number. As soon as she heard my voice, she asked sweetly, "Brett honey, when are you getting that cute ass of yours up to Tennessee and how are you feeling? You know that I love you, don't you. Well, don't you?"

"Kathryn, I've know you loved me from the first time you smiled into my camera. To answer your first question, I would like to pull out of Texas tomorrow and head on up to Tennessee for some of that sweet southern loving. But now I've got to run or I will be late for dinner."

I hung up, hoping she was not offended that I terminated our call so abruptly, but I didn't want to get into the who, what and why of my current situation. I realized that something had happened to me in the course of those two phone calls. I no longer felt that I could trust my own judgment. Some force was tearing my normally clear-headed, decision making into a 1000 shreds of doubt. Despite Sister Alice's assurances, I questioned what had happened in Kelly's big bed. Was that padded restraint cradle a platform to the blessed world or just an altar of degeneracy?

When I was in the Light, there was no right or wrong. But on this earthly plane right and wrong were a common occurrences, like changing channels on the television. I wondered, if there were no moral instructions posted in the heavens, why was it such an issue in the gravity laden atmosphere of Earth? Absorbed in my musings I walked into the kitchen. Kelly was just sliding the Porterhouse steaks under the broiler and Rain finished placing the wine glasses on the table. When she tried to light Aunt June's black candles that sat in equally strange dark candelabras, her left breast pushed against one of the wine glasses, threatening disaster. She pulled back just in time.

When she heard me behind her, she whirled around, glared and barked, "Everything is so fucking black around here. I wonder what Kelly's aunt was into."

I figured that Aunt June's choice of illumination was just a flickering introduction to the exquisite bondage session awaiting her guests in the boudoir. Kelly interrupted those thoughts when she came into the dining room carrying to the table a large silver platter filled with succulent broiled meat and roasted chunks of russet potatoes.

We sat down on the designer chairs, which matched the dining table. They were the work of Robin and Lucinne Day, two Brits who set the standard for modern furniture design in the 1950s, although their pieces were rarely seen on this side of the Atlantic. I wondered how Aunt June had acquired them.

Kelly filled our glasses and we toasted to friendship. As we clinked goblets, I looked into her eyes and saw a different person from the woman who had come to visit me at the hospital. She had the look of a predator about to pounce on innocent prey, although I didn't think that I was her intended target this evening.

I tried to explain the significance of our dining furniture to my dinner companions, but my words fell on deaf ears. Kelly started to talk about her rehabilitation skills with young women, and Rain wanted to hear more about the how and why of addiction.

The meal was delicious and Kelly kept pouring hefty amounts of the deep purple wine into the redhead's glass. At first I loved the way Rain's full and moist lips caressed the crystal goblet, pursed like a plump baby's lips in pursuit of its mother's nipple. But as Kelly continued to pour wine, it became repetitious.

By the second bottle we were all a bit knackered and Kelly launched into a bawdy story about lesbian love affairs behind convent doors. She was on a fishing expedition to see if Rain would swallow the bait.

She surprised me by saying, "That kind of stuff turns my stomach." Then she reached over, touched my arm and softly purred to Kelly, "I would much rather have a piece of his hard meat than your prickly tongue any day of the week."

I didn't enjoy the game of sexual badminton and said, "I'm off early in the morning for Tennessee. I think I'll head for the bedroom and rest up."

As I was leaving the dining room, Rain shot me a pleading don't-leave-me-here-alone look. Kelly, on the other hand, smiled as if I had just given her a pot of gold.

Ten minutes later I heard raised voices and shortly after, the front door slamming. I waited for a moment and the bedroom door opened and a distressed Kelly marched in with a glass of wine in hand. She started to shake and cry at the same time.

I wasn't ready to let her off the hook and said sarcastically, "It's not often one gets to become part of a Greek comedy. I can't remember ever having so much fun watching perversion float across a Day table."

Kelly replied, "I don't know what you mean by that."

"I was referring to the Greek island of Lesbos and why you really had to leave your vocation to Christ."

The color drained from her face. Kelly swallowed hard and her strained voice was barely a whisper. "I was not thrown out of the convent for my sexual desires. I hid my wantonness well and only revealed it to those who needed what I could give them. No, Brett, I left the order because I felt that my marriage with Christ was melting away like a cheap candle. One can't serve two masters, so I choose lust over Catholicism. That all changed that day I ran you off the road and into eternity. Now I want to serve only you until I die. I will no longer be beholden to the desire of my flesh unless you want me to be and then all bets are off!"

I folded her into my arms, smoothed her worried brow, and held her until all her tension dissipated.

Then I said, "Let's go to bed," and Kelly nodded like a little girl.

Just before we drifted off to sleep, I whispered into her ear, "With my knowledge you will learn to see in a pure Light. Follow me and I will lead you through the magic of death. But this time around you will be aware that death is life and life is death, and you will know that both energies issue from the same source."

As the words poured out of me I realized that they came from a conscious knowledge that I had brought with me through the eons. I kissed my newest ward on the cheek and fell asleep.

Day 36

Over a breakfast of muffins and coffee, I informed a rejuvenated looking Kelly all about the love I shared with Kathryn and my belief that there was room in our circle for her.

Kelly's eyes grew larger, filled with unasked questions.

I took her hand and said, "Kelly, love is a type of energy and we human beings have the ability to tap into that energy. But when we do, it commands total attention. The energy of love travels on different frequencies. One lower vibration translates into infatuation, another governs sexual attraction. These lower vibrations require taking care, for they can lead into darkness. Kelly, through Kathryn and me you will take our combined strength and use it to become who you really are."

I paused to give her time to digest this. Then I asked, "Sister of sweetness, won't you come together with Kathryn and me to experience the purest rhythm of love."

Kelly slipped out of her chair and slid to the floor. Kneeling, she placed her head sideways in the cradle of my lap. Looking up slowly she mouthed silently, "We are one." Then she slowly returned her head to my lap.

I hugged her tenderly and said, "I will call in a day or two."

Before I left I gave her my new telephone number, in case she needed to get in touch with me.

I made it to Little Rock in less than two hours. Memphis took another two hours of hard driving and then, just east of Memphis, I left the frenzy of the Interstate for a more peaceful road. Continuing on, I lovingly thought of U.S. 64 as "the artery to Kathryn's heart."

Around dusk I stopped in Lawrenceburg. The Shell gas station had a lot of character and the old man, with cigarette in hand, leaning against the shabby white wall, had a certain look that called for closer inspection. With his hand wrapped around a Nehi grape soda bottle, he reminded me of old Joe from the *Bat Cave Diner*. But I didn't have time to explore him as a subject to photograph because I wanted to call Kathryn.

When I got hold of her and told her where I was, she could not believe I was so close to her house. "You just wait there in that old gas station and I will come down and get you," she said and continued in the same breath, "Brett Tempest, I just love the hell out of you and I can't believe you are here in Tennessee."

Exactly 23 minutes later Kathryn pulled into the old Shell station and jumped out of her Audi, leaving the motor running. I had barely time to register that she was wearing a pair of jeans, a red and blue flannel shirt and fluffy slippers before she flew into my arms.

Then she said, "Now, Brett, you just follow me to my little ol' house. I hope that pretty bike of yours will be all right on a dirt road. I am five miles off Highway 43 and the last mile is on dirt."

I said. "Don't worry. This bike is a *Valkyrie*."

She gave me one of her quizzical looks. But before she could formulate the words that always followed that expression, I had already straddled the bike, snapped down my visor and pushed the starter button.

I smiled to myself as the big engine hummed a new tune. I even received a thumbs-up from the good ol' boy leaning against the gas station wall.

Kathryn's house turned out to be a very nice log cabin at the end of the road, near the small community of Webber City. I braced myself before entering because most log homes I knew looked like taxidermy museums, a tribute to dead animals, with moose, elk, lion, deer and bear heads mounted on the timbered walls. But I was pleasantly surprised. Kathryn's place was quite the opposite. The few items on display were affectionate mementos from her past. The interior consisted of three main rooms, a large kitchen-dining room combination, a living room with two skylights and a wood burning stove. A small bedroom was off to the right.

Seeing my glance, Kathryn informed me, "That contains a half bath as well."

I poked my head into her bedroom. It was nicely furnished with a queen sized four poster bed, finished in dark cherry veneers, and a dressing table and chair of the same dark color.

The place was warm and cozy, and all the walls were hewn from oiled logs that were perfectly sealed. The overstuffed furniture had been picked for comfort, not elegance. The dining area had a Shaker bench style table, designed with a philosophy of function over comfort, but Kathryn had added soft cushions to the hard wooden seats. The occasional furniture was of nice quality, too, no doubt taken from inventory at *The Peddlers Pride*.

The first of Kathryn's many art objects that caught my eye was a framed first edition Remington lithograph depicting a weathered cowboy on a horse. The masterful way in which the artist had rendered this scene almost made it come to life. Most of the other pictures looked like naive, Pennsylvania Dutch painters, but I did not recognize any of the artists.

While I was looking at an old kerosene lamp, Kathryn came up behind me, put her arms around me, locked her hands together over my chest, and said, "Brett, we need to have a little talk because I had another dream about you the other night."

Putting my hands on top of hers, I said, "Let's first unload my motorcycle and then pour us a spot of Blanton's fine bourbon whiskey. It's been something of a haul for me to get here as fast as I did."

Twenty minutes later we were sitting close together on her sofa toasting our budding and ancient love affair. Kathryn's green eyes sparkled like emerald crystals. She looked more beautiful than ever before. I pulled her to me for a deep, soul stirring kiss. Tasting Kathryn's sweetness nourished my love for her and rekindled my desire. As our tongues explored each other's mouth, we helped one another discard our clothes and let our naked bodies experience the bliss of new love.

Afterward we lounged in each other's arms as the fire softly faded into glowing embers. At some point I reluctantly untangled myself from love's embrace and placed another log into the stove. I topped off our drinks and we repaired to the bathroom for a nice hot bath. Soaking together in the tub was the perfect opportunity to tell each other everything on our minds.

Kathryn wanted to start first but I had difficulty concentrating because I was watching the ebb and flow of the water wash over her partially submerged nipples, changing their normal deep red color into a softer magenta hue. As the sudsy liquid retreated, it left miniature soap bubbles on her soft nipples. Like a fascinated child I kept moving my body to create a tidal effect.

Kathryn, realizing what I was doing, said, "Would you stop that rocking and listen to what I have to tell you?"

I settled back against the tub and promised, "You have my undivided attention."

Staring ahead, as if reliving her dream, she started, "Brett, last night I awoke in a state of fright. It wasn't scary, like when you run into a mountain lion. This was fear of the power of the unknown. The dream I had was not a weird nightmare, it was more like a vision. I saw you surrounded by three women and I was one of them. The others were responsible for carrying your child. I know it sounds funny that two would bear one, but that is what I saw. I knew indisputably that we were there to take care of you and you would take care of the world. You weren't empowered to heal any diseases or poverty, or anything like that. You were here to heal the spiritual cancers that have been ravishing our world for centuries."

I shifted uneasily, absorbing the vision.

Kathryn put her hand on my arm and continued, "I saw you mend people's hearts with no more than a smile. Your words of wisdom were so uplifting and eloquent that modern day scribes recorded your every word for future generations. Brett, your obligation to mankind is to pave a road for the unborn by removing people's blinders. It's what they have been waiting for. That's why we have to protect your offspring, so it can carry on and make whole what you have started. The old guard of priests, preachers, rabbis, mullahs and evangelists will come together to try and kill you, just as they killed other prophets."

I was amazed by the complexity and depth of her vision. I took a long pull of my whiskey.

Before I could say anything, Kathryn continued, "That was my last vision, Brett. My first happened a few days ago. The two were essentially the same with one major exception: You were not in the body that I am looking at now. You were more of an essence, an expression of your life force. You materialized from that dream and into a vision. You see, Brett, I had asked God to bring me a lover and, instead of a Casanova, he sent me His ambassador."

A part of me hoped that Kathryn's divination was wrong. I didn't know if I would be strong enough to shoulder the responsibility of changing my life, let alone the world. Another side of me embraced her vision with open arms and I knew in my heart of hearts that she had seen my destiny.

I switched sides with Kathryn, so she could lean back and listen to me without the faucets poking her with its chilly touch. I told her all that had happened to me, every bit of information that I could recall.

When I got to the part about buying her a ring to celebrate our fictitious engagement, she stopped me and said, "Let me go and freshen our drinks. I have something to show you."

I added hot water to the tub and tried to let my burning mind unwind. By the time Kathryn returned and handed me another whiskey, I had achieved a state of relative calm. Then she showed me a description of a ring that she had torn out of a magazine.

I almost choked on my drink. It was from *Helzberg Diamonds* and was the exact ring, down to the carat weight, color and clarity that I had picked out for her while lying in a coma—or, as I saw it, in another dimension.

Kathryn shocked me even more when she said, "I saw you putting this exact ring on my finger in a dream I had the first night we slept together."

Now I knew it was time for her to know everything about the spiritual road we were traveling together. I even told her about the earthly Kelly Porter and my ejaculation into her stretched open womb. Surprisingly, Kathryn simply nodded as if she knew about it already through her own visions.

I went on for so long that I had to add hot water to the tub twice more in order to keep us comfortable.

We finally left the tub and got into her comfortable bed. I felt spent but she took my face in her hands and asked, "Make love to me like it's our honeymoon."

In our hearts, it was; and I did.

Day 37

My first awareness as I awoke the next morning was a blend of aromas of coffee from the Ivory Coast and Nicaragua. The African flavor was the more dominant, and I kept my eyes closed as long as I could, reveling in the anticipation of a good cup of roasted joe.

When I finally relented, I saw a woman standing before me, a glowing vision of adoration, holding two cups of steaming coffee. As she handed one of them to me, another smell, heavy with apples and cinnamon, drifted in from the kitchen. It not only warmed my heart, but also made my mouth water—Kathryn Baily was baking me an apple pie!

I no longer had any doubt that this fine woman from Tennessee would be with me, in one form or another, far beyond the realms of time. Looking at her, the uncertainty that I had felt in Kelly Porter's bedroom two days earlier dissipated like a puff of smoke. Kathryn had restored my faith in myself.

For breakfast Kathryn had prepared a batch of scrumptious griddle cakes with crispy bacon, and for the *piece de resistance*, a slice of Southern apple pie. We ate slowly, savoring every bite, and feeling the irresistible attraction we had for one another sparking between us.

When I felt that the time was right, I looked at her with serious intent and asked, "Kathryn, are you comfortable with someone else giving birth to our child?"

She smiled and said, "Of course I am, and I have a warm feeling about Kelly, too."

I reached under the table and caressed her knee. Then I asked, "Do you remember the time you wanted to go on a road trip with me, and I had a bit of trouble with that?"

She nodded yes.

"Well, Kathryn Bailey, how would you like to go on a little road trip down to Texarkana?"

"I would love to and have already planned for it. I sold my share of *The Peddlers Pride* in anticipation of you asking me to be with you."

I was rather shocked. "How did you know that I would ask you to come with me?"

"Brett, don't be silly. A woman knows these things. When I sold my half of the business, I never in my life felt so liberated. The irony is that when I bought in a few years ago, I never felt more secure. So what is worth more, security or destiny?"

I continued to be amazed at her ability to trust her instincts and risk it all. "I guess you had no choice but to do what you did," I said.

"Brett, you got that right. After my enlightenment, I have only one choice and that is to be with you. Now, do we take our Audi or ride the *Valkyrie* to Kelly's place?"

I weighed the options and decided, "Let's take the Audi and on our way back we can stop in Memphis and get you some proper leather riding clothes for our road trip to D.C."

"Sounds like a plan to me. We can store the motorcycle in my shed. You don't have to worry about that pretty traveling companion of yours. She will be safe and sound until we get back."

That decision made, I finished breakfast and we got up to get ready to go. After showering I put on my new clothes.

Kathryn took a look at me and said, "Boy, Kelly really did a nice job on your wardrobe, didn't she?"

She'd done it again, putting two and two together on her own.

"How did you know that Kelly Porter picked out the clothes for me?" I asked.

"Brett honey," she said, "you told me last night in the tub, and besides, a woman knows when another woman has had a hand in dressing a man," adding mischievously, "or in undressing him, for that matter."

I shook my head in resignation while Kathryn chortled happily.

We were just about ready to put the *Valkyrie* in the shed when Kathryn said, "Close your eyes. I have a little surprise waiting for you in there."

I felt a little silly but humored her. I heard the key slipping into the padlock, the click of the bolt being released, and the wooden door swinging open with a squeak.

Kathryn whispered, "Honey, you can open your eyes now."

Something gleamed in the darkness of the shed. As my eyes adjusted I realized it was a six-foot, bronze cross. I immediately recognized it to be the work of the Italian master, Alberto Giacometti, one of my favorite artists. Giacometti was not only a superb sculptor, he also possessed a wonderful control of hand on paper, and his drawings were almost as exquisite as his three-dimensional creations. I remembered a quote of his in an art history book, "It's impossible to finish. The more a sculptor tries to finish, the more he has the feeling of starting all over again."

I was stunned. I could not believe I was looking at one of his remarkable works here in a shed in the back woods of Tennessee. I turned to Kathryn and asked, "Do you know the significance of what we were looking at?"

"Brett honey, I don't know anything about this piece other than it came from an old man who walked into the store a week ago. He told me that I needed to have it and to pay him whatever I felt was a fair price."

"What did you pay him for this piece?"

"Everything I had in the cash box—223 dollars. He refused to take a check for anything more. He said that what I had on hand was more than enough for him and that his job was now complete."

I was dismayed. "Kathryn, listen to me! We have to get in touch with that old man and return this piece to him or pay him a hell of a lot more money. Let's go inside and call him and straighten this out. I really feel bad about this."

Kathryn put her arm on mine. "Brett, there is no way I can find him. He did not leave a number and did not want a receipt for the piece. He did say that he knew that it would end up in the right hands and he was happy about that. He spoke with a funny, German sounding accent. He definitely was not from these parts, I can tell you that."

I still wasn't convinced and paced back and forth in the garage.

Looking at me with a worried expression Kathryn implored, "Brett, I bought this piece for you and the old man knew in his heart that it would end up in our house. Honey, did I do wrong in buying this big cross?"

Suddenly a sense of serenity came over me, like the wind dying down and calming a sea of agitated waves. "Kathryn, I don't think that you had any control over it being right or wrong," I said. "This sculpture came to us from a much higher plane and it will stay with us, just as the old man wished it to."

I took a closer look at the cross. It was in pristine condition. The clear signature etched into the base at the back was dated 1956—the year I was born! It bore no body, but nails were driven into the metal sculpture where the hands and crossed feet should be.

Kathryn let out a little squeal and said, "The sculpture and you are exactly the same height."

I swallowed hard. Then I noticed, etched into the bronze at the top of the cross right above where the crowned-head would be, these words in Italian, "Nell'anno del Signore, 2016" or "In the year of our Lord, 2016." I knew instantly that the cross was a symbol of creating and death, referring to my beginning and ending.

A mortal chill ran through me and I pulled Kathryn into my arms to borrow some of her warmth. Her eyes reflected the fear I felt. She intuitively knew that the time she and I had together on this Earth was limited.

I pulled her to me and whispered, "My love, we will be together until forever disappears and that will be the beginning of our second day together as one."

She looked deeply into my eyes and replied in a voice so low that she had to put her lips against my ear, "I have already been with you since the beginning of time. It's just that this moment we are sharing now is so much more than just us, and I am mad because I want you all to myself. I love you, Brett Tempest, and always will. Now, let's get going."

We managed to squeeze the *Valkyrie* next to the Giacometti by turning the cross in a sideways position and locked the shed.

When we got in the Audi she handed me the keys and gave me a few pointers about using the multimedia interface which controls entertainment, satellite navigation, climate control, suspension configurations and all the other accessories she had bought. The car was fun to drive with its Tiptronic gearbox and smooth and fast shifting, although it didn't have as much immediacy and vivacity as the *Valkyrie*. But the ride was much warmer, considering the temperature outside hovered around 50 degrees.

I took the opportunity to catch Kathryn up on everything that was awaiting her in Washington, D.C., and more immediately, what to expect when we arrived at Kelly's place. We stopped in Memphis for a late lunch of ribs at a little place that Kathryn knew, and continued on, making good time.

Somewhere near Arkadelphia I called Kelly to give her a heads up that we would be at her place in about an hour. I was actually looking forward to the meeting between her and Kathryn.

When we got there I was not disappointed. The two were a classic example of how beautiful women size one another up. Both used the "quick scan" method to note any flaws that could be used as ammunition at a later time, if needed.

Kelly had dressed in a skin-tight, black pants outfit and wore a cute black beret that gave her mahogany colored hair a soft, alluring quality. Looking a bit like a black leopard, she reminded me of young Cyd Charrise.

Kathryn had put on a purple and black, diamond print, knit dress by Benny and Hizzin that set off her figure very well. I knew the names of the designers because she had mentioned them when I had complemented her on her choice of clothes this morning. The hemline was three inches above her knees, displaying her black stockinged legs to their best advantage.

Both women looked sexy as all get out. If I had been refereeing, I would have called it a draw. But my heart and desire was with Kathryn.

I suggested to Kelly, "Why don't you give Kathryn a tour of the house and all of its wonderful period furniture while I fix myself a drink and make some phone calls?"

Kelly smiled uncertainly and said, "I'll be glad to give you a Cook's tour."

Taking hold of Kathryn's hand she started off towards the dining table.

I went to the well-stocked liquor cabinet, found an opened bottle of Blanton's and poured myself a two finger shot. The line about the phone calls was just a ruse to give me some time alone. I amused myself watching the burning logs in the fireplace, hoping that the two women would connect on their tour of the 1950s and early 60s treasure trove.

Twenty minutes later they returned to the living room arm in arm and in a much better mood than when they had left. I could tell that Kathryn was impressed by what she had seen. I was pleased that they had put aside whatever possessiveness of me they harbored and had connected on a deeper level.

When Kelly saw my tumbler of whiskey, she blurted out, "Hey, big guy, aren't you going to offer a couple of beautiful ladies a bit of that poison?"

I bowed expansively. "Neat or on the rocks, what would be your pleasure?"

They both opted for ice cubes. I fixed them their drinks and we toasted to the force that had brought us together.

Then I told them, "Things are becoming clearer to me and I feel that the Creator has chosen each one of us to help in the unfolding of our final destiny."

When I glanced at Kathryn I knew that she agreed with my words.

Kelly put her hand on my shoulder and said, "I have never been more sure of anything in my life as I am about joining you two in body and spirit."

Kathryn held out her raised glass, inviting us to clink glasses with her. She said, "Brett is my life blood and I shall always be at his side. Kelly, you are my sister in this consecrated alliance. Let's drink to a compact we make with each other that can never be broken."

We drank up and then, on cue, prompted by some mysterious directive, threw our glasses into the fireplace at exactly the same time. The remnants of the liquor exploded into flame, creating a bluish purple circle of light, which hung above the logs for a just a moment. Then it transformed into a clear circular window that floated in the air and finally dissipated into orange and blue tongues of fire.

I looked at my partners and said, "We just saw what our symbol of purpose will look like."

We came together in a tight, body melding hug. I felt electric currents arcing among us. Both Kelly and Kathryn felt the same. We all knew that powerful forces were aligned with our coming together.

Kelly brought out a new set of glasses and we sat down at the table. While I poured another round of whiskey, Kathryn took the lead in her inimitable, candid way. "So Kelly, what's this all about with your desire for women?" she asked as if making ordinary conversation.

Kelly pouted and then answered somewhat defensively, "I was in the convent for about seven months when I was called into the

Mother Superior's private room. It was odd to be called into her presence after lights out. Her chamber was dark and only had a red votive candle burning on the small bedside table. Sister Margret was lying without her habit on top of the white sheets that covered her bed. She was naked!"

When Kelly paused to catch her breath, her lips drawn tight, Kathryn left her seat and came around the table and stood behind her. Bending down she gently kissed Kelly on top of her head.

Thus strengthened, Kelly continued, "On the bed next to the Mother Superior's body was a small metal pan that contained various oils. She beckoned me to stand next to her. Then she handed me one of the bottles and asked me to rub the oil into her 'pain.' I had no idea what she meant by that and asked her to explain. Sister Margret took my hand and guided it to her womb. But it was not her need that caused the pain, it was the crudely carved cross above her vagina, partially healed but still oozing puss. I worked the healing oils into the wound and found that I was becoming more aroused with every rotation of my hand on her warm skin. Sister Margret pushed my hand down until my fingers found her entrance and before I could think, my lips traced my finger's journey and I consumed Sister Margret's love for me.

These visits continued. At first they were separated by weeks, but before too long, they became almost nightly. Once I had the taste of woman in my mouth, it became intoxicating and demanding. My position in the sisterhood was to teach wayward girls the righteous path. But I found so many willing young women that I got caught up in the tempest of lust and had to leave the order to excorsize the demon of desire that was flowing through my body. My decision to leave religion was reinforced when Brett Tempest entered my life. I am now on a new path. I am aware that I will occasionally get a thirst for the softness of female flesh, but I know in my heart that I can always quench that thirst by drinking from the cup of Light."

Kelly looked like a great weight had fallen from her shoulders. Her face glowed with relief and newfound strength. She raised her glass and said, "So, I propose a toast to the one who is inside me."

After we clinked glasses and took a sip and continued, "Kathryn, I want to also tell you that I felt you with us when I conceived. I know it was you, because I saw you coaxing the life giving semen into my womb."

With that revelation Kelly took Kathryn in her arms, kissed her tenderly on the cheek and added, "I will always love you for that."

I looked at both women and felt my heart go out to them as waves of love emanated from deep within their beings cleansing my heart and nurturing my soul.

Taking Kelly and Kathryn by the hand, I asked solemnly, "Can I count on both of you to always love and cherish me and, more importantly, each other so that the flame that we are going to light will be eternal? I need your promise that in the years to come, you will raise our prodigy with love that can only come from the pure of heart. After I leave this world, you need to keep the love you have for me burning with the knowledge that you will be joining me in the endless bliss of eternity."

In answer, Kelly and Kathryn led me to the bath and undressed me while the water filled the tub. They disrobed, guided me into the soothing, hot liquid and gently bathed me and rubbed cleansing oils into my body. After I got out of the tub, they dried me with soft towels and ushered me to the bed and joined me.

That night we slept together in peace, our minds and bodies entwined with the unbreakable bonds of love, created on this day of revelation of the body and liberation of the spirit. It was a new beginning for all three of us.

Day 38

The next morning over breakfast we discussed my plans to move to the Washington, D.C. house. Surprisingly, Kelly had no objections.

"I am as free as a bird and Texarkana doesn't ring my cultural bell," she said. "I think our nation's capital will be a great place to start our journey of enlightenment."

I was thrilled to hear that.

Then Kelly said, "I think it's best if I sell this house so we can all live together with you."

Kathryn reached out, took her hands, joined them with mine, and said, "This feels right."

I felt a fire of energy start in the pit of my stomach and spread through my fingertips into their hands. I was transported into another dimension and watched as the force coursed through me and galvanized the women, raising goose bumps on their arms.

Kelly said, "Did you guys feel what I just felt?"

Kathryn replied, "Yes, it was like a warm, comforting hand massage that spread through my whole body."

They turned in unison to me wanting to know if I had felt the same vibrations.

Returning to our present reality, I smiled and said, "I am glad that you enjoyed this little gift."

Before I could elaborate my cell phone rang. It was Lydia. Her voice sounded as excited as I had ever heard her. "I just got the photographs and I am tickled pink," she burst out. 'Shave-Ice' definitely will make a wonderful addition to your book on America. And who is that gorgeous creature wrapped in those lovely scarves?"

I replied, "Her name is Kathryn Bailey. You'll meet her in person in a few days."

My revelation took the wind out of her sails. In a distinctly cooler voice she asked, "Are you bringing her home with you?"

"Yes, Lydia, I am bringing her home, and she is sitting right next to me. I would like you to say hello to her."

I handed the phone to Kathryn trusting that her soft and melodic voice would melt the wall of ice that my British assistant had put up.

While, they were talking, Kelly asked me, "Would you like the furniture after I sell the house. You seem to love it."

"I would be honored to put it in the North Carolina house. In fact, we can redo the entire interior to match it."

The thought of having my Durham home as another strong base was exhilarating. It meant we could continue our quest from solid foundations stretching from D.C. all the way to North Carolina.

A beaming Kathryn Bailey handed the phone back to me. When I got back on, Lydia's voice bore no trace of frost. "Kathryn, sounds as lovely as she looks, and I am truly looking forward to meeting her in person."

"Well, that sounds good to me," I said expansively. "To be honest, I have been away from my lovely and very special British lass far to long for my own good."

Lydia actually giggled. "Drive safe and stay warm," she said. "The weather in Washington is cold as all get out one day and as lovely and warm as a baby's bum the next. Just come home safe."

I was about to end the call when she sputtered, "Oh my God, I almost forgot, Bernie Cornfield called from Malibu and wants the Picasso Vollard Suite. He thanks you for the 'more than fair price' and will transfer the money sometime today. By my calculations you just cleared $1.1 million dollars. Not bad for a day's work."

204 – Michael Judge

And with that she hung up the phone.

It was time for us to leave. Kathryn hugged Kelly good-bye and I wiped away her tears, whispering in her ear, "You'll be with us before you know it."

She waved after us as we got in the Audi and headed back towards Tennessee. The clouds were dark grey and heavy, promising rain. In my eagerness to stay ahead of the impending downpour, I almost did not stop at Christus St. Michael's, but Kathryn insisted on seeing the hospital where I had my "recovery."

When we walked inside, Sister Mary Alice was waiting for us at the front desk. How she knew that we were coming was a mystery.

Without introductions, Kathryn walked right up to the old nun, put her arms around her and kissed her on the cheek.

Mary Alice looked at Kathryn and said, "So, you have come to serve. The vision is now almost complete."

I smiled and said, "There are now two women who will always be at my side."

The old woman replied, "Blessed One, there is another that awaits you by a mighty river, and she will bear half of the whole." Her eyes sparkled as she continued, "I am so glad that you brought this woman to see me. All of you will be in my prayers. Your mission is larger than the Earth, and one day your teachings will warm hearts and blaze a path all the way to the Light. Now go in peace."

She made the sign of the cross with a wrinkled hand and I noticed a circle ring on her bony fingers. Then she was gone, as if she had never been there.

Kathryn held my hand as we left the hospital and we resumed our travels. She did not say a word until we were 30 miles past Texarkana.

Finally she asked, "Why have I been chosen to be part of this re-birth? What have I done in my life that made God's light fall on me, and why did you fall in love with me when you could have any woman in the world?"

"I fell in love with you because you were chosen and your warmth is part of my life. Without you, my road would be cold and long, but with you it is a joy and there is no obstacle that we cannot surmount together."

When she leaned over and kissed my cheek, I felt her love vibrate all the way down to my toes.

Kathryn then voiced the very questions that had been swirling in my mind since we left the hospital. "Brett, what did that old woman mean by, 'bearing half of the whole'? And what did she mean by, 'The Two shall become One'? That has something to do with my dream, doesn't it?"

"Funny you should ask. I don't know, but I'm sure we will soon discover the answer to that conundrum."

Time passed quickly and before we knew it, we were pulling into the parking lot of the motorcycle dealer in Memphis. An hour later we were back on the road with Kathryn's brand new riding gear stowed in the rear of the Audi.

Back on U.S. 64, we were cruising towards Kathryn's house and almost passed the motel where we had spent our first night together. Without saying a word, I pulled over. The proprietor didn't recognize us when I checked us into the same room.

As soon as we got there Kathryn started to undress me as I undressed her. Our eyes never left each other. We fell onto the bed of our beginning and made love. We took our time in a comingling of peace and desire, and reached our peak at exactly the same time.

In passion's afterglow Kathryn held my face in her hands and asked in a hushed voice the same question she had asked 25 days earlier, "Brett, will you take me with you?"

This time I did not hesitate. "Yes!"

Two hours later we left and drove the few remaining miles to Kathryn's house. We cooked a wonderful spaghetti Bolognese dinner together and I found a half-gallon of red Gallo wine gathering dust on the floor of the pantry. It was still good, and we enjoyed our meal with candle light and talked about the future.

We decided to have the Giacometti sculpture, along with Kathryn's clothes, shipped to our home in Washington but to keep her cabin as a get-away for when we needed it.

Later when we took a bath together, facing each other in the tub, Kathryn asked, "How did it feel when you were making love to Kelly?"

"It was good because her soul was pure," I replied. "If it hadn't been, she wouldn't have been sent to us. She was a virgin, Kathryn, and that night was her offering to us from the Light."

"What do you mean?" Kathryn sounded hurt.

"Because, my special one, everything that you women do with me, should be felt and shared as a gift, for we are all one and the same. I do not plan to have sex with anyone but you. With one exalted exception: to create our child of the Light."

My words soothed Kathryn's bruised feelings. Her foot found my genitals and she stroked me ever so gently with her toes while making love to me with her eyes.

Later as we lay in bed together, I gave Kathryn the complete run-down on how to ride double and the art of becoming one with the bike.

She tickled my ribs and said, "That should be a piece of cake, since I am already one with you."

Day 39

In the morning it looked like the weather gods were going to bless us with a rain free day and mild temperatures. The forecast indicated we would start in the upper 60s and reach into the lower 70s the further southeast we traveled.

It was a joy to have Kathryn's help packing the *Valkyrie*. We were more excited than on the day I left my Durham driveway to begin this odyssey.

As we pored over my maps to determine our route, I asked Kathryn, "Would you like to take the Blue Ridge Parkway up to the D.C. area?"

She was concerned about where we would spend our first night. I thought that Asheville, North Carolina would be a good place. "We could visit the Biltmore Estate, America's most famous castle of decadence," I teased.

"Why, Brett darling, if we stay in that citadel of dissipation and you go for your nightly pee, how would you find me afterwards, with so many bedrooms?"

"Kathryn, my dear, I would use my nose to lead me right to that sweet smelling honey pot of yours."

"Oh, baby, make love to me right this moment! I can't stand it when you talk sexy to me."

I didn't need a second invitation and we made love right on the kitchen table. Our torrid and lustful indulgence almost resulted in our getting a late start.

As we were ready to head out, I remembered that I had completely forgotten to pay Kelly for my clothes. When I called her to apologize, she started laughing.

"Lydia called me two days ago and made a wire transfer into my checking account," she explained. "Brett Tempest, what would you do without us women to take care of you? Lydia said that you never remember money or any other mundane things, and it would be up to us to keep you on track."

Kathryn pulled on my arm and asked for the phone. Excitedly, she filled Kelly in on our impending road trip to Washington. Now we were definitely late and I wondered if we ever would get going and make it from the fertile fields of Tennessee to the power pavements of Capitol Hill.

I snatched the phone away from her and said, "Bye, Kelly. Got to go."

Before Kathryn could retaliate, I mounted the *Valkyrie* and started the engine. It roared to life, drowning out any possibility of conversation. Kathryn joined me on the metal maiden, and we were off.

By the time we reached U.S. 64 East, Kathryn was riding like a pro. I'd known she'd be a natural and it felt great having her hug me with her arms wrapped around me from behind.

Our first stop was at *Country Boy's* in Winchester, Tennessee for two slices of Butterfinger cheesecake. There really is nothing like dessert for breakfast! While enjoying our calorie laden treat, Kathryn asked something that I found quite endearing, "Brett, can we go to places on this trip that you have never been to before, either alone or with someone else? I don't want you to think I am some old southern bitch. It's just that I want every minute we spend together to count, so I can fill my scrapbook of memories with only you and me together, and nobody can ever take that from me."

I went out to the bike, brought the map back and unfolded it on our table. "OK, my darling, let's discover new territory. And did I tell you that I love you?"

Pushing the red plastic water containers out of the way, Kathryn covered my hand with hers and murmured, "You know, Brett honey, you are starting to sound just like me and yes, you told me this morning."

We determined that we would drive to Cleveland, Tennessee and take U.S. 11 North toward Knoxville and all the way into Virginia.

That decision made, we finished our Butterfinger cheesecake and resumed our trip.

Past Knoxville we entered the mountain Bible Belt. The area is a Christian stronghold, an Evangelical fortress, where the most exotic manifestations of faith are snake dancers speaking in tongues and dunking Baptists hanging around the river banks. I could feel the fear of the unknown vibrating through these hills. Anyone not of the accepted brand of Christianity was doomed to damnation. Catholic priests, rabbis and imams were the representatives of Satan. Since nuns were similarly mistrusted for teaching false doctrine, I sent Kelly a mental picture of what we were sensing in these hills.

We started to notice advertisements for a tent revival posted on various buildings and poles on the side of the road. I thought we might stop and get a little insight into true Christian fear tactics. The revival was to take place between Church Hill and Mount Carmel, Tennessee at 8 p.m. We decided to drive a little further north first, to Kingsport where we would spend the night.

We found a Hampton Inn and got a room with a king sized bed and the usual amenities. After we unloaded our bags, we rode the now sleeker *Valkyrie* back south 15 miles until we came to a large meadow filled with trucks and older cars. We parked near the front of the large old circus tent. A 10-foot, bloodred cross had been sewn onto the front canvas.

We walked inside in full motorcycle leather regalia. The place was packed with about 200 people of all ages. Immediately, we caught the attention of the head holy man, a self-styled "country healing preacher" who went by the name of E. Buck Jenkins.

He greeted us with a toothy smile and these beguiling words, "Welcome, my leather clad sheep, into the fold of our Lord."

I had hoped to slip quietly into the congregation of Tennessee Baptists, but now every eye in the tent settled on our road duds and slightly disheveled appearance. Preacher Jenkins had his usher find us two seats right up front, treating us out-of-towners with courtesy and respect. But I reckoned the real reason for our front row seats was that he hoped we would be easy targets for him to extract our sins, not to mention the cash from our wallets. Kathryn took hold of my hand as we sat down. I was hoping to witness a few "healings" and maybe some sort of staged levitation.

The Reverend Jenkins started off by blasting a local church for having a Saturday pancake dinner and encouraging members of its congregation to speak in tongues in order to raise money. He pontificated, "It is not my place to scorn other churches, but me and Mrs. Jenkins have never put ourselves before our flock. We do not cotton to gimmicks for the Lord."

I took a good look at the preacher's wife who was standing behind him. She was a gaunt woman with her hands folded in front of her. Her eyes never left the floor. She had shoulder length, curly brown hair and, judging by her skin, was in her 40s even though she looked 60. Her long, black dress reached from the base of her neck to just above the ankles. The only ornamentation she had allowed herself was a silver pendant in the shape of a dove floating just above her right breast. Although she was hard to read wrapped in her plain robe, I knew in my heart that she did not believe in what she was doing with the reverend.

My thoughts were interrupted by her husband's penetrating voice. "Now I want everybody who has brought their Bible..." He paused significantly and cast an admonishing look at Kathryn and me, who obviously had failed to come appropriately prepared, before continuing, "...to turn to Psalm 23."

I remembered that verse as an old standby for fleecing customers hungry for religion and waited for his pitch.

Sure enough, the reverend went right to it. "The Lord is my Shepherd, I shall not want. You people who belong to Jenny and my flock shall not want!" he intoned. "Of course, some of you have more than others, and some give more than others. What do you suppose Jee-sus sees when you have an extra hundred in your wallet and don't give it to him? You are not giving. You are buying your place in heaven. Do you think that slackers and cheaters use the golden path to heaven? No, the path of gold is made from gold." He pointed to an older woman sitting three seats to my right and thundered, "Like the path for sister Grace sitting right here, who just gave ten thousand dollars!"

A chorus of "hallelujahs" rang throughout the tent.

The Reverend Jenkins went on, "Do you think that your ten dollars will buy less of the golden road than sister Grace's generous gift? No! That is the right answer. So dig down deep and let Jee-sus know that he did not die in vain for your sins." He paused to let that sink in before continuing at a lower volume, "Now I have been told that brother John Sibley has been struck deaf by forces of the devil. Will someone bring Brother John up to be anointed by the grace of the Holy Ghost?"

A couple of guys dressed in dark, ill-fitting suits guided an older man up to the stage. The reverend started speaking strange and unintelligible words in ever rising intensity. But to the people sitting behind us those words were a new testament.

I heard one woman say, "Brother Jenkins speaks in the best tongues in all of Tennessee."

I was glad that poor John couldn't hear the gibberish the preacher was yelling at the top of his voice. But after a good slap on his ears, John turned and faced us and said joyfully, "I can hear, I can hear. Thank you Brother Jenkins," and walked off the stage a new man.

After Mr. Sibley's miracle, the reverend treated us to two more equally miraculous healings. Then he started the process of separating the members of his flock from their money by offering memorabilia in exchange for heavy donations. Tee shirts with decals of a dove went for a $100. For $500 you got a gold writing pen with a miniature version of the same dove, glued on just above the clip.

The pièce de résistance, commanding a whopping $1,000 donation, was in the words of E. Buck Jenkins, "A solid silver dove to wear on your blouse or jacket, showing the world that you are one with the Holy Ghost. This fabulous piece of jewelry was hand crafted by Brother Jacob Heltzberg, a Jew, who found his salvation in Jee-sus right here in this tent."

The ill-fitting suits passed the plate around and money started to pour in. The tee shirts, gold-dipped pens and silver dove pendants disappeared faster than donuts at a police station.

When I had heard and seen enough, I asked the woman next to me if I could use her Bible. Then I stood up and asked the Reverend Jenkins, "Could I share a passage from the Evangelist John?"

He nodded, pleased.

I turned to John 2:13 and read, "And the Jews' Passover was at hand, and Jesus went up to Jerusalem. And found in the temple those that sold oxen and sheep and doves, and the changers of money sitting: And when he made a scourge of small cords, he drove them all out of the temple, and the sheep, and the oxen; and poured out the changers' money, and overthrew the tables. And said unto them that sold doves, 'Take these things hence; make not my Father's house a house of merchandise.'"

The reverend flushed red with fury, pointed his finger at me and shouted, "Shame on you for trying to stop these people from getting into heaven!"

As he launched into his tirade, I planted my feet firmly on the dirt floor and pointed back at him, feeling the energy leave my finger. His mouth kept moving, but no audible words came out.

I walked up onto the stage, faced his congregation and said, "There is no place for fear in my house and you cannot buy your way into the

Light. Only love will take you to heaven. You who come seeking an easy road and use the wallet instead of the heart will be cursed to many lifetimes of being a slave to money. But those who find love for others, you are true children of Light. If you look into your hearts right now, you will know which one of us is telling the truth and which one is fishing for money, using the lie of a golden road as bait. I only have love for you and if you love me in return, we will share eternity. Now, leave this place of greed and don't return."

Then I walked over to the dumb-struck preacher, touched his lips with my finger and restored his voice to him.

He started yelling at the mass exodus of people leaving the tent, "This man's a fake! A disciple of Satan! He's just trying to trick you into going to hell with him."

But it was too late. The tent soon emptied except for the Reverend Jenkins, his wife and his handful of employees.

I looked at the broken man standing in front of me and said, "You and your kind have ministered cruel injustice for thousands of years. I have come to change the order of things and bring humanity back to the Light. The people you have been bilking for so long will now become your archenemies and you will be destroyed by your own lie."

I left the stage and took Kathryn's hand. She was stunned and shaken by what had happened. There were rivulets of tears on her face, but as we walked out of the tent together she glowed with pride.

Day 40

The next morning, after the obligatory cup of coffee, we decided to warm up the bike while loading her. It was chilly outside and as we left the lobby's entrance portico, we were met by seven people standing about 20 feet away from the *Valkyrie*. They had, surrounded it with flowers. Some carried more flowers, others held Bibles. They were looking at me expectantly, waiting for me to say something to them.

I asked, "How did you know that we were here at the Hampton Inn?"

One young man stepped forward and handed Kathryn a bouquet of flowers, saying, "I followed you here last night."

I was surprised to see Mrs. Jenkins standing among the group. She came forward, grabbed hold of my hand and begged me, "Please forgive me for cheating on the Lord."

I put my hand on her chest and felt the throbbing between her breasts, and projected my love into her heart. She brought my hand up to her face, kissed my palm with trembling lips, and slipped me a small card with her name and a phone number handwritten on it. Then she slowly backed away to the rear of the small gathering.

I pointed to the flowers ringing the bike, "When we are finished here, take them and go to the graveyard. Place them on graves of people you don't know or, more importantly, someone you disliked while they were alive.

They shuffled awkwardly trying to keep warm.

Kathryn took it upon herself to invite them all to join us in the hotel breakfast room for coffee. On the way in, I went to the desk and gave the clerk on the morning shift 20 dollars to cover the coffee and donuts we would consume.

After we sat down at the tables, the first question came from the young man who had acted as the scout for the rest. "Does God love homosexuals?"

I looked at him kindly. "What is your name?"

"Jacob Heltzberg."

"Well, Jacob, do you think that God made a mistake in creating you? And if so, can you explain to me how God is capable of making mistakes?"

He stared at me a blank look on his face, waiting to hear more.

So I continued, "Jacob, your body is of no importance—'from dust to dust.' Now, if you feel that dust has more importance than your soul, then yes, you are a mistake of God. But if you know in your soul that dust is just dust, then God did not make a mistake in allowing you to exist. You see, our bodies are only made of a few minerals, and everything on this earth with the exception of your soul is made up of atoms that are in constant motion. Sometimes they move in one direction, as in you, or in another, as in Jenny Jenkins. All that matters is that when your body returns to the Earth, your soul starts a new journey. If your heart is pure, that journey is towards the Light, and if your heart is darkened by fear, greed, hatred and mistrust, then your next incarnation will be in a place of darkness."

Jacob nodded eagerly and then burst out, "Every preacher in every church I have attended in search for a truth I can understand has told me that it is an abomination against God to desire another man. Do you agree with that?"

"Let me ask you again. When God arranged the energy to create desire, did he make a mistake, or is it organized religion that has made the mistake? The only transgression through desire is letting it become more important than your soul, for desire is fleeting and your spirit is everlasting."

I continued to chat amiably with the group and answered many questions.

At some point I said, "It is time for us to go. It was a treat to be able to spend time with you."

As we headed outside to warm-up the *Valkyrie* again, the men and women thanked me.

Jacob looked longingly at me, as if I had just handed him a get-out-of-jail-free card. Seeing his hungry glances, I wondered if I was now his new object of desire. As he stepped backwards, his leg touched the hot engine of my *Valkyrie* and she burned a hole into his designer jeans. He was unhurt and walked away quickly without looking back.

An older woman approached me opening her purse. She started to fish out some dollar bills.

I held up my hand. "Please keep the money for yourself. It has no value in getting you to the next world, despite what the Reverend Jenkins had told you." Then I turned to the others, "We are finished here for now. Kathryn will give you our number, if you so desired it."

All but one wrote down the number of my cell phone down. When they'd left, only one person stayed—Jenny Jenkins.

"May I visit with you privately?" she asked

I smiled and nodded. "Why don't you come to our room?"

As we stepped inside, she asked, "Are you the Second Coming?"

I replied, "The one who comes after me will be the new Light. I am here to burn down the old and build the new. My mission is to enlighten and pave the way."

Then I looked into her gray eyes and said, "Please take your clothes off."

Kathryn caught her breath and shot me a stern glance, but I quieted her with a wave of my hand.

Jenny stood in the middle of the room shaking and with trembling hands, let her dark dress fall to the floor. Standing in her white cotton bra and panties she looked at me and waited.

"Undress completely."

With tears running down her face, she unclasped her brassiere and freed her small, scarred breasts. Then she stepped out of her cotton underpants, revealing a crudely carved Calvary scene with the initials E.B.J. just above one of the three crosses. This abomination was etched deep into the skin above her shaven genitalia.

Upon seeing the obscene engraving, Kathryn let out a deep sigh and said, "That sadistic bastard should burn in hell."

I said, "This is only the doorway to his depravity," and took Jenny into my arms and kissed away her tears.

Kathryn cried out, "She has been whipped by a strap. Her back is a mass of welts."

Between sobs Jenny said, "It's to atone for my sins, to cleanse me."

Kathryn ran her soft hands over the deep welts trying to make them go away.

Jenny then told us a tale of pain and debauchery, which included the Reverend Jenkins forcing her to perform fellatio on other men and having them urinate on her while he watched and masturbated himself to a climax. She concluded with an appeal, "Mr. Tempest, it is too late for me, but my daughter is still pure. After I caught Buck trying to seduce her with his twisted words, I packed up a few of her things and sent her down to stay with my sister on a houseboat in New Orleans. But Beverly and her husband Charles have five children of their own, and they have all been crowded into that old houseboat since they lost their house and everything they owned during Katrina. I have to find someplace else to keep my little girl safe."

I felt a surge of understanding pass through me.

Jenny gripped me with her feeble hands, pulled me to her naked body, and beseeched me, "I beg of you to help me with my little Michelle."

"How old is your daughter?" "Michelle is thirteen and will turn fourteen on December 17. I know that God has sent you to lead her to salvation."

I held her at arm's length and said, "After you hear about my mission and everything that led to it, you will see that Michelle is to be a part of the world's salvation."

Kathryn went into the bathroom and returned with a dampened washcloth. She proceeded to clean off Jenny's tears and helped her get dressed. Then she took her to the edge of our still disheveled bed and sat down next to her. Holding Jenny's hand, she nodded to me to begin.

I told Jenny everything from my departure in Durham, North Carolina over a month ago to my arrival in this hotel room in Kingsport. I didn't leave anything out, nor embellished any part. By the time I brought my story to its conclusion, Jenny was in rapture. She knelt before me and started to speak in tongues, offering herself and her daughter to me, and I understood every word.

When her spirit returned to a more settled plane, I asked, "Can we reach your sister by phone?"

Jenny nodded and said, "She has both a landline and a cell phone."

I sat down next to her on the floor and we made a plan to bring Michelle back to us. I figured that it was about 330 miles from Kingsport to Washington, D.C. If we jumped on I-81 and took it up to I-66, we could be crossing the mighty Potomac River and ride into Washington in about six hours. We decided to have Beverly take Michelle to the Louis Armstrong New Orleans International Airport, where Lydia would have a will call ticket waiting for her to fly to Ronald Reagan National Airport in D.C.

I felt that we would know if Michelle was chosen within a day or two. If she wasn't, we would keep her with us and get her into a private school either in D.C. or Durham. Jenny agreed and said that she would work with Lydia and would have Michelle in Washington tomorrow.

I had another idea. "Jenny, it would be good for you to move into my house in Durham. You could start a new life there and leave the beatings and humiliation of E. Buck Jenkins behind."

Jenny looked at me like she had met a saint. Undeterred, I continued, "In the meantime, it might be a good idea to book this room for another day, so you can use it as a safe place from where to organize Michelle's travel plans."

By the time I finished Kathryn had already picked up the house phone to make it happen.

For the first time a small smile appeared on Jenny's face, and when Kathryn and I said our good-byes just before noon, we knew that her life had changed for good.

We stayed on U.S. 11 for a short jaunt and then joined Interstate 81 at the Virginia border. The sunny weather was holding and the roads were relatively empty all the way to Interstate 66 near Front Royal. By then we were less than 70 miles from D.C. The *Valkyrie* was running smoothly and I was pleased that I had finally broken it in all the way.

At a quarter to six in the evening we crossed the Potomac River on the Fourteenth Street Bridge, and 15 minutes later we pulled into the alley behind my house on Third Street S.E.

I was disappointed that the small garage I used for my Jaguar and motorcycle was locked. My own keys were long gone, lost somewhere in a junkyard in Texarkana. It was time to hunt down Lydia. Having stopped only for gas and a couple of restroom breaks, we were tired and hungry. We hurriedly unpacked the cases from the *Valkyrie* and placed them on the top stoop by the back door.

I walked around to the front of the house and took the five steps down to Lydia's basement apartment. By the second knock my lovely and trusted friend opened the door, threw her arms around my neck and kissed me. I was surprised. It was the first time she kissed me on the mouth instead of the usual peck on my cheek or forehead and I became mildly aroused by the warmth of her soft lips.

Dismissing that feeling, I said, "Kathryn is waiting with our luggage at the back door. I have no keys to the house."

After introductions and hugs we finally made it inside. Lydia handed me a new set of keys and announced, "Michelle Jenkins will be arriving at Reagan Airport at 11 tomorrow morning on US Air."

Then she left us to our own devices.

I suggested to Kathryn, "Why don't we quickly change our clothes and walk up to Pennsylvania Avenue to get something to eat. Then I'll give you the full house tour."

She agreed and we started to carry our cases to my bedroom upstairs on the third floor. Kathryn immediately fell in love with the master bedroom, with its exposed, brick covered walls displaying museum grade art, including an 1864 Renoir oil painting of a lovely female nude in repose on a dark blue, silk settee.

The large, raised platform bed also served as panorama seating—I had designed it to double as a three-sided sofa. The headboard was about two feet from the exposed brick of the back wall, which had a large picture window that looked out on the street below. An immense skylight in the roof created a marvelous glow throughout the room, although it was fading by now. At night the skylight allowed an unobstructed view to the heavens above. Kathryn stood speechless in the middle of the room, slowly turned around and simply said, "Wow."

While we were changing our clothes, Kathryn kissed me and said, "Brett, you are the most amazing man I have ever met and did I tell you today that I love the hell out of you." As we were about to leave the bedroom, she added, "I think Lydia is attractive in that wonderful British way and doesn't she have strikingly beautiful skin?"

After that breathless declaration all I could manage was, "I guess so. Now let's go and eat before I have to take a bite out of that lovely arm of yours."

We walked up to Pennsylvania Avenue, turned right and made our way to one of the oldest pubs on the hill.

The *Hawk n' Dove* had been opened by Stu Long and Mike Lange in 1967 and was still going strong. The food was typical bar fare:

burgers, stews, chili and hot roast beef sandwiches. But if you don't try their hot cream of crab soup, you will surely miss one of the best she-crab soups this side of the Chesapeake Bay.

We settled at a corner table and ordered two Hawk burgers with fries and a pitcher of beer. Kathryn kept looking around expecting to see Bill Clinton or some other famous political luminary walk through the door. I explained to her that Sunday night in D.C. is no time to go celebrity watching, but to no avail. My southern belle kept scrutinizing everyone who walked through the front door.

After we finished our meal and most of the beer, we took a walk to the Capitol building. The vision of incandescent lights bathing the dome topped by the bronze depiction of Lady Liberty was magnificent and better than any dessert we could have had to complete our wonderful evening. Ever the tour guide, I informed Kathryn, "By decree of Congress no structure in D.C. can be higher than the woman who stands on top of the Capitol dome."

Our pleasant walk was rudely interrupted when we reached Third Street just south of Pennsylvania Avenue. A pair of street drunks appeared from the shadows of an alley and demanded money. One of them brandished what looked like an ordinary table knife. I moved Kathryn behind me and put out my hand like a traffic cop stopping an oncoming car. I felt a stream of unseen energy leave my body and watched it render the two thugs helpless.

The armed mugger dropped the knife to the sidewalk. It made a clinking sound as it hit the hard concrete. The other man took his hand from the torn Army surplus, fatigue jacket he was wearing and offered to shake mine.

He slurred apologetically, "We've made a terrible mistake, mister."

By then his partner was on his knees begging, "Please don't send him to the fires of hell. I know who you are, mister. I promise I won't drink anymore and I won't steal from anyone ever again. Just don't hurt me, mister."

While the kneeling bum was making his case, his partner took off running south towards C Street. I gestured for the man before me to get up and leave, and he disappeared in no time.

As the threat of danger vanished into the night air, Kathryn came out from behind me and asked, "Brett, have you always had that effect on people?"

My forehead furrowed as I tried to understand what had just happened. "Not that I recall," I ventured. "This power came out of the Light. But I have no idea how to control the energy that emanates from within me and that scares the hell out of me. I think this force has been given for me to hone and pass on to my progeny. Then it will turn into a dynamic power, which has not been seen in this world since the time of the Christ."

Kathryn smoothed my brow, gave me a kiss and said, "I am just tickled pink that I get to share it with you."

I smiled, hooked my arm in hers and said, "Kathryn Bailey, welcome to Washington."

Day 41

For the second time in three days, the smell of freshly brewed coffee tickled my nostrils as I awoke. I wondered if Kathryn was going to make this a regular morning ritual. I could get used it.

Opening my eyes, I saw her sleeping next to me. When I turned, there was Lydia looking fresh as a daisy in her dressing gown, smiling at me. She asked me, "Did you remember that you had an 11 a.m. pick up at the airport?"

I yawned. "What time is it?"

"A little past nine."

Kathryn must have heard us talking because she groggily murmured "Good morning" to both of us.

Lydia asked her, "How do you take your coffee?"

"With a little sugar and a lot of milk."

"Would Half and Half do?" When Kathryn nodded affirmatively, Lydia continued, "Don't you guys expect this service every day because it's not part of my job description. Now, you two have got to get a move on or that poor little girl will have no one to meet her when she arrives. Brett, why don't you take my car? I don't think the three of you will fit in the Jaguar. Or, maybe Kathryn and I could go together and you can catch up on that pile of paper work I left on your desk."

"That sounds good to me," I said and looked at Kathryn to see if she was game.

Kathryn smiled and, giving Lydia a wink, said, "Sure. It'll be fun to compare notes."

Leaving, my trusty assistant said, "I'm getting dressed. I'll be out front at 10:15 sharp.

After we finished our coffee, Kathryn took a shower and slipped on a pair of jeans, a tee shirt, and a lavender wool pullover. She completed her by now familiar casual look with a pair of tennis shoes.

I donned a similar outfit, except my sweater was rust colored. As I put on the new Italian shoes that Kelly had bought for me, I thought, *Now would be a good time to call my favorite defrocked nun.*

I put the cell phone on speaker, so that Kathryn could participate in our conversation. Kelly's voice was bright and cheerful. "Brett Tempest, I am so glad that you arrived safe and sound in D.C. I have some good news for you."

"And what would that be, Miss Kelly?"

"I sold the house!"

"That's wonderful!"

"I need to know where to send the furniture. Also, would you like that big old bed?"

"I think it will be too big for any of the bedrooms in my Durham house."

At that point Kathryn broke in, "Oh Brett, can't we find room for that wonderful bed? I loved sleeping on that silk football field."

Kelly responded, "I could have it disassembled and shipped out with the rest of the stuff." She paused and added, "You want Aunt June's Fiestaware, too?"

"You bet!'" I said excitedly. "And the Bakelite flatware as well, if you don't mind."

"You got it. By the way, I will be in Washington within two or three days at the outset. How does that sound, Mr. Tempest?"

"We can't wait to have you here with us."

After we said our good-byes, Kathryn and I headed downstairs. Lydia, with British punctuality, was double parked in front of the house at exactly 10:15. She lowered the window of her black Volvo station wagon and held out a handmade sign with "Michelle Jenkins" written in giant letters. I gave her the thumbs up as Kathryn got in on the other side. Lydia took off at her usual brisk pace, acquired from years of driving in London. I figured that they would be across the bridge and at the airport before I had finished my second cup of coffee.

I moseyed into the wood paneled office. The massive, walnut partners' desk Lydia and I shared sat in the center of the room with two matching, dark, wine colored leather chairs on either side. I sat down and tackled the pile of paper work that needed my attention. An hour later I had signed three letters of provenance and purchased two parking spaces in the parking lot of my bank, which was conveniently located just up the street. By the time Lydia got back from the airport, I had almost cleared my side of the desk of paperwork.

I heard the front door open, followed by a youthful voice saying uncertainly, "Boy, this is sure nicer than that old house boat down in New Orleans. I don't think I have ever seen a house this tall before."

Then Kathryn came into the office, ushering a young girl ahead of her. She was dressed in a dark blue and black, plaid wool skirt, a white Peter Pan blouse buttoned up to the neck, blue knee socks and black Oxford shoes. About 5'3" tall, she had bright blue eyes and dark red, shoulder length hair, the kind that flames in sunlight. Her face was covered with freckles. She still had boyishly slim hips and was just beginning to show the first signs of developing breasts. I knew in an instant that I would never let E. Buck Jenkins touch this child again.

I got up and said, "You must be Michelle. Welcome to my house. Let me show you where you are going to stay."

She looked at me with fearful eyes while I took her small leather suitcase and led the way to one of the guest rooms on the first floor.

Looking around at the crimson and white walls and decorations, she broke into the first smile since her arrival. With eyes sparkling, she asked, "Is this where I will be staying?"

I nodded and said, "Yes."

"This is the most beautiful room I have ever seen in my life!" she sputtered. "I love how everything matches, right down to the pillow-cases and shams. It even has a crimson skirt surrounding the bed!"

Michelle did not notice the five Rembrandt etchings in dark red, wooden frames, which hung in a row on the white wall opposite the queen sized bed. I made a mental note to explain their significance to her when the opportunity arose.

When she opened the closet, she gawked and said, "This will be the first clothes closet that I won't have to share with someone else."

Kathryn was so touched that her eyes misted and her lower lip started to quiver. I put my arm around her and drew her close.

Just then Lydia came in and announced in a loud voice, "With the new administration coming in, the traffic around the Hill is like a *Key Stone Cops* movie. I just watched one guy with Illinois tags crash right through a police barrier. That twit almost got himself shot."

Her brusque statement was a welcome bit of comic relief and al-lowed Kathryn to gather herself.

While she dabbed her eyes, Lydia gave me one of her looks and said quietly, "Brett, we need to talk!"

I knew that tone of voice brooked no argument. I told Kathryn, "I need some time. Would you take a walk with Michelle and show her the big-ass library up the street?"

"You mean the Library of Congress?" Kathryn said, giving me one of her raised eyebrows looks.

I mouthed, "Please."

She nodded in understanding and said, "Come, Michelle, I want to show you something."

After they left the house, Lydia and I went up to the kitchen and sat down. She leaned forward, rested her elbows on the table, put her chin on her hands and said, "Now tell me everything."

As I related my amazing story, omitting nothing, her expressions changed from mild scoffing to doubt to incredulity. When I ventured into the deeper regions of my metaphysical experiences, I could tell I was about to lose her regard and trust in my mental faculties, so I said, "Hold on a second."

I quickly went upstairs, retrieved Sister Mary Alice's letter and handed it to her. Lydia's tightened face relaxed as she read. By the time she got to the end, tears welled up in her eyes.

What Lydia said next took me by surprise. "Brett, from the way you described Kelly Michelle, I realized that as a young girl she and I could have been twin sisters. I'll have to dig up some of the old photographs of myself when I was around her age and see what you think."

She came over to me and kissed me tenderly. Then she held my face between her hands, looked at me in a way I had never seen from her before and said, "I am yours to do with as you wish and I will never again doubt your words. Brett Tempest, I love you and have loved you from the first day we met in that wonderful little chapel at Georgetown University. Now, what can I do to make this journey of yours easier for you?"

I answered, "Lydia, I need your strength and fortitude with me always. I know and have known that you are a major part of this miracle. Please don't stop loving me, as love is the well from which I draw my strength. I must warn you, though, we will come under attack from every direction, for people can't let go of the status quo, even if it is poisoning them."

Suddenly, Lydia screamed and pointed to the letter lying on the table. The script was fading until it had completely disappeared, leaving a blank, white sheet of paper.

Stunned, Lydia said, "All that is left now, is your word."

I felt momentarily at sea, overwhelmed by waves of anxiety washing over me. Trying to find an anchor to the so-called, real world, I asked Lydia, "Would you take care of getting Jenny Jenkins out of the clutches of Reverend Jenkins and get her to Durham as soon as possible?"

I realized that she felt much the same about Jenny's situation as I did when her eyes burned with fierce intensity. "I will," she said with steel determination in her voice.

After she'd left, I picked up the mysterious paper and turned it over. It was just as empty on the other side. Had it been written using some kind of disappearing ink? Considering everything that had happened, I didn't think so.

Remembering that I had a phone number for Sister Mary Alice, I pulled my wallet from my back pocket and extracted the yellow Post-it she had given me. It was a wasted exercise. The scrap of paper was now blank on both sides, too!

I sat trying to regain my equilibrium when Kathryn and Michelle returned from their brief excursion, wide-eyed and excited. Kathryn exclaimed, "I had no idea the inside of the library would be so big."

"Yes," I commented, "it contains not only the largest collection of books in the world but also some beautiful works of art."

Kathryn asked, "Do you know who painted the wonderful mural of the seated woman between the two window arches?"

"As a matter of fact, I do. That mural is called 'Erotica' and was painted by Randolph Barse. But I love the mosaic 'Minerva of Peace' by Elihu Vedder even more."

Michelle wrinkled her forehead and asked, "How do you know about all this stuff?"

I replied, "I like to read and do research on things that intrigue me, and that building and everything in it is one of my great loves. I visit it all the time. It is a true Phoenix rising from the ashes. You see, in the War of 1812, when the British burnt down the Capitol building, they destroyed our original national library of more than 3000 books housed there. Thomas Jefferson offered his entire personal library of over 6000 volumes, at the time the largest collection in the United States, to replace it. So in an odd way the British, by burning down the Capitol, were responsible for creating a new, even bigger library. I can tell you about another great building here on Capitol Hill if you –"

But Kathryn raised her hands and interrupted, "Enough, enough! I'm starving already and I know our little friend is too, aren't you, Michelle?"

"You bet, I love this city and don't ever want to leave it."

I called down to Lydia, "We're going to *B. Smith's*. You have the only car that will fit us all in!"

Her laughter echoed from below. Then she shouted, "Does that mean that I am the designated driver again?"

"No, my love, I'll be doing the driving, unless we call a cab."

Kathryn said, "Let's take a cab. That way we can really let our hair down!"

I threw up my hands in mock surrender. "Okay, Lydia, you heard her!"

"Aye, aye, boss," came the cheeky reply from below.

By the time we got ready, a Diamond Cab pulled up at the curb outside and took all of us to *B. Smith's* in Union Station. With the presidential seal on display over the arched doorway and the stately sconces in small alcoves in the marble walls, the place quite possibly was the most elegant dining room in all of America!

Awestruck, Michelle looked around the towering ceilings and grand archways and asked, "Who is B. Smith?"

I said, smiling, "Why don't we save that explanation for dessert."

I looked over the menu and ordered one of Chef James Paige's specialties, "the Swamp Thang," a combination of mixed seafood over southern style greens in a tangy mustard seafood sauce. Lydia, having eaten here many times before, did not bother with the menu and asked for black-eyed pea soup as an appetizer and the grilled lamb chops with mint-flavored jus as her main course. Kathryn went with the Maryland crab soup and an entree of apple roasted BBQ ribs in a sweet and spicy sauce with red beans and rice.

When Michelle looked at me for advice, I ordered her a starter of catfish fingers in a Guinness tartar sauce, roasted free-range chicken with sautéed spinach, and macaroni and cheese on the side.

For drinks, I selected two bottles of a Duckhorn Decoy Meritage along with two bottles of Pellegrino.

Although disappointed that there was no Dr. Pepper, Michelle gamely said, "I'll be fine with 'the bubbly stuff.'"

During dinner Kathryn and Lydia kept looking at Michelle, sizing her up to see if she belonged in our budding group. I already knew the answer.

Finally Lydia said, "As beautiful as Michelle is, she does not look the way Brett described the first Kelly Porter. What do you think, Kathryn?"

"Well, I see some similarities, but you are right, Lydia. She does not match the vision Brett described her to me."

At first Michelle fidgeted in her chair much like a dancer confined to a wheelchair. But as the two women continued to scrutinize her, she retreated like a turtle disappearing into her shell.

Her relief was palpable when I said, "Why don't we talk about this esoteric stuff when we get home?"

Then I ordered two desserts for us to split—a white chocolate mousse cake and a dark chocolate cake—and launched into an explanation to Michelle's earlier question.

"B. Smith was one of the most admired black models in the United States. Her eyes were like magnets and worked so well in magazines that she was in demand for over fifteen years. Then she started this restaurant. Sadly, in recent years B. has started to lose her thoughts a bit and will soon close this great venue."

Michelle started to mist-up and asked, "Why would God want to hurt her like that?"

"God has nothing to do with the onset of Alzheimer's. It's chemical in nature and happens to some people when they get older."

Michelle started to rub her temples until Lydia took her right hand in hers and pulled it softly back to her lap.

Stuffed to the gills, we took a taxi back to the house. On the short ride home, Michelle who was riding up front, turned around and told us, "That restaurant is the prettiest place that I have ever been to or even seen in the movies. And I just know that B. Smith is going to be all right."

I loved her innocence and honesty and resolved again to protect her from harm.

After the three of us tucked Michelle into her bed, we decided to have a nightcap up in my bedroom.

Lydia said, "I want to change into something a little more comfortable. I'll meet you upstairs."

I stopped at the wine and liquor closet in the kitchen and picked up a bottle of Grand Marnier and three large snifter glasses, while Kathryn continued up the stairs to the bedroom. When I got there, I found her in naked repose in the middle of the bed. Her eyes danced with desire and she beckoned me with a curling forefinger.

In a sultry voice she said, "We have a few minutes before Lydia returns, so come here and make love to me. I have wanted you inside me all day."

As tempting as her offer was, I found the strength to decline and poured three glasses of the orange tinged liquid instead.

Then I sat down on the soft seat by the bed nearest to Kathryn. Looking at her loveliness, I asked, "How come you are not wearing your beautiful jeweled barrette tonight?"

Her answer sent a chill running through my body. "Brett darling, that piece just up and disappeared from my jewelry box. I have looked high and low for it for five days now, with no luck. I can't imagine what could have happened to it."

At that moment Lydia called up to our room, "I'm tired and going to bed. I'll see you in the morning. Good night."

We spent the next two hours in the softest caresses of lovemaking I had ever experienced.

At some point, Kathryn whispered, "Brett darling, why couldn't I be the one to carry your child?"

She repeated this question two more times.

I finally told her, "Kelly is carrying our child of Light because we are all connected in the spirit. But, Kathryn, you are my chosen one. You are the woman I want as my wife."

Hearing that, Kathryn's reserve fell away and she started to laugh and cry uncontrollably. As I tried to comfort her, I felt my own fears rise up, questioning if I was strong enough to perform the cosmic tasks I had been given, despite my human frailty. I did not share this with Kathryn, however, because I knew she needed me to be the tower of strength for her at this moment.

When we finally regained control, she said, "Brett, I love you with all my heart and deep within my soul, but you are here for the world and not just me. What happens in marriage is that one gets lost in the other's intrigues and insecurities and I don't want that to happen to our love. You now have Lydia and Kelly as well as me, and the three of us have become one. Each one of us loves you with all of our hearts. I believe that all three of us are on this earth to take care of you and fulfill your needs. I am thrilled that you asked me to marry you, but that would take away, or at least tarnish, what Kelly and Lydia feel for you. So, my love, if there is to be a marriage, then let it be with all of us so that the circle will be complete."

Day 42

When I awoke the next morning, I was alone in the bed. I showered, dressed and followed the tantalizing aromas downstairs into the kitchen. There I found Kathryn, Lydia and Michelle huddled in conversation at the breakfast table.

When she saw me Michelle stood up, still wearing her Poo Bear pajamas, and came into my arms. "Mr. Tempest," she said. "I just heard that you are the father of a child who will grow up to become the new Savior and that I will be part of this wonderful experience. Mr. Tempest, I love you with all my heart and will serve you and the baby until I die."

I backed up a step and looked deeply into her eyes. In a flash, I saw her life from conception in the back of an old church right up until this moment. I felt her confusion and shame when her corrupt father placed his tobacco stained fingers into her still pure vagina. I felt her pain as she watched in horror the beatings and burnings he performed on her mother. I experienced her joy at being part of the new life to come. And finally, I felt her unconditional love for her new family. I knew that Michelle and her mother were to become the record keepers of the events and words of the new millennium.

I placed my hand on Michelle's chest and felt the fire of love transfer to her from my spirit and consume her being in a communion with eternity.

Shortly after I finished breakfast the telephone rang. Lydia answered and handed me the receiver. It was Jenny. She was close to

Durham but didn't know how to get to my house and no way of getting inside without a key.

While I gave her directions and told her where the spare key was hidden, Michelle was dancing and bouncing up and down around me, unable to contain herself. When I held the phone out to her, she grabbed it like an eager panther cub lunging for meat. Then she told Jenny everything that had happened since her arrival. She finished by saying, "We are now children of the Light and our circle will never be broken."

Lydia took the phone and informed Jenny about the financial arrangements that she had made for her. Then she passed it back to me and I said, "I'll be bringing Michelle to Durham today. We'll be leaving in the next hour or so."

After I hung up, I noticed Michelle looking uncertain. Part of her yearned to be reunited with her mother, but another part did not want to give up her new room and lifestyle.

I assured her, "You will always have your room here and you will always have your own room in Durham. So, you are now a two-home girl. What do you think of that?"

Her beaming face was a better answer than any words she could have uttered.

I had first thought of taking Michelle to Durham in the Jaguar, but then it occurred to me that it might be my last opportunity to take a road trip on the *Valkyrie*. My world was undergoing such radical changes that soon my time would no longer be my own.

Kathryn helped Michelle get dressed in her new leathers, which were a bit large for her slight frame but would do fine for the 225-mile trip.

Lydia told Michelle, "You looked pretty damned cute in those exotic Italian leathers." She took the girl in her arms and gave her a big hug and kiss good-bye. Then, she turned to me, gave me a soft kiss and whispered, "Drive safely."

Kathryn helped us pack the bike and then wrapped her arms around me. "Promise me you'll ride with the angels and come back soon."

I mounted the black and yellow *Valkyrie* and waited for Michelle to climb aboard. Once she was firmly ensconced in back of me, I started the big bike and pulled out of the alley with a roar, heading south on Third Street. Michelle gripped my leathers as if hanging on for dear life, but after we crossed the Potomac River and joined the I-95 south, she started to relax and put her arms lightly around my hips. When we reached Fredericksburg, Virginia, I pulled into a rest area to let Michelle stretch her legs and use the restroom.

As I watched her walk to the one-story building, one of her thoughts came into clear focus in my mind: *I hope he doesn't think that I am one of these stupid women that has to pee every ten minutes.*

I chuckled, enjoying her girlish concerns, a mixture of worry and judgmental opinions. But when I saw her walking towards me with her red hair catching the early afternoon light, she looked like an angel. I liked what I was seeing and knew that she would grow into a fine woman.

Once we reached Petersburg, Virginia, we joined Interstate 85. Heading west we encountered even less traffic and rode through a corridor of trees that lasted all the way to Durham. We drove right to my house on Broad Street where we found Jenny's rental Buick in the small driveway that led to the garage. I drove the motorcycle next to her car and shut off the engine

As we walked to the front door, I felt Michelle getting nervous in anticipation of seeing her mother. Before I could get my key in the lock, Jenny opened it with a huge smile on her face. Michelle dropped her saddlebag and ran into her arms. It was heart-warming to witness them come together like two lost souls who hadn't expected to see each other for a long time.

While they were getting to know each other again, I unloaded our gear and brought it into the house.

The place was in the first stages of remodeling. The walls needed painting and decorating. Kelly's furniture hadn't arrived yet and the rooms looked empty and uninviting. Once everything was finished, including the kitchen and bathroom upgrades, and fully furnished, I imagined this 30-year-old home would look like a million bucks.

Jenny came up behind me, interrupting my reverie, and said, "I am so glad to see you. Thank you for letting me stay here. It means the world to me and Michelle."

I acknowledged her gratitude with a gentle nod and said, "You know, I have plans for you and Michelle. I want to sit down and share them with you soon."

Just then Michelle walked up to me and said, "I'm hungry!" Her overly demanding tone of voice seemed to echo for me from another dimension.

"That's a good idea, but I think I cleaned out the refrigerator before I left for my trip," I said. "Why don't I pick us up a little something to eat and bring it back to the house?"

I called *Cinelli's Restaurant*, which was just down on Broad Street, and ordered two large New York style pizzas with sausage and mushrooms. Then I went to my bedroom and ditched the leathers in favor of my old standby clothes—jeans, tennis shoes, button down shirt and a leather jacket. I figured it was a good time to give the car parked in my garage its first run in some time and let a mother and daughter have their first face-to-face talk in over a month.

Before I left on my big cross country trip I had put a trickle battery charger on my perfectly restored, red 1960 MGB roadster and she started right up. It felt good tooling around this college town again. I loved being in Durham ever since I had been an undergraduate at Duke University back in the early 1980s. The place was close enough to D.C. that it took less than four hours to escape the hustle and bustle of the big city for a more relaxed atmosphere.

The restaurant was less than a mile from my house and I knew I would get there long before the pizzas were ready. I decided to take a little spin down Ninth Street to check out the crowd of students, yuppies and assorted pseudo bohemians that always congregated at the restaurants and shops. I wondered if my new spiritual perspective would change my feelings and was glad that I still enjoyed the sight of the colorful denizens that gave university environments their special, unique atmosphere.

My timing for getting to *Cinelli's* was perfect and I walked out with my two pies inside of a minute.

Back at home, the two starving females made the first pizza disappear in less time than it takes to tie one's shoes.

By my third slice I was able to concentrate a little more on Jenny Jenkins. Now that she was out from under E. Buck Jenkins's control, she seemed less tense. Her voice was mellifluous and she was no longer afraid to show her soft femininity. After a few seconds of my scrutiny she became self-conscious, however, and reverted to her former self. Perhaps she felt I was sizing her up to see if I meant to keep her as a member of my small group and found her wanting.

Her insecurities floated across the table in the form of a question, "Brett, I'm used goods. Do you really want me in your spiritual circle after what I have been through."

I tried to reassure her, "How could I not want a fine woman like you to lend her talents and knowledge to help get my message out?"

"Oh, Brett, do you really mean that? If you do, there are many things I can do to help you realize your mission, I just know it."

Michelle piped in, "Mom was the one who made it all work while Dad sat on his ass or was out chasing loose women. I hope he dies for what he did to Mom and me!"

Jenny was taken aback by her daughter's vehemence and was about to chide her, but I held up my hand and said, "You have every right to be angry, Michelle, I would feel the same way in your place."

I was pleased to see her tense shoulders and tight lips relax.

I got up from the table, fetched a bottle of Jack Daniels and, holding it up, asked Jenny, "Would you like to join me in a little libation?"

She looked at me for a long moment and said, "It has been a while since I had a drink with a man. But yes, I would love to have a one, or even two, with you."

Michelle yawned and asked, "Where am I going to be sleeping tonight?"

"Let me show you."

I led her down the hall to one of the bedrooms she would occupy. She sighed in disappointment when she saw the minimalist furnishings.

On the spur of the moment, I brought her to my bedroom and set her up in front of the television with the other pizza.

"Eat what you want and save the rest for breakfast."

Michelle smiled at me and said, "Even though this place isn't as nice as the house in Washington, I know I will love it here." Then she gave me a big hug.

By the time I got back to the kitchen, Jenny had cleared the table.

"Why don't we retire to the living room and enjoy our drinks with a little music," I offered.

I poured us two glasses of bourbon and found a CD of Paul Simon's *Graceland*, which always raised my spirits. When she heard the first notes of, "The Boy in the Bubble," Jenny started to tap her foot and said, "This is one of my favorite albums. How did you know to put this on?"

"I didn't. It just happens to be one of my all time favorite albums, too."

We touched glasses and drank to Paul Simon and all the joy he has brought to this world. "When I was young, his song 'Kodachrome' was influential in getting me interested in photography," I explained.

Jenny didn't seem to follow what I was saying. I noticed that she was wearing one of her long, dark dresses that did nothing for her appearance. So I asked, "Why do you wear those old fashioned dresses when you have a lovely, slim figure and should be proud to show it off?"

She blushed and said, "Buck picked out my clothes for me. He said that the Lord did not want to see me in clothes that aroused men. He would not let me wear anything outside the home that might be considered provocative by his parishioners; but in the bedroom, he had me dress in all kinds of kinky outfits."

"Well, you're finished with that kind of hypocritical, Puritan nonsense. It's time to start to be proud of what God has given to you and let your body breathe again. I want you to get rid of all of your clothes. Everything has to go, down to your socks and underwear. Tomorrow you will buy yourself and Michelle new clothes. You can choose what you want to wear. Don't worry about money. Lydia will take care of it."

Jenny lost her composure and started to cry—great, heaving sobs of release.

I put my arm around her shoulder until she regained control. Looking at her intently, I said, "Jenny, my love, you are now free to be who you always wanted to be. I see in you a woman who loves life and has been stifled for so long you have forgotten how to have fun."

She nodded, her face looking solemn and spent.

I stood up and offered her my hand. "Well, then I think it's time for you and me to dance."

She lifted her tear-stained face, smiled and said, "I would love to dance with you Mr. Tempest."

Just then "Crazy Love, Vol. II" was just starting to play. I pulled Jenny to her feet. I held her close and we started to sway to the rhythms of the song.

Jenny took a step back, unbuttoned the first few buttons of her grandmotherly dress, pulled her skirt above her knees and started to skip around the room in a carefree and lighthearted manner. The music and our vibrations beckoned to Michelle in my bedroom. She suddenly appeared in the doorway. Her eyes lit up and she clapped her hands. Then she skipped over to her mother and the two of them danced around me until the end of the album.

240 – Michael Judge

We all ended up on the sofa together, laughing at nothing and everything. I knew at that moment that I had just freed the genie from the bottle. These two really were fun loving souls, who needed to play and enjoy life.

While Jenny took our glasses to get a refill, I said to Michelle, "Prepare yourself. Tomorrow morning you and your mom are going shopping for a whole new wardrobe for both of you."

Her eyes sparkled with joy and she looked as a happy 13-year-old should. She slid across the sofa and gave me a kiss on the forehead. Releasing her from the bonds of her father's perversions had taken only a matter of days. Now it was time to work some magic on her mother.

I could tell that Michelle was quite exhausted beneath the euphoria of her newfound freedom. So when Jenny returned, I said, "It's time for Michelle to go to sleep."

She didn't protest much when her mom and I took her to her room and tucked her into bed. I knew that she would be asleep by the time we turned off the light.

When we got back to the living room and our drinks, Jenny said, "I will always remember this night. I'll be yours forever." She took a sip and continued with a new found sense of serenity, "I don't need to be married ever again. You have shown me that I can be free and I want you to know that you are all that I need in my life. Michelle and I will always be here for you. When I am with you, Brett, I don't hurt anymore."

I said, "Kelly has conceived and will need you to be there for the child."

"Brett, what are you saying? I am down here and she is up in Washington. How can I help with the child from here?"

"You will go where I need you to go. Sometimes it will be in Washington and sometimes here in Durham. I want you to start to plan for a large gathering of people so I can give them the same hope that I have given you and Michelle."

In a most earnest manner, Jenny said, "Brett, I will do everything I can. You must know that I have not stopped thinking about you since that night at the revival. Did you know that before I left Tennessee people wanted to know where they could hear you preach?"

"Jenny, I am not a preacher, I am a messenger who has come back to this Earth to turn on the Light. You must tell the people that our meetings are not about what is already written, but about what will soon be a new gospel. I feel that you and Michelle are the ones who will record what our Creator wants me to tell his children. Right at this instant, I am here to tell you, Jenny Jenkins, that the only sin you can commit is the sin of fear. I know the things that so-called preacher made you do and the pain you suffered from those terrible acts of perversion, but I will now protect you and your daughter from him. You two are now free and pure in the eyes of the Creator."

I had given her a lot to digest and watched as she accepted it all slowly. When her mind radiated with clarity, I got up and I said, "Now I want to take a bath and go to bed so I can get an early start to go back to D.C."

Jenny stopped me and said, "I will draw your bath and wash your body, and then it will be my pleasure to tuck you into your bed."

True to her word, she let the water run into the tub. Then she removed her ugly dress, and standing in her white cotton underwear, watched as I stepped over the side of the tub and slid into the warm water. She poured my almond scented, pure Castile liquid soap onto a damp washcloth and started to wash me as she would wash a baby.

By the time she finished every inch of my skin was cleansed. I emerged from the tub dripping and Jenny dried me with a large bath towel. Then she led me by the hand to my bed. When she had pulled the covers up to my neck, she leaned over me and kissed me so tenderly that it felt like a cloud had touched my lips.

I heard her whisper in my ear, "I love you today and I will love you tomorrow and I will love you to the end of days."

I closed my eyes and just before I started to float in dreams, I was relieved to visualize Kelly and Kathryn walking through my house in Washington, safe and sound.

Day 43

I would have liked to get an early start, but I knew that it would be sometime in the afternoon before I could leave to go back to Capitol Hill. There was simply too much to do—returning the rental car; getting a new car for Jenny and Michelle; and of course, shopping for new clothes.

When Michelle heard about my grand plan, she squealed with delight and asked, "When are we going to be doing all of that?"

I told her, "First, the good news. We are going to Whole Foods and put you guys on my account so you can get some good organic food in your stomachs. The bad news: Someone has to stay home because my MGB only has two bucket seats, so who goes and who stays for the food trip?"

Michelle opted to stay and start to clean her new room.

Jenny threw a light jacket over her jeans and sweatshirt and was ready to go in a flash. We decided to return the rental first, get groceries and finally buy a car. Then we would drop off the food and pick up Michelle to shop for clothes. It was a lot to accomplish, but we got a good start. We managed to check off the first two items on our list in just under an hour. Buying a car for Jenny and Michelle took a little longer, since the first two car lots did not have what I was looking for.

I finally found the perfect vehicle for them, a 2008 Chrysler Pacifica Wagon, big enough to haul all kinds of stuff, yet easy to maneuver around town. It was painted a deep wine red color and trimmed out in tan leather with all the right options and had low mileage to boot.

I negotiated what I thought was a good deal and put it on my American Express card. Jenny followed me home in her new car and whenever I looked in my rear view mirror, I could see her smiling.

Michelle must have been waiting for us by the window because she bolted out from the front door just as we entered the driveway. She ran right by the Pacifica and jumped into the MG. Then she asked, "When will you take me for a ride in your great red sports car?"

"Do you like your mother's new car?"

"Everybody has one of those. Your car is sexy."

"Maybe after we go shopping we will take it for a little spin."

Satisfied, she slid out of my car and jumped into the Pacifica. For a while I watched her and Jenny try to figure out how everything worked. Then I went inside and called my brother in Washington.

I worked out the details of getting Jenny and Michelle new identities without any hassle from Tommy. In fact, when he heard some of the unpleasant details and that their tormentor was a preacher involved, he went ballistic, ranting on about the hypocrisy, destructiveness and horrors of organized religion.

When he had calmed down somewhat, he said, "Don't worry. I will have those two buried so deep that nobody will be able to find them."

Then he added something that sent a chill through me, "People like Buck, whatever the fuck his name is, should not be left to stain this Earth. I might just go down to Tennessee and pay him a visit myself."

I knew my brother well enough that, once he'd made up his mind, nothing could dissuade him. So I just said, "Thank you. I'll have to tell you in private what an incredible experience I've been through."

We agreed to try and meet next week at our favorite place, the *Off the Record* bar in the Hay Adams Hotel, which fronted 16th Street just across from Lafayette Park and provided D.C.'s best view of the White House and the Washington Monument.

Tommy ended the call, saying, "By then I should have the paper work ready. Drinks will be on you, little brother."

The next call was to my Washington house and Lydia answered. "Kelly arrived today."

"How is she?"

"Fine, although she brought some bad news with her. Sister Mary Alice passed away the day before yesterday."

She sighed and continued, "I am sad for you. I know she meant a great deal to you. Is there anything you want me to do, like sending flowers?"

I was about to give Lydia the go ahead when I realized deep in my mind that it would not be necessary. "There is nothing to be done." I said. "I believe that Mary Alice completed her work on this Earth and has gone home."

Lydia must have heard the sadness in my voice because she tried to lighten things up by changing the subject. "Brett, have you ever noticed how Kathryn can string more sentences together than a tobacco auctioneer on speed?"

"Yes, Lydia, she is a real motor mouth," I replied and laughed. "But you've got to love her, she is unique in the entire world."

"Actually, one of the nice things about your being gone is that she and I have grown closer," Lydia volunteered. "But when are you coming home? I need your energy and strength."

"Sometime later this evening or mid-morning tomorrow, depending on how my shopping excursion with Jenny and Michelle goes."

I could sense Lydia's relief when she said, "Oh good. You know, I can almost feel the baby in Kelly's stomach." Then she added in a voice tinged with caution and desire, "Brett, I would love to give birth to one of your babies. Good-bye."

She hung up before I could formulate an answer. My mind was spinning and I grabbed a quick shot of whiskey to calm my nerves and hammering heart. Lydia's statement had plunged me into a whirlpool of turmoil and confusion and it took me a while to regain my equilibrium.

When I went outside Jenny was behind the wheel and Michelle had staked her claim to the front seat, so I got in back and we were off on the great clothes safari. Jenny was a great driver and had no trouble following my directions to the Northgate Mall.

When we got there, I turned them loose with one of my credit cards and I found a nice quiet spot to sit and gather my thoughts about Lydia Gordon's revelation. I settled on a little bench near the entrance close to where we parked, closed my eyes and let the afternoon sun bathe my face while considering Lydia's place in our circle.

In the middle of my reverie Michelle's face entered my mind along with her thoughts and mental images. I had to smile at the concerns of a young, still innocent young girl: *God, please make Brett love my new clothes, I want him to think that I am the prettiest of all. I will just die, if he hates these dresses and pants...I know he will really like my green Mickey Mouse sweatshirt. I would love to go to Disney World with Brett....*

Suddenly, Michelle's image flipped and I saw Kelly Michelle Tempest skipping out of the *Planet Blue* boutique in Malibu! An instant later the image jumped back to Michelle and then skipped back and forth until I felt lost and no longer certain where I was.

Then I heard Michelle calling out to me. I opened my eyes expecting her to be standing right next to me, but she was not there. When I looked around, I saw her about 50 yards away, skipping along next to her mother and swinging a rather large shopping bag. I knew then that my telepathic power was also a gateway to other dimensions of reality. I wondered what it would further teach me about my mission.

On the way out of the mall, Michelle sat in back with me and announced, "I want to model all my new clothes for you."

I knew I had to disappoint her and said, "I'd love to see them, but I need to get back to D.C. while there is still some light left."

Michelle started to tear-up. Suddenly, her emotions burst and poured out of her. "I love you so much for everything that you have done for us," she sobbed. "Please, please never leave us, and I know we will never leave you."

I took her hand and pulled her gently to my chest and in a soothing voice said, "I already know that the two of you will be with me until the end of time, but it sure feels good to hear it coming from you." I decided to change the mood by adding, "Michelle, you will look so beautiful in your Mickey Mouse sweatshirt. I hope you'll be wearing it when I see you again."

Her eyes became big as saucers. "How did you know that I–?"

I laughed and said, "I just do."

Not another word was said until we reached home, but I could read their thoughts of wonderment and reverence.

After heartfelt good-byes, I got back on my *Valkyrie* and headed to D.C. The ride was uneventful and gave me a chance to get ready for the final leg of my journey.

Just before I reached the Virginia border, I had a vision that unraveled the mystery of Sister Mary Alice. I saw her as an incorporeal being in another dimension and realized that she had taken her earthly form to be a messenger for the Creator of Light. I also understood that the entity known as Mary Alice and I would someday cross paths again in the great radiant cosmos and that eventually we would become one in the Master's Light.

I wondered what adventures and challenges I would face until then and felt confident and unafraid. Mary Alice's energy stayed with me all the way to Washington.

I decided to enter the city via Chain Bridge where the Potomac is at its most beautiful and mighty. Cresting waves crashed against the huge boulders around the supports, spraying white foam far into the air, but I felt calm.

I was almost across the bridge when the last words uttered by Mary Alice came to me again, "Blessed One, there is another that awaits you by a mighty river and she will bear half of the whole and the Two will become One." All of a sudden I understood their meaning with searing clarity.

When I got to the house and walked in through the back door, I was greeted by the three women ordained to share my destiny. Smiling, they blocked me from going beyond the foyer. Kathryn put a blindfold over my eyes and they gently guided me upstairs to the second story. When we arrived at what I figured was the formal living room, they pulled to a stop and restored my vision to me.

I was awestruck. In the corner of the room stood the Giacometti Cross glowing in light. Its luminous presence in my house reached to the core of my being and made me tremble with wonder and reverence. As my eyes found the etched numbers "2016" in the middle of the bronze cross section, I knew that they represented my epitaph.

Kathryn followed my eyes and felt my emotion. She sidled over to me, put her lips to my ear and whispered, "I will love you until the end of the past and the birth of the future."

I contemplated the sculpture for some time in silence. Then I turned to Kelly. She looked fresh and wonderful. I hugged her and she let me know by the way she molded her body to mine how good it made her feel to finally be home.

The telephone rang before I could get to Lydia. As she left the room to get it, Kathryn came to me again for an affectionate embrace and I yielded to her soft comforting.

I heard Lydia call out, "Kelly, it's for you."

Then she was back in the room and came into my arms. Breathing softly into my ear she murmured "Now I am yours to keep."

Then she kissed me and beckoned Kathryn to join us. As she settled into our loving embrace, a sigh escaped her.

Kelly came back into the room with a look of shock and bewilderment on her face. In unison we asked, "What is wrong?"

Stuttering a bit, she said, "That call was from Madelyn Karri. Sister Mary Alice has disappeared from the hospital morgue. Now get this, nobody else at Christus Saint Michael's hospital has ever heard of Sister Mary Alice, and there was no record of her body ever being in the hospital's morgue."

I smiled reassuringly at her and said for the benefit of all, "Sister Mary Alice was a messenger from another reality. When her job was finished here, she simply returned home. Her words disappeared from that letter at the exact time that she left us. There is no need to fret about any of this. It will all become clear to you in the near future. In fact, you will continue to communicate with her from time to time."

They seemed to accept my explanation, so I suggested, "I think it's time for a little refreshment."

Kathryn responded, "I think we should all go upstairs to the master's bedroom. Why don't Lydia and I gather everything we need?"

When Kelly and I got there, she said, "I love this house and this painting, Brett. Is that a real Renoir or great copy? I've never seen anything like it outside a museum. In the convent we had Sister Wendy's *History of Art* book, but the plates didn't show the intricacies I see here in your painting."

I chuckled and said, "That book is one of my favorites. But to answer your question. If you mean 'real' as in 'not a fake,' then yes it is a real Renoir. But if you mean 'Is it real?' you would have to ask Sister Mary Alice."

Still gazing at the painting, Kelly asked, "Do you think I'll look like this or more like a Rubenesque nude later in my pregnancy?"

I replied, "No matter what your shape, you will always be a raving beauty to me."

With a radiant smile Kelly came back into to my arms.

I said, "I want to take a shower and clean off the road dust off my leathers."

Kelly helped me take off my boots. After four hours on the road, the shower felt heavenly and I emerged from the warm spray clean and

250 – Michael Judge

refreshed. I slipped into a thick Turkish robe trimmed in deep blue with gold piping and slid my feet into a pair of matching slippers.

I had no sooner walked through the door than Lydia put a tumbler of Blanton's in my hand and said, "Welcome to your harem. It's bloody well time you came home to us. We were beginning to wonder where your loyalty was, weren't we, ladies?"

I decided to be a good sport and joined Kelly and Kathryn's laughter while gently pinching Lydia for trying to put me on the spot.

For the next hour we sipped our whiskeys—Kelly abstained because of her pregnancy—and talked about many things.

Then, out of the blue, Kathryn dropped a bombshell. "I was wondering when would be a good time and place for the four of us to come together in marriage. Since it would not be fair for Brett to marry just one of us, I feel that you should do the right thing and take all of us into a marriage circle. Now what do you think of that idea, Mr. Tempest?"

I swallowed hard before answering, "I think that before you ask me that you should check with the others how they feel about polygamy and breaking traditional laws?"

"Darling, I already have and we are all in agreement that we want to be your wives by your decree."

I put my hands on my hips and said, "Well, my lovelies, if that is your choice then so be it. But you know that I do not put credence in pieces of paper or religious or secular officials giving us permission to commit to one another."

Lydia said, "I think that we should commit to it right here and now and stop mucking about."

Kathryn and Kelly readily agreed. Then they turned towards me for instructions on how we should perform this ritual of the heart. I did not have to think long about what I had to do. I extended my hand to Kelly and gestured her to sit beside me.

She looked at me with her piercing eyes and said, "I am ready and thank you for choosing me first."

I took her hand and said, "I chose you, Kelly, because you have made a great commitment to our Circle of Light, and now I want to see if you have the same allegiance to me as a man as you have to me as a teacher of men."

Looking deeply into her essence and spirit, I encountered a curtain of darkness from her past lives. I saw her desire for women and lust directed towards me along with fear of rejection. But her strengths— passion and compassion—which coexisted with her newfound loyalty would easily open that veil and let in the new Light that would become her beacon into eternity. By agreeing to conceive life, she had satisfied the rules of Karma, thus setting her free! I saw the love she felt for me and became intoxicated by the many levels of adoration she wrapped around me, illuminating my own being.

I had to discover one more thing. Gently, I probed deeper into her psyche and found the answer to my unspoken question: Would she harbor resentment if another bore a second child? What came back was pure acceptance. Kelly knew that she was one with her Sisters of the Circle.

I kissed her moist mouth and said, "Thank you for the love you feel for me. Kelly Porter, will you marry me?"

She smiled sweetly and said, "Yes."

"I am glad."

Kelly got up, looked at Kathryn, then back to me and said, "Your Kathryn is also our Kathryn and she is the natural balance between Lydia and me."

Kathryn gave her a dazzling smile and came over to me. Her radiance shone brighter than a thousand suns. She found a comfortable place on my lap, ran her fingers through my hair and said, "You have made me the happiest person in the world."

I looked into her soft emerald-green eyes and replied, "I do not need to examine your mind and soul. I have known you for many eons and experienced countless lifetimes with you in preparation for this birth of Light. There is just one thing I want to know. Kathryn, darling, why did you create this marriage scenario when you and I decided not to get married?"

She twirled a lock of my hair around her finger and answered, "Sweetheart, the Circle of Light is far greater in the whole than any one individual. You and your appointment with the Divine are the only things that matter. The three of us are part of you, so why shouldn't we be as one and soar like a *Valkyrie*?" Then she added, mischievously, "Besides, where else are you going to find three good-looking broads willing to take care of your every need, and I mean every need, for the rest of your life?"

She gave my hair a playful tug and hopped off of my lap. Then she extended her hand to Lydia and led her to me.

Lydia was carrying what appeared to be a photo album. Her lithe body vibrated with barely contained energy. Yet she smiled at me cautiously as she sat down next to me like a piece of silk falling from the sky.

I understood her awkwardness and felt it myself—we were contemplating a huge change in our relationship. I took a deep breath, reached out for her free hand, and asked, "Are you absolutely sure about this?"

Her reply startled me. "My dearest, I have been yours since you first smiled at me that day we met in Georgetown. Now, I understand why God put me on this earth. My love for you has grown over the years from infatuation into a warm earthly affection, and now, all boundaries and restrictions are gone. Brett, I love you as a woman loves a man, I love you as a disciple loves a prophet, and finally, I love you as a helpmate loves a partner. You have come to make darkness crave the Light and I am part of your radiance, and that luminosity has turned my desire for you into God's desire for me."

She opened her silk wrapped photo album and presented it to me. I started to turn the pages from front to back looking at black and white pictures of Lydia from the time she was a baby to when she reached puberty. One caught my attention: Lydia standing by the sea, squinting into the sun. She could not have been more than 13 and looked exactly like Kelly Michelle Tempest. They were one and the same!

I put the album down, pulled her close to my heart and asked, "Lydia do you know why you are here?"

She answered me with the words of Sister Mary Alice "Blessed One, there is another that awaits for you by a mighty river and she will bear half of the whole and the Two will become One."

I put down the album and said, "We will keep it as a memento of your time on this earthly plane."

It was time to tell my loves who they were and what they meant, not just to me, but more importantly, to the world. I sat on the cushioned settee by the foot of my bed and beckoned to the women. They gathered around me, lounging comfortably on the bed and the settee. I could feel their collective breath bathing my skin like a soft, warm breeze and smelled their intoxicating beauty.

"It is time to reveal our joint history," I began. "Each of you and I, as well, have visited this planet before in other incarnations. All of us came to the Earth from an astral world to bestow love and happiness on a savage world. You three were the daughters of Zeus and Eurynome and collectively became known as the Three Graces. Your gift to mankind was joy, enchantment and elegance. You were inseparable and always acted as one. The early scribes sometimes placed you erroneously among the Muses, but you were not part of them. The wonderful thing you created with your combined energy was universal love. You were responsible for the great love shared by two of the earth's overlords, Eros and Aphrodite, often described as deities, which they were not. They were visitors from a more advanced civilization and seemed as gods to their less developed human cousins."

At this point Lydia interrupted, "Why did you say at the beginning that this is a joint history?"

"Lydia, in that incarnation I was known as Hephaestus and my gift to humanity was art in all of its manifestations. You might say that I was the carpenter of creativity. Today you see in Greece the remnants of those blessings. I chose Kathryn, who went by the name of Aglaia, to join me, for her energy was a conduit to deliver imagination to mankind. But since the three of you were as one, I mated with all of you as one. There was no difference as our love was a cauldron of energy that lit up the world around us."

Kelly asked. "What name did I use?"

"Your name was Euphrosyne and you, Lydia, were called Thalia. All of you look pretty much today as you did then."

Kathryn's question had more far-ranging implications. "Why did we leave Earth?"

"Mankind developed an ever-increasing feeling of self-entitlement, and that energy robbed us of our abilities to communicate in the purest sense of the word. Our powers were siphoned off even further by humans choosing greed over charity, lust over tenderness and power over humility. It tarnished our love for humanity. The Earth turned into a prison. Some of us simply returned to the place of our heritage, others stayed and intermingled with humankind trying desperately to foster change, but we failed. Eventually those who stayed lost their powers for good and were no longer able to cross into the fourth dimension."

Kelly's body melted into my side as she asked, "What happened to us?"

"Well, we went back home and on to other lives and places."

"Brett, what did we call our real home?"

"Eden."

They expelled a collective sigh.

My next revelation for the Graces was of a more earthly nature. I stood up and said, "This union we are about to form must be of an immaculate nature to become an example for our future disciples. Therefore, we must practice celibacy in our lives together with one great exception."

They started to fidget and their questions invaded my thoughts. I mustered my psychic strength and calmed their minds so they could absorb what I had to say.

"Sexual abstinence makes one depend on virtue and respect rather than climatic chills to magnetize the relationship. If we stay pure in our Circle, then we will be able to see clearly what help others will need. There will be no hidden agendas entering our Circle of Light by way of sexual desire.

Now to answer your most important shared question so far: Sister Mary Alice came here to deliver the proclamation that we were to bring into this world two babies, who together will become one. That is the meaning of her message 'And the Two shall become One.' I have seen clearly that Lydia is to carry the second child, and she will be the only exception to our rule of celibacy. The child created from the union with Lydia, will be a female. She and her brother together will have a joint power heretofore unknown on this Earth. Their giving of Light will lead mankind to a higher echelon, where wars, pestilence, greed, jealousy, lust and famine will only be known through history books. All human beings will once again mingle with their brothers and sisters from Eden and you, my Graces, will once again dance to music from Apollo's lyre.

Now, what other questions do you have?"

Kathryn made the first inquiry, "Brett, when will we bring our union of Light into being?"

"Kathryn, I feel that we should form this union as soon as possible and that we should include Jenny and Michelle in the ceremony. I really shouldn't use the word ceremony. That is not what will join us together. It is more of a personal bond of commitment. In any event, I believe that we should make our start in Durham."

Lydia piped up eagerly, "When and where will this child be created?"

"Lydia, you need to answer the first part of that question yourself for two reasons. First and foremost, when will you ovulate, and second, when will you be ready to make love with us? As for where, I want this child to be conceived in North Carolina and I want the conception to take place on Kelly's bed, with all of us present together."

Lydia smiled and whispered almost to herself, "As it should be."

Then Kelly asked, "How do you see these babies being delivered and where would you want their entry to this world to begin?"

Her question was a little more difficult and required me to go deeper into my visions for an answer. "The babies will come into this world in the water. I want them to be born here in this house in our golden bathtub. I also know that these divine beings will be born at exactly the same time at 8:18 in the evening on the seventh of July."

There was a moment of silence as my Graces contemplated the future impact they would have on the world.

Then I said, "We will leave in the morning for North Carolina. Lydia, please call Jenny and have her and Michelle prepare for our arrival."

Day 44

Lydia drove with Kelly in her Volvo and I took Kathryn on the back of the *Valkyrie*. The ride was a bit on the chilly side as we encountered an early harbinger of wintry weather. Stopping only twice, we made it to Durham in about three hours.

The Jenny who answered the door looked different than the woman I had left the previous morning. Before I could comment on the wonderful change in her appearance, Michelle flew down the steps and into my arms. Kathryn moved in behind me and gave Jenny one of her patented Southern girly hugs. Then we switched partners and it was my turn to feel Jenny's warmth penetrate my riding suit.

I took the time to admire her new clothes. She was wearing an elegant, off-white cashmere sweater, trimmed in purple and tight at the bosom. Her knee-length, black leather skirt added to her allure and let the world see her fine legs. On her feet were a hip pair of leather "Mary Jane" shoes that I could have sworn I had seen before.

When we went inside, I was delighted by the new look of my old house. Kelly's furniture had arrived and transformed the interior from a drab shell into a showcase of American and British design. I couldn't wait for Lydia to feast her eyes on Robin and Lucinne Day's creations. A more cautious driver than me, and deeply aware of the important passengers she was ferrying, Lydia did not arrive for another half-hour.

While Kathryn and Michelle huddled in the kitchen for a pow-wow, I took the opportunity to have a talk with Jenny. I led her into my bedroom and sat her down on the giant bed, which occupied almost the entire space. There was no room for any other furniture. I joined her, took her hand in mine and began to talk about my mission.

"Jenny, you and I have come here to enlighten humankind, me as the teacher and pathfinder and you as the disciple. Our spiritual journey won't be easy. The transformation of humanity will start and finish in the heart. Fortunately, we don't have to invent everything from scratch and can follow a time-trodden path."

She looked at me wide-eyed but not surprised.

I continued, "Everything has come to pass billions and billions of years before, and all that transpires is a circle, an eternal repetition wrought by the Creator of Light. The Divine One is love and where there is love there is no room for hatred. Hate comes from the darkness inside man and love is from the luminous Creator.

I love each and every one of you as I love myself, and you, Jenny Jenkins, are very special to me. Now, let me tell you what is going to happen tonight."

Jenny smiled and said, "I already know that you are going to marry the...the Three Graces. Brett, we are so happy about this that Michelle and I made a feast for your wedding."

I brought Jenny close to me and held her until she wept with the feeling of the spiritual Light coursing through her being.

We were just leaving the bedroom when I heard Lydia's car door slam outside. In the same instant Michelle darted from her room, ran to the front door and flung it open, just as Lydia was about to knock.

Kathryn came over to me and whispered, "Spend a little time with Michelle. She needs to hear from you what we have planned for her and Jenny."

As Lydia and Kelly came inside, she added, "All of us need to go and buy something to wear for the evening. Why don't you and Michelle go out for a little talk? Be sure and tell our little girl that I am going to pick out a great outfit for her. And, Brett, have I told you lately just how much I love you?"

I decided to kill two birds with one stone and took Michelle for a spin in the MG.

As we drove along Michelle told me, "I love this car so much. When I get older, I'll get one just like it."

I couldn't help but laugh at her innocent desires. I said, "This car will be yours after I leave this earth."

"Yea, when will that be? When hell freezes over?" Realizing what she had said, she covered her mouth and looked at me with uncertainty.

I leaned over, kissed her cheek and said, "It won't be long. That is why you must listen to everything that I teach you in the time we have together."

I stopped to get some gas in Carrboro, the town next door to Chapel Hill. While I filled up the car, Michelle ducked into the small convenience store to go to the bathroom. While she was in the restroom, I could feel her thoughts once again. This time she was anxious and worried about the future. When she returned to me, we took a little walk around the store. I put my arm around her shoulder and pulled her a bit closer to me. Then I told her about her place in our Circle of Light. When I got to the part about her being everlasting, she put her arms around me and kissed my cheek.

"Thank you for giving me eternal life," she said.

I stopped her and said, "You are a creation of the Light and therefore a child of the everlasting. I didn't do it. I only helped remove your human restraints."

Michelle still looked worried, so I elaborated until all the confusion had left her and she was beaming with the Light of Creation.

When we got home, the house was filled with joy, excitement and an abundance of flowers. The aroma from the colorful blossoms filled me with happiness and created a feeling of harmony in my heart. The women were all busy with preparations, delegating to me the job of being a contented observer.

I decided to help things along by filling the house with festive music. To start things off, I chose Handel's *Water Music*, which has always conjured up a feeling of celebration for me.

Finally, the time arrived and everything was in place. The women had set the table with a large bouquet of flowers in the middle and placed several bottles of champagne in ice buckets around the house. They had also had turned off the lights and put out a myriad of candles for illumination. Their flickering flames projected marvelous patterns on the ceiling in rhythm to the sounds of Chopin's *Nocturnes*.

My three Graces were draped in the sheerest silk, tinted in pale yellow and infused with soft purple. They were not wearing store tailored dresses, but had formed continuous pieces of silk to their bodies and girdled them with muted silver ribbons. They wore nothing underneath, nor did they have anything on their feet. Jenny and Michelle appeared wearing elegant slips of white silk with no lace highlights. They shimmered in the soft candlelight and added dancing sparkles to the patterns on the ceiling. Their garments were held in place with thin silk straps that caressed their bare shoulders and, like the Graces, they wore nothing underneath or on their feet. All five women had their hair up and tied to their heads with purple ribbons. I had chosen a white muslin shirt and matching pants and went bare-footed, too.

We formed a circle in the living room with Michelle standing directly behind me. Jenny made her way to Kathryn and stood in back of her. I moved into the middle of the ring as the Graces approached holding hands.

When they stood before me, I began, "As we engaged in commitment thousands of years before, I re-commit myself to you in body and spirit. My love for you is boundless and will continue to grow in the Light. I need you to make me whole, for what you possess is greater than anything of this Earth. Our bond will last forever and we will pave a road for the Two that will become One. This road will be the route for humankind to travel all the way into the Light.

Kathryn Bailey, I give you my love forever.

Kelly Porter, I give you my love forever and accept stewardship over your gift to mankind.

Lydia Gordon, you have my love through time without end and I will, together with you, bring to this world the other half that will make everything whole.

Now, my sweet ones, gather yourselves tightly to me and let us become one, without separation, forever throughout eternity."

Kathryn and I reached out at the same time and brought Jenny and Michelle into the circle. They would record for posterity, how true love was about to change the world.

After we shared the champagne and finished dancing, we all knew that it was time.

Jenny and Michelle took Lydia to the bath and cleansed her with scented oils and perfume. Kathryn and Kelly removed their silk coverings and placed them in the center of the bed. Then they lay down on either side of the silken altar.

I removed my clothes and positioned myself in the center and waited for Lydia.

Emerging from her bath, she looked beautiful in the flickering light that emanated from the two candles held by Jenny and Michelle, her lovely handmaidens.

When they had escorted Lydia to the bed, they placed the candles on the wall sconce mounts on either side of our platform of love. Then Jenny and Michelle slipped out of the room as quietly as they had entered.

I moved to Kelly's side of the bed in order to make room for Lydia.

Kathryn bent over Lydia and tenderly kissed her on the mouth. As she slid back ever so slowly, she repeated "I love you" over and over.

Kelly, looking serpent-like, slithered across me and covered Lydia's body with her own. Then she kissed her in a tender and loving way and moved to a position by my side.

Lydia looked into my eyes and whispered, "My love, come and make our union whole. Help me bring into this world for whom it has waited so long. "

We rocked back and forth as Kathryn and Kelly ran their hands over our moist bodies and whispered words of tender encouragement.

I started to loose myself in swirling passion. Lydia's breasts were thrusting into my heaving chest. I pulled her tight to me and felt the beginnings of my seed starting its journey towards engendering a new life.

Kathryn and Kelly, feeling our passions escalate, wrapped their bodies around us to be part of the creation.

Ever so slowly everything in our world started to change.

Lydia Gordon melded into Kelly Michelle Tempest and then back into herself again, and kept shifting back and forth, again and again, with each stroke of my inflamed penis.

As both of us started to build toward a mutual climax, bathed in a flurry of lights and loud whooshing sounds, my lives were slowly intermingling around me. The reality of one moment was changing in a whirlpool of color from another time. Every hue and shade in the rainbow was present in this passionate vortex.

Then the sucking, whirling mass of color turned into a deep purplish black that seemed to reflect my face back to me. Gradually a speck of bright yellow emerged from the black and purple. The yellow continued to cover the black until a full third of the circle was in the color of the sun. I heard Lydia screaming my name over and over again.

Suddenly, in the spinning vortex I saw my own face starting to materialize from the rotating circle of lust and love.

I felt heaviness and a throbbing pain in my left arm. The pain was becoming increasingly intense and my arm unbearably heavy, so much so, that it brought me out of one dimension of time and space and into another.

Circles of blackish purple became my being, as I fell from one existence into another. I was here in North Carolina, but in yet another dimension of time. I was straddling worlds and inhabiting them at the same time.

I watched as the freshly enhanced metal turned slowly from purple to black and then yellow, only to start again.

Sweat started to materialize on my forehead and every revolution of the golden cloth gave the glassine pigment more verve which, in turn, rewarded my eyes with a profusion of blazing yellow and eternal black.

My mind gradually emerged from the hypnotic spell of the three Graces to the swirling cloth fabric and the fading purplish circle it had cast. Standing back and looking at my handiwork, I now knew that I was finished with this job.

Epilogue

My left arm still shaking from the ordeal, I managed to slither it into my pocket and steady it enough to extract my gold pocket-watch. I couldn't believe it was 2:23 and I just spent, what felt like a lifetime, preening the *Valkyrie*, for her road trip. But I wondered in mystification—haven't I just finished the last road trip on the *Valkyrie*?

Acknowledgments

I want to acknowledge and thank the people who helped me over the course of the journey creating this work.

Above all, to the person who's encouragement and feedback seemed to be the glue of inspiration, my wife Amanda.

To my dear friend and fellow artist, Francesca Tiffin, who took the time to help me negotiate the minefield of words, which became the pavement of *The Last Road Trip*.

And to Chris Angermann, who has the ability to mold himself into the story behind the story. He is without peer in his editing ability.

"Judge" by Judge

Michael Judge

Accomplished author, photographer, artist, promoter and gallery owner Michael Judge has led a whirlwind life creating visually striking images seen throughout the world. His work can be found in major international collections and museums, among them the National Museum of Architecture in Poland and London Contemporary Art in England. The list of collectors includes President George H. W. Bush, the estate of Senator Edward Kennedy and Senator Robert Dole. A native of Washington, D.C., he has lived in Spain and Poland, as well as in California, Montana and Florida. He now makes his home in the White Mountains in Arizona.

He holds the distinction of having been the only artist chosen to create the 1976/1977 Congressional Calendar for the Bicentennial of the United States of America, 10 million of which were distributed worldwide. His work has also appeared in *The Washington Post, FOTO Magazine, Fotographia Magazine, Polish Radio and TV, NBC News, NBC TV, Perspectives Magazine, Margin Journal, Photo/Graphic Magazine* and *The Malibu Times*.

He produced and directed three 30-second film spots for NBC Radio, which aired on WKYS in Washington, D.C. Two of the three spots garnered an Addy Award for Excellence.

His memoir, *Captured Horizons, An Artist's Journey*, received an impressive second place in the 2009 Independent Publisher Book Awards.

For information, inquiries or interviews
visit *www.michaeljudgestudio.com*.

www.ingramcontent.com/pod-product-compliance
Lightning Source LLC
Chambersburg PA
CBHW031117030726
47496CB00002BA/584